Photograph

and the

Atomic Juggernaut

D1453229

Paperback: ISBN 979-8-9867772-0-7
eBook: ISBN 979-8-9867772-1-4
Library of Congress Control Number: 2022945632
First paperback edition: October 2022

Development Editor/Copy Editor: Amy Reeve
Additional Editing and Proofreading: Cleo Miele
Covers by MiblArt and Nessgraphica

Jackowick Publishing
Bordentown, NJ 08620
michaelblatherwick.com

The characters and events in this book are fictitious. Any similarity to real persons, living or dead, is coincidental and not of any intention or inference by the author.

Dedicated to Robert Allen, a true friend and my copilot exploring the mysteries of New Jersey and seeding the daydreams of something bigger. It breaks my heart that I can't share this with you, but you live on every day when I turn up the volume and hit the gas.

"This CD is really good."

Prologue

I killed your father."

Colonel Samuel Jefferson Sr. drew a long, shallow breath. His hospital suite was reminiscent of a guest bedroom out of a home décor catalog, generic decorations and modest colors, not a sterile and clinical space like seen on a television medical drama. The minimal machines hooked up to him were compact and quiet, only the whispers of electronic tones and a ghostly hum. His tenure in the military had afforded him a high quality of care during his end stage of life. His thinning gray hair maintained the tight cropped cut of his military service and he wore a button-down shirt rather than a coarse hospital gown. Even at this stage, dignity was important to him.

The afternoon hour was deep, and the shadows began to form in long gray masses on the tile, creeping like black snakes from the flowers on the windowsill toward the girl sitting across the room in the wooden guest chair with faded orange cushions. She wore a simple dress, more suited to a little girl than one on the verge of adolescence. The colonel had picked it out himself; he wished to keep her embedded in the fantasy of youth rather than the oncoming reality of adulthood.

"Come closer, Dana. This is important. I may be a villain in this story, but I am not the only villain. And you may be the hero." He smiled with a slight wince of pain. "Even if you are still just a little girl." His eyes, a mixture of yellow and pink from age and disease, focused with a hint of the steely-blue iris of his youth before returning to the gray that had settled in over the last decade of his life.

Dana Jefferson sat up, confused by her grandfather's confession, and, using her feet, dragged the chair to the side of her grandfather's bed. The smell of simple soap overpowered the musk of his cologne, the antiseptic plastics, and a trace of cigarette smoke from someone who had been in the room prior to her visit. He reached out a frail dark spotted hand that she accepted into hers. She examined their matching skin tones. His hue had been weathered into a deep tan forged through years of sunlight; hers was the mix of her mother's coffee and her father's ivory.

"Dana, I am so sorry for what I am about to burden you with. As you know, I have made my career . . . my life . . ."—he paused and looked into her eyes without blinking—". . . *our* life about the preservation of our liberty and our nation. Do you understand that?"

Dana nodded. Her grandfather had raised her since her father died, which was preceded by her mother's death from a swift terminal illness. Before then, all three generations had lived in her grandfather's comfortable, but not extravagant, large rancher in New Mexico. She learned how to properly unfold and raise the American flag on the tallest pole with every sunrise at the front of his property along the canyon road. On the morning after her mother passed, she had raised the flag to half-mast only to be rebuked by the colonel when he returned home with her father.

Her grandfather continued. "As you know, I spent my time working on engineering—you understand what that means, right? We built things. We improved things. We made things safer for our soldiers abroad so that they could ensure we were safer at home."

"Like the balloon camera?"

"Yes, the balloon camera!" He let out a short dry cough as he started to chuckle excitedly, his yellowed eyes opening wide at her appreciation of his invention. "We didn't just use that camera for taking pictures of mountains and rivers for mapping. That camera also contained a small charge, or, rather, an explosive. We would send those cameras out to be intentionally discovered and shot down. We would allow the insurgents to take it back to their camp and—"

"You killed them?"

"Yes. My projects were *malevolent*," he replied. He misread the stillness on her face as miscomprehension of the word, not acknowledgment of the deed. "That means they were very bad and harmful. I am what is known as a casualty engineer. Everything I built was meant to . . . kill."

He felt her hand twitch in his, so he softened his grip. She recoiled her hand.

"My life's work, Dana, was a very special weapon. So special that it required your father's hands to create my dream." He stopped and turned his gaze to the flowers on the windowsill, which were growing darker as the setting sun backlit their silhouette, making their shadows more jagged as they reached the wall across the room.

"The device was breathtaking. If you'll pardon my flair for the dramatic, my last years have afforded me the opportunity to branch out beyond the binary responses of giving and receiving orders."

She did not realize that, despite withdrawing her hand, she leaned in closer with every pause in his story.

"I made something terrible, a nightmare . . . it proved too dangerous during testing. We didn't intend to travel the path we took. We had protocols that were not tested because of the many pressures." His throat tightened as his confession continued. "There were too many parties whispering offers of large sums of money into our ears."

He slammed his gaunt fist onto the bed, and then drew his closed hand to his chest. Dana bolted upright in her seat, as she had never seen this inclination to violence and outbursts from her usually restrained grandfather. She remained silent as a light breeze from the open window cupped her cheeks with cold invisible palms. He paused before he spoke his next words with a low somber tone, hanging on each word.

"I gave your father cancer because we needed that wretched weapon to be ready. I am so sorry."

Dana began to slowly retreat in her chair. This was too much for most twelve-year-old children to process, but her acuity with grown-ups was ahead of her peers. She exhaled one word, the last she'd ever speak aloud to him.

"Why?"

"Dana, my beautiful Dana. We needed men to test it before it was ready. I told your father that the safety shields were ready, but I knew that we had radioactive leakage. I knew putting him inside that machine would be a long, slow, painful death sentence. I was promoted after that. I received a *promotion for killing my own son* . . . AND A DOZEN MORE MEN!"

An attendant from outside the room peered in when he heard Dana's grandfather shouting but then slunk back behind the portal window. Her grandfather lowered his voice below speaking but above whispering.

"I am not asking you to vindicate me or change my legacy but to safeguard others. Your father and I discussed this before he died, but it was my burden to complete the mission, and to right our wrongs. It appears I will not be able to complete the mission, Dana." He lifted his chin and straightened his shoulders to as if he was standing at attention while stranded in his bed. "I had made preparations, but I did not anticipate that my health would descend this rapidly before you turned eighteen. Here."

He reached into his shirt pocket. His fingers struggled as he pulled out a piece of paper.

"There is a safe deposit box back in New Jersey where your father and I worked on this evil machination. You may access it when you are a legal adult; the contents are yours. You will find all the information you need, as well as, my dear, the last of your father's plans. Something designed for war but with the hope of wonderful civilian uses."

She kept her eyes down as she took the folded piece of crisp white paper. She could see the ink bleeding through the back in a few places. One spot grew in size but faded in color as a tear saturated the document.

"Do you know that I used that balloon camera to take pictures of you? I have some exceptionally beautiful photos of your eyes; those wonderful hazel fingerprints you see the world through. They soften my heart every time I look at them, and they hardened my resolve to tell you this story one day. Every eye is unique, and both of yours are extraordinary." He winked at her. She faked a smile.

"Do you still like roller skating, my dear?"

Her lips parted as she raised an eyebrow. Dana and her mother would roller skate in the house when Colonel Jefferson and her father had been away on their extended trips. It was typically forbidden inside, especially in the parlor, so they went to great lengths to hide their secret roller derby activity, even going so far as to polish the floors to hide the scuffing from their toe stops.

His rough cheeks retracted into a smile, his capped teeth catching the last reflections of the sun before it surrendered to the horizon.

Dana tucked a strand of her full black curls behind her ear, stood up, and, without saying a word, weakly hugged her grandfather. She turned and paused so he would not have the satisfaction of seeing the tears that welled in her eyes, and she walked out of the room with the wish to never see him again.

Her wish was granted that night.

Chapter 1

Futures – Jimmy Eat World

For a Tuesday night, the Stroudsberg Inn was busier than usual. Being one of the few bars in the middle of the Pine Barrens, a million-acre swath of forest cast across southern New Jersey, dictated that most patrons were a steady crowd of well-worn contractors, local business owners brokering side hustles, and a rotating cluster of singles who cross-dated with regularity. Dana Jefferson enjoyed her work behind the bar as well as the steady tips and the requisite free advice she doled out. The youngest bartender by age and tenure, she still knew a good number of the patrons by actual name or nickname, even if it was one she kept to herself. The rednecks who harassed her because of her peanut-colored skin were few and far between, and she could count on the other staff to escort the most racist patrons outside.

Dana checked her hair in the mirror behind the bar—not from vanity, but to confirm her thick black waves were in place after running back from the walk-in cooler. She smeared the sweat on her forehead with the back of her hand and studied her reflection, mocking herself with a flirty wink and dimpled smile. Her teeth flashed blueish white from the neon sign to her left, but her light-brown eyes still sparkled back in their true hues. "You are so hot, you're going to make *at least* ten bucks in tips tonight," she whispered to herself, "so we don't have to choose between toothpaste and underwear." Her smirking reflection faded.

She walked over to the end of the bar and retied the knot in the front of her flannel button-down before pulling a bottle opener from the pocket of her waist apron.

"Hey, Paula, another one?"

A short woman in a faded black T-shirt and light-blue satin jacket sitting at the bar in front of her nodded, shaking her long braided brown ponytail. Paula was Dana's teammate on the Asbury Angels, a roller derby team out of Asbury Park. Dana had moved to New Jersey a year ago with only a few bags and a steamer trunk in her rusty blue Ford Bronco. An only child, she had spent her adolescence rotating through a handful of boarding schools across New Mexico and Arizona, sponsored by the trust fund her parents and grandfather had established prior to their deaths. Making friends in a new state as a twenty-three-year-old had been a challenge, but the Angels had given her the first semblance of family since she was a child. Paula became the first of her many sisters on the team and looked up to Dana despite being her elder by several years.

"I was talking to Mary Beth, and we got the next practice dates set. Looks like we may be sharing the park with those whiners from Cape May," Paula noted dryly. She reached into her purse and pulled out a photocopied sheet. The teams in the league often shared facilities and costs for practice, fermenting a sisterhood of skaters that went beyond the matches. Dana enjoyed meeting the other team members before the rough-and-tumble of an event, especially since the rosters frequently changed as women moved from one town to another. The only drama was often the result of someone dating and then breaking up with a fellow skater, something Dana was now personally familiar with.

Dana reached for a glass and poured herself a ginger ale from the dispenser. "Are your folks having Sunday dinner?" she asked. Dana appreciated the weekly invite to Paula's house and the banter of her family around homemade casseroles and potato salad. As one of her few friends in New Jersey, Dana had latched onto Paula's parents and sister as a surrogate family whenever she could shoehorn her way into familial events. She didn't mind being a fifth wheel if there was a warm meal and corny jokes from Paula's mom.

"No go on dinner this week; we're going to my uncle's down in Cape May. I'd let you tag along, but he's a little, you know"—she thumbed her nose into the air—"*proper*, my dear."

"Must be nice to have that kind of money in the family." The friends sipped their drinks in silence as the conversation steered into an uncomfortable lane. Dana let Paula take the wheel to drive the next topic.

"Have you talked to Angela recently?" Dana sensed that her friend approached the subject with caution as she dipped her fries into an excessive mound of ketchup on her plate.

"No. Not recently." Dana looked for any misplaced items on the bar, hoping to dodge the follow-up question she was sure would crash into the conversation.

"So, not since you two broke up? Nothing?" Paula pointed an accusatory fry at Dana.

"Nope. I said my things, she said her things, and luckily we had our own places, so only the exchange of toothbrushes and a shirt or two was necessary." Dana found a pile of napkins that looked not quite aligned and began to straighten the stack. She loathed talking about breakups. She was a proficient heartbreaker, rarely single, and had left a trail of former boyfriends and girlfriends behind her. Unfortunately for her partners, her priority was not her relationships; rather, it was tracking down the long trail of clues left by her family. If she discovered another lead, she found herself severing ties and moving on romantically and geographically. When she had landed in New Jersey on the trail of the most recent breadcrumbs, she took a shot with Angela but found the relationship challenging to maintain as both teammate and girlfriend.

Dana leaned in after patting down the pile of napkins and taking a quick survey for any empty glasses on the bar. "Paula, I have to admit, Angela and I were just a bad idea. I mean, she's great, and oh my God, she's gorgeous, but I had to rip the Band-Aid off before we got too deep. And I do feel bad. She was more into me than I was into her." She smirked. "I do miss seeing her brothers on a regular basis. Family full of jocks and they always had some story about a prank war during baseball season or some rowdy tale about a cheerleader." She wagged her bottle opener and winked. "Or three."

Paula held up her glass in solidarity before chugging the rest of the contents.

"Yes, indeed, she is a looker. I mean, I don't, you know . . ." She struggled as her words sought the politest route. ". . . I just date guys, but girl, she is smoking hot."

"Looks aren't everything. I'm old enough to know that." Dana glanced back at the bar and up at the clock. "I have to close out a few tabs. I'm only here until ten. Be right back."

The barroom was slowly thinning as the late dinner and happy hour crowd filled their gullets, and Dana began her check-ins. One of her recent favorites was an older single guy named James who ordered a pitcher and bacon burger every Tuesday and Thursday. She sauntered over to his table where he slumped a bit more than usual on his stool.

"James, are you alright, big guy?"

He looked up with heavy eyelids, more buzzed than usual.

"I had a long day. Skipped lunch to make my quota at the yard." He fumbled and subsequently dropped his wallet. "So, I think I was already running on empty."

Dana looked past him out the window to his old compact car in the parking lot, and then down at his keys. She slowly slid them off the table into her pocket and felt the lump of folded dollar bills next to them. She could buy new underwear and pay the electric bill later. *I'll just have to work harder on tips next week*, she reasoned.

"Cab fare is on me. Just remember it next time."

As Dana walked back to the bar, Paula hopped off her stool and tapped a small pile of bills under her glass. She began to button her jacket, its colorful embroidery of "Asbury Angels" stretching across the back.

"See you at practice. Don't forget the schedule, sweetie!" she chimed as she trotted to the door. "And hey." She paused for dramatic emphasis. "Call Angela or just get an ice cream or something. We can't have our big brawler going soft on us. Or going full road rage with a broken heart!"

Dana reluctantly held up an okay sign with her hand as Paula left. Her tip jar count left her in the positive by only ten dollars after paying for James's cab fare and comping Paula's drinks. She said goodbye to the cooks and grabbed her leather coat as she snuck out the back door. Dana glanced at the tag inside the black worn leather as it fell under the lamplight in the lot. The faded "S. Jefferson" written inside by her mother sparked a warm smile. When she had packed the coat for her first day of boarding school, she hid it at the bottom of her suitcase, unsure if she was allowed to bring her mom's handmade jacket, complete with tuxedo tails, and slightly embarrassed by the sloppiness as it engulfed her small thirteen-year-old frame. But all these years later, in the cool New Jersey evening, it fit snuggly, accentuating her broad shoulders, a proper uniform for any imaginary upcoming battles. She retained few possessions from her earlier life stages, but those that she kept, like the jacket, were more valuable than all the tips she had ever earned.

Her truck sat parked in the far back corner of the lot to keep prying eyes away from the large backpack tucked in the footwell of the passenger side. She leaned on the hood for a moment as she unfolded a sheet of paper with a list of road names from her back pocket. The first ten were crossed off, leaving another twenty to go. The next on the list was a county road number, followed by a second number indicating a mile marker. She studied it before opening the truck door.

"Are you girls ready for another run?" she inquired of the bag next to her. "I think maybe we'll have a little more fun and do a little less detective work tonight."

0:00   3:13

Chapter 2

When You Close Your Eyes – Night Ranger

S on, you need to keep your eyes *off* the road. That's the trick."

Nick Andrews never liked driving at night in the Pine Barrens, but his dad was easily spooked by deer and critters on the back roads. Heading home late together from overtime work for the electric company meant miles of unlit two-lane roads that were often populated by more opossums than pickup trucks. Nick was grateful for the job—albeit as an hourly fill-in—especially when career choices without a college degree across the county were limited. His dad, Mitchell, had pulled a few strings to get him in the door.

"If you leave the headlights and interior lights off, after about five minutes your eyes should adjust, especially on a cloudless night like tonight." Mr. Andrews tapped the windshield to acknowledge the deep navy-blue sky above them. The white paint of the hood glowed slightly under the stars.

The old dented Ford F150 rattled sporadically as they moved through the woods. Nick alternated between squinting and widening his eyes as the lines in the road began to swell and grow with his dilating pupils. The best way to avoid blinding a deer at two in the morning was as his dad suggested: to drive with no lights on, at least for the next half hour, when the stretch of road would be devoid of streetlamps.

"Are you and the guys going out to play paintball this weekend? Or is Saturday motocross?" his father asked as he unscrewed a thermos of decaf coffee.

Nick shrugged. He had neglected participating in either activity for months, but his dad hadn't noticed. Between the overtime shifts he took to save up tuition money and his intermittent courses in electrical engineering at Ocean County Community College, Nick was exhausted. The little free time he had in his schedule was spent with his on-again, off-again girlfriend, Lindsey. Being a lineman in the Pine Barrens meant climbing poles on a daily basis and swapping out box parts for homeowners who often mistook him for one of the many locals trying to steal parts for the scrapyards, which was often the reason he was called out in the first place—that and removing the occasional burnt glove of would-be thieves who were not able to ground themselves properly.

"I'm not going anywhere this weekend. Just studying." Nick tensed as he anticipated the possible and probable topics that would come up next.

"You can go out, you know. Look, I've been saving up my OT, and we can use that toward next semester so you can cut down on the work and pick up an extra class or two."

"Appreciate it. Right now, I just want to get to bed." *Here it comes*, he thought.

"So, you and Lindsey . . . are you guys in a rough patch?" Nick felt the sarcasm in his father's voice needle into his ear canal. He did not want to talk about his girlfriend—or ex-girlfriend, depending on the day of the week, especially with his old man after a grueling day of labor.

"We were supposed to go to her cousin's birthday party last weekend, but there was a schedule conflict. I don't think we're going to hang out this weekend." The silence shrouded him as he waited for a follow-up question that did not materialize.

The truck barreled through the blue-black darkness as the forest gave way to a more thinly populated section. On the right, the trees were about half the height of the woods on the left. According to a local urban legend, decades ago a forest fire was blocked by the newly paved and widened roads as it blazed across the county.

The new pavement and extended shoulders were wide enough to stop the spread and saved countless homes but stunted the growth of the burned section. Today, the shorter tree line that had grown in let in some moonlight, just enough to allow for shadows and shapes to be visible at a greater distance down the road. Nick continued to squint at the inky soft forms ahead. A tiny blot in the distance stood out.

"Hey, Dad, do you see something up there?" Nick nodded his chin toward the blackness far down the road. He dropped the speedometer about ten miles per hour as they both stared at a shape moving along the center line about a half mile ahead. "Should we hit the headlights?"

"Not yet, kid, keep back a bit. Might be a bear. About the right height for an adolescent."

The speedometer ticked down another hash on the dial as Nick assessed the object's rate of speed. Whatever this thing was, it was moving with intent and skill, prowess and power.

"We're not getting closer, and we're holding the same speed. How fast do bears run?"

"They're pretty fast. But thirty to thirty-five is pushing it outside of a sprint. He must be after something fierce. Do you hear the growling from here?"

Nick rolled down the window. As soon as the air seal of the window broke, a chilly wind blew his hat off his head and into the back of the truck cab, ruffling his short blond hair. A faint metallic set of tones crept in with the cool air. It was a low rumble, not heavy but thick, like a loose low guitar string rattling with distortion. Nick cautiously depressed the gas pedal, and the tone started to rise from the Doppler effect as they closed the gap with the figure ahead.

"That's not a bear," Nick whispered. The darkness was interrupted by tiny flashes of light coming from the bottom of the shape as it wobbled in tiny arcs back and forth across the lines. "Sparks! Dad! Dad! Do you see?"

"I do. I don't know what the hell that is. It's moving side to side over the double yellow. Is it . . . dancing?"

Nick saw the sparks in greater detail as they erupted, flaring in a tiny storm on the road each time the figure changed direction. Rhythmic and repetitive, the swerving pattern belonged to a now visible biped, but the shape was too dark in the achromatic night to make out more detail.

"I'm catching up to it," he murmured as a new flurry of sparks shot out, outlining what looked like two ski boots mounted to wheels. The pickup heaved forward unevenly as it decided between gears. Nick banked to the right side of the lane as they closed the gap and pulled up next to . . . a woman on skates.

At forty miles an hour, they matched her speed, holding the truck parallel to her. What looked to be black curls played with the darkness and were pinned back by her hairband, and a clear plastic shield similar to shooting goggles rode on her hairline. She wore a cropped leather jacket with long tails in a tuxedo style, and her forearms were excessively padded from elbow to glove. Her dark irises stared back at him. She pulled one earbud out of her ear as she laughed, yelling, "You almost caught me!" She flashed a gigantic smile in direct contrast to Nick's agape mouth.

Her slim-fit cargo pants were tucked into a pair of large plastic and metal boots, with extended shin guards attached to kneepads. The spasms of sparks illuminated more details of the skates as she swerved away from the truck. The four slim wheels on each skate were built out of coiled metal around a core wheel, like a two-inch-thick guitar string, growling and grinding at dizzying speed.

As suddenly as they caught up to her, she shot ahead of them in a firestorm of sparks, the metallic tones converging into a distorted chord. Nick hit the headlights and then the high beams as she rocketed ahead, her oversized roller skates grinding against the pavement as she abruptly swerved left onto an unmarked side road. He slammed the brake pedal down to the floor mat and skidded the screeching truck to a stop almost perpendicular to their travel lane.

"Well. That was something," Mr. Andrews declared as he stared at Nick, one hand still holding the sun visor he had grabbed for stability and subsequently ripped from the header, his other hand clutching the coffee thermos that was now half empty from spilling in the cabin.

"Dad, did you—"

"See? Yeah, she was like a . . . *photograph.*"

"Photograph?"

"Yeah, that girl's like a photograph. That's the only way you'll catch her."

The father and son sat silently for another moment before Nick reengaged the gear shift to continue home.

3:13

Chapter 3

Somnambulist – BT

Nick stared at the ceiling in the dark. *Such a cliché thing to do*, he thought to himself as the fan in his bedroom droned. He had spent the last two hours trying to make logical sense in his head of the events that had transpired on his way home, and of the mysterious girl with the beaming smile, despite the impending alarm clock that would erupt in thirty minutes to let him know it was time to get up for class. Sleep was finally pressing on his eyelids when the alarm rang, making him question if what had happened was all a dream.

"Nick, breakfast! Get in here and stop thinking about girls on roller skates."

Nope, not a dream, he reprimanded himself.

Nick sat up and looked around the room. He had taken down his posters that had been on his walls since high school a few months ago after he turned twenty-one but could still see the pin holes, tape remnants, and sun-faded rectangles on the far side over his desk. His engineering books were organized on his shelf in alphabetical order by subject. Despite his thin finances, he chose not to resell them. One day they might be fun relics for his children to peruse, as he enjoyed paging through his mother's old schoolbooks. He looked down at his feet. He had fallen asleep in his work boots as usual and began his ritual of taking off his shoes before putting on his clothes for the day.

Down the hall, across the rancher's length, was one large room containing the kitchen, dining room, and family room—the open floor plan his mother had requested before she died. His father had done the work himself to convert the space per her wishes, including the handmade bookshelves, and Nick had cherished his first self-managed project laying out the electrical plan and doing the wiring himself before he joined the union. Every outlet was also fitted with a USB port, and two recessed lights, one on each side of the room, ran off a small solar cell he had installed on the roof on each side of the skylight. The Pine Barrens provided diverse weather across the year, so having a set of solar-powered lights in case of a thunderstorm, blizzard, or hurricane seemed like common sense to him. But the more likely recurring power issue was the occasional drunk driver taking out the power line pole at the end of the street, which also ensured job security.

"So, what the hell did we see last night? Was that a next-gen hoverboard?" his dad asked.

Nick sat down at the table and folded his toast into triangles.

"No way. Something like that would have hit all the big boy sites," he said as he took a ravenous bite of his breakfast. "The tech blogs, the human-interest rich-folk-gawking, the financial pages. I bet I could run a search and not find anything close to that unless it was written about by Bill Cooper or Isaac Asimov." His voice faded. "They were so cool looking." He picked up his glass and saw that his dad was standing at the counter, head bent low.

"You sound like your mom. You got all *her* brains, and *my* beautiful hands. Make money with your brain because your hands won't last forever."

"Neither will my brain," he countered to his father. He regretted the words as he momentarily recalled the day his mom told him the definition of meningioma. Nick put his water down but kept his hand on the glass, drawing small circles with his thumb. He cleared his throat to bridge the silence that hung between them. His father, unfazed by the comment, moved back to the looming mystery.

"Do you think that girl was with the military? We're really not too far from the base and reserve complex." He was talking about Joint Base McGuire-Dix-Lakehurst, an amalgamation of army, navy, and air force facilities that employed many of the locals in civilian and enlisted roles. Nick had learned at a young age how to identify the aircraft, day or night, as they flew in and out on training missions and deployments, sparking the birth of his interest in engineering.

"I doubt it," he said, pointing his toast crust at his father. "They'd be doing that stuff under lock and key, and anything with speed goes out west to the desert. Salt flats or dry lakebeds. Places like that."

Nick stood up and grabbed his backpack and laptop from the couch. He paused to pick up a shopping bag from a high-end menswear store that contained a dress shirt with the tags still attached.

"I'm going to run. I have to return this shirt Lindsey bought me, and I have to get to campus early for lab time. This laptop screen is too small for the specs for my assignment." He grabbed the keys to his truck from the hook by the door. "I'll see you at work around noon before shift starts."

"Son." Mr. Andrews intercepted him at the door. Nick looked down at his feet, preparing for another lecture on bad girlfriend choices. "Let's not tell anyone about last night. I mean, someone else had to have seen her. Let them talk first. I don't need anyone at work thinking I'm out of sorts." Nick understood the implications. His dad's coworkers had questioned his behavior during and after his wife's illness, and Nick saw he held on to his sanity one day at a time. He glanced at the bag in Nick's hand. "And that's a nice shirt. You might need that for a job interview. You should keep it."

Nick nodded back at his dad. His father's eyes were the same blue as his mother Josephine's, as well as his own. Mitch's rounded jaw and soft cheeks contrasted with his mother's angular features, including the pointed nose and chin that Nick saw every morning in the mirror. He was his mother's child, and he knew each day that his father felt joy and pain seeing her in him.

Nick plodded out to his faded red Ford Ranger pickup next to his dad's white F150 in the gravel driveway. Once behind the wheel, he thought about the mysterious girl they had seen, the wonderful machines on her feet, and the bliss in her smile as she soared into the night. He looked at his calendar appointments on his phone: school, work, study, and Lindsey. Repeat. He opened the phone's browser to the shopping app.

"You can't catch a photograph without a camera," he said softly to himself as he scrolled through the images of new and refurbished equipment. He clicked on a highly rated wireless camera and selected the next-day shipping option. With a small smile, he pulled out of the driveway and headed toward the college computer lab.

Chapter 4

One Night in Bangkok – Murray Head

Dana studied the patrons seated at the bar and the ones standing at the high tables near her section. The crowd was thick once again with packs of working-class comrades and middle-aged married couples out on their Friday date night. If anything stood out, it was the lone young man sitting by himself, a short pile of neatly stacked file folders on the bar in front of him. She didn't recognize him personally, but his short blond tousle of hair and runner's frame had become as of recent a frequent fixture, albeit never in her section where she could prod him with charming banter for tips. She elbowed her coworker Grant, who was a long-time employee of the Stroudsberg and knew most people in the surrounding area.

"Hey, do you know that guy?" she asked with another nudge. "He's been in here recently, a few times now."

Grant ran a hand over his receding hair and laughed in his deep booming voice.

"I think I do. Handsome, right? You interested? I think he was dating Lindsey Chandwick," he stated and then assumed a slightly British accent with his confirmation, "*of the Cherry Hill Chandwicks.*" Dana smiled with a shrug, indicating her lack of name recognition. "Her dad's a dentist from a long line of noble tooth pullers. They have a lot of money. That guy"—he nodded toward the solitary young man at the end of the bar—"was dating above his station in life, in my opinion. My little brother went to school with him. They used to meet up for paintball together. Nick Andrews. I think that's the right name."

Dana raised an eyebrow and pulled her bouquet of black curls into a loose bun. She tightened the knot of her flannel button-down tied at the waist.

"Let's see what the big nerd is doing." She retrieved her bottle opener and flipped it in her hand on her way behind the bar. She planted herself in front of Nick and gave the opener a final flip to grab his attention. "Let me guess, Blondie, a Miller Lite?"

Nick looked up from one of the folders on the bar in front of him. He opened his mouth but only inhaled.

"You've been in here three times over the past week. You order a Miller Lite, look at your homework or whatever that is, and then leave after thirty minutes. So, am I right?" She tapped the opener next to his pile.

"Sure. Yes. One. Please." He slapped the folder closed.

"You can drink when you want, but if you're here to ask me out, that's not going to happen." As she leaned on the bar, her dark curls liberated themselves and swung in front of her shoulders. Her unblinking hazel eyes bore into him.

"Oh sure. Sure." He swallowed a stutter and cleared his throat as he broke the intensity of her gaze. "I got a different question for you, though, when you bring that beer back."

"Ask me now. Let's get it over with." She beckoned with a flippant wave before ostentatiously cupping a hand behind her ear. He slid the folder across the bar and tapped it with two fingers. She looked at the closed folio skeptically and pulled a bottle from the cooler under the bar.

"Is this you?" Nick slid a finger between the cover and the pages, indicating that she should make the reveal herself. She popped open the bottle first and lifted the manila flap. There, in black and white, was a bird's-eye view of a blurred woman in the center of a road, a trail of sparks and lens flare behind her on the image. Dana pursed her lips.

"Okay," she lowered her head and brought her face within a few inches of his, her eyes locking with his. "I got enough creeps in here. You finish your drink, Blondie, and then you leave."

Nick closed the folder but held her gaze.

"I saw you a couple of weeks ago. You passed my truck. Well, it's not my truck, but I was in it. But anyway . . ." He paused. "Can I see them? Your skates?"

Dana pulled back. She felt trapped, her secret now exposed by a stranger, even if he did have a kind face and would lose to her in an arm-wrestling match by her own estimate.

"I don't know what you're talking about, but like I said, there are enough weirdos and stalkers in here. Want another example? Don't look, but that guy at the table under the window? The guy in brand-new work clothes and expensive tactical boots? He's been in here three times this week like you, just staring at me. Only orders from the other waitstaff. You can go over to him, ask *him* for a date, and hop in his Mercedes or whatever he drives." Nick glanced quickly, then looked back at Dana.

"For a guy in nice clothes, he sure drives a broken-down beater," Nick said with a forced laugh. "Every time I pull up, he's looking under his rust-bucket Bronco, probably watching the oil leak." Dana kept her eyes locked on Nick as her confident façade dropped and the color drained from her cheeks.

"I'm the only one with a rust-bucket Bronco here."

Nick glanced back at the man under the window. He had the build of a linebacker or tight end, and his pant legs were pulled over his boots, which were impeccably clean. A water and a beer sat untouched on the table as he tinkered on his phone. His haircut was a military regulation flattop, and his face was clean-shaven and whisker-free, odd for ten o'clock on a Tuesday night. Nick lowered his voice to a bar-level whisper.

"Every time I've been here, I've seen him looking under that truck. Every time. I even went over once after he went inside to see if it had a leak or flat tire." Dana did not blink as he concluded. "Every time I've been here. *Every time.*"

Dana darted her eyes back and forth between the man in the corner and Nick. Of the two men suddenly stalking her, at least she knew the name of one, thanks to Grant, and his motivations were literally laid out before her in black-and-white photography paper. She pulled a pen and notepad from her waist apron and scribbled a short note: *back door dumpster 3 minutes.*

She tore the sheet and slid it to Nick. He turned the paper over and puffed his cheeks as he looked back to her face. She winked twice. He downed his entire beer and walked out the front door.

Dana peeked out the employee entrance and waved at Nick as he milled in a circle.

"That truck?" she whispered.

"Yep, that's the one." Nick pointed to a blue decades-old Bronco with liberally applied primer paint.

Dana jogged over and knelt in the muddy gravel next to her vehicle, with Nick following and doing the same. She poked her head under the front bumper, shifting her focus back and forth from the truck to Nick.

"If you guys are in cahoots, that's a bad idea. I should tell you I'm from a military family, and I'm in a roller derby league, so I have absolutely no qualms about putting you face down in the . . . shit . . ."

In the reflection of a small puddle under the front suspension was a faint glowing red dot. Nick pointed at it and then traced a line back up to the suspension, ending at a small plastic box the size of a 9-volt battery with a tiny red LED, partially covered by a piece of tape attached to one side of the box.

"Holy Ghost, will you look at that," she whispered while reaching a hand toward it.

"Don't touch it—let me think for a minute. For now, get back inside," Nick suggested. "Keep working. At closing time, I'll pull up back here and drive you home." Dana gave Nick a sideways glance and arched her eyebrow. He mirrored her with own attempt at flexing his brow.

"Do you trust the guy who wants to ask you about your roller skates or Mister 'On the next episode of *Murder She Wrote*' who put a tracking device on your car?" he asked.

"You do have a point, Angela Lansbury. Be at the back door at twelve thirty, and like I said, any funny business . . ." She pointed back and forth between her fist and below his belt buckle.

Nick nodded.

As she walked back inside, she glanced back, unsure if they were now in on this together, or if he was part of some larger conspiracy. She saw Nick grab the tracking device and scan the parking lot.

He jogged to a lone yellow compact car with out-of-state plates and attached it under the front fender with the remaining bit of tape. She gave him a thumbs-up and shut the door.

Punctually, at their agreed rendezvous time, Dana was at the back door with a large blue canvas backpack on one shoulder as Nick pulled his truck around.

"Was he still inside?" he asked as he opened the door for her.

"No, Captain Creepy left about a half hour ago. Go out the back of the lot." She shoved her bag into the cramped space behind her seat. "There's a delivery entrance we let the big trucks use. It lets out about fifty yards down from the driveway."

Nick pulled on to the road and started driving toward his house. Dana looked down at her apron, neatly folded in her lap, and smiled.

"You didn't ask me where I live. Or my name. You want that punch now or when we get to your storage unit filled with bodies?"

"Oh my God . . . Nick. I'm Nick Andrews. And I just assumed my house would be a safe bet. I'm not really thinking clearly right now." She was relieved he said the same name Grant had told her. She placed one foot on the dashboard.

"Dana. Dana Jefferson. Call me DJ and I'll drop-kick you."

"Full disclosure: I live with my dad, I go to community college, I work for the electric company, and I just want to see your skates." He scanned the rearview mirror. "And now I'm curious who else is stalking you." He returned his gaze to the road. "Besides me."

She watched the corners of his lips curl up at his joke and allowed herself to reciprocate the expression.

Nick turned on the radio at a low volume. A classic rock station hummed in the background as the truck rolled over the cracked asphalt in the darkness. The only other soul on the road was a fox that ran into the opposite lane before changing his mind and returning to the safety of the woods.

"You must want to see my skates pretty badly to set up cameras to stalk me," she said.

"The lonely hobbies of a lineman. I put the camera on one of the electric poles after my dad and I saw you the other night. We were the idiots in the truck without headlights? Remember?"

"Ah, yes. I go skating late at night on the roads when there's no traffic. And I don't skate when I see cars, I just dive into the woods and let them pass. It's the only way I can road test Laverne and Shirley."

"Your skates are named Laverne and Shirley?" he interjected.

"Yes. Skating's my hobby, and I built my own. I'm a tinkerer. Except for auto body repair, as you saw in the parking lot." She watched him flick on his turn signal as they approached an empty intersection. *Attention to safety, probably not a murderer,* she concluded.

"You know, my dad came up with a nickname for you. He called you Photograph. He said that was the only way to 'catch a girl like that,' or something to that effect."

"Photograph. That's funny. Better than DJ." She looked out the window and watched the trees passing for a few minutes. Nick put on his blinker and pulled into his driveway. As Nick turned the ignition off, Dana grabbed his forearm lightly.

"Here's the rules. I am sleeping in *your* room and locking the door, thank you. You said you live with your dad, so tell him you know me from school and my car broke down. You don't mention the skates. You don't look in my bag. You wake up at six and drive me back to my truck."

"Sure thing."

"I'm serious: you don't mention the skates. If your dad brings it up, he's mistaken. That wasn't me. He's mistaken."

"Sure, okay."

Dana released her grip on his arm.

"Don't. Mention. The. Skates. Have you mentioned them to anyone else?"

"No, no, no. No! My dad didn't even bring it up the morning after we saw you."

"Before we go inside, I need to know how you tracked me to the bar, Community College Boy."

Nick uncurled the photos from his jacket and handed them to her. Dana took the good-faith gesture.

"I had a hunch you'd be in that area. The roads are long and straight around there, based on the grid maps I use at work. Power lines, property lines, roads. Anyway. Then I just guessed that you might be someone local, and there's only a few bars around."

"You're a clever boy," she noted, "and in my experience, clever boys are nice guys. Is there anything else you can tell me that won't trigger me to kill you in your sleep in a proactive strike?"

"I've spent a *lot* of money on beer in the past few weeks." He weakly smiled. "Don't tell my dad."

"Fair enough," she laughed.

"And just so we're clear," he countered, holding up his hands, "you're not going to rob us, right? Help yourself to the pantry, but we're not exactly *rich folk*."

"You and me both, buddy. *Nick*."

He opened the truck door silently and gingerly took out the house keys to avoid any rattling. He held the door for Dana after unlocking the deadbolt. As they walked into the dark house, Nick pointed to the bathroom door and made a formal gesture toward his room with a bow. She smiled at him while nodding and closed the bedroom door, which was followed by the click of the lock. Light snoring from his father's room droned in the background.

Nick sat down on the couch, set the alarm on his phone, and, for a change, pulled off his boots. He lay back, staring at the ceiling, and admitted to himself that she was probably the most attractive girl he'd met in a long time. He hadn't dated anyone other than Lindsey since high school; college classes and work kept him busy enough. It would be nice to hang with someone new, even as a friend . . . but, really, he just wanted to see her skates. He imagined the blueprints and technical specs for such amazing devices as "Laverne and Shirley."

As he closed his eyes, he heard a door lock unclick. A moment later, he felt Dana's breath on his ear.

"Tomorrow, can you show me those electrical grid maps?"

Chapter 5

Mr. Crowley – Ozzy Osbourne

Wearing his usual stoic expression, the man who had made a recent habit of sitting by the window at the Stroudsberg Inn scrolled through his phone, flipping through grainy photos of a small mass followed by a trail of sparks. He ran his fingers through his flattop and scanned the bar before leaning under the table to adjust the semiautomatic handgun strapped inside his boot. His second gun concealed under his arm didn't bother him as much as the boot holster, especially when seated on the barstool at a high table. He adjusted his pant leg again to ensure the ankle holster remained hidden.

He looked up and noticed that the female bartender was no longer behind the counter. He suspected it might be her break as he reran his mental head count of the patrons and staff visible in the room. He stood up to his full height of six feet two inches and walked out the front entrance to place a call from the parking lot.

"This is Ninety-Nine. I put a new unit under the asset's vehicle tonight. They keep falling off. Last night someone ran over it in the parking lot. I'm going to need something higher quality."

"We are not going to be handcuffed by a piece of over-the-counter tech."

"Yes, Mr. Rhodes."

"When the rest of the unit pulls in tomorrow, we'll have the additional hardware. Tail the new tracker tonight, and we will circle back on the asset extraction with the full team."

Ninety-Nine scanned the parking lot and saw a blond man in a Carhartt jacket walk around from the back of the bar. He noticed the young man's knees were covered in mud.

"Ninety-Nine, I am sure you do not need to be told this again but I must reiterate: We need the asset alive and that means not in critical condition. She's useless if she's unconscious or with her face swollen with a broken jaw."

"Affirmative. Have you made contact with the purchasing group?" Ninety-Nine salivated at the prospect of the payout that was looming over the mission as much as the satisfaction of completion. The opportunity afforded by Mr. Rhodes was a personal and professional apex.

"Yes. The parties are ready to pay upon delivery. I cannot stress enough the importance of the asset and the mission." Static momentarily spat out of the phone. "The spoils of war are not the keys to the kingdom but the keys to the treasury."

"Affirmative. Once I track her tonight, we can set the plan for extraction."

Ninety-Nine heard the line click as he finished his sentence.

Tom Pannet pulled over on the side of the road about three miles from the Stroudsberg. He pushed up the sleeves of his light-blue nylon windbreaker and searched through the trunk for a tire iron for the spare. As his usual luck would have it, it appeared he had run over a nail in the parking lot. He only noticed something was wrong after driving a few miles into the darkness of the Pine Barrens. Walking several miles back on this stretch of road seemed like a bad idea. There were no streetlights, just dark dense pine trees menacing the road with jagged shadows. Tom was a self-described "risk-avoidance specialist," and the boldest decision he had made in years was to get a yellow car, which he considered "flashy."

Not finding the tire iron, he decided to jack the car up to prepare to remove the wheel anyway, hoping a good Samaritan might stop to assist him if they saw the hard work was done, although he understood the reluctance of strangers to help someone with out-of-state license plates. He placed a magazine under his knee to avoid soiling his pleated khakis and, with an effort punctuated by several loud grunts, jacked up the front wheel a quarter inch at a time. As the tire had just cleared the pavement, he noticed the dull parking lights pulling up from behind. A well-polished black boot stepped out of the black Dodge Charger parked behind him, attached to a tall muscular man with a haircut reminiscent of the military or police.

"Hello! Oh, thank you. I don't know what happened. Well, I do, it's a nail, but anyway, I don't have a tire iron apparently."

"I have one in the boot," the stranger offered with a faint Australian accent.

"Come again?"

"The trunk." Ninety-Nine popped his trunk and grabbed the cross-shaped iron.

"Are you from Australia? I've never met a real one before. Wow, that makes you sound like a mythical creature! My name's Tom. I'm from New York." Ninety-Nine grunted an affirmation as he kneeled next to the car.

"Call me Sydney, then."

"Well, Sydney, thank you so much. I already jacked it up. I can do the iron myself," Tom offered as he kneeled beside the jack and ran his hand across the tire. "There's the nail. Right here. You can see it. It's right in front of that flashing light. I guess that's the new car sensor they use for monitoring efficiency?"

Ninety-Nine stooped down behind Tom and tilted his head. He noted that the tracking device was blinking in time with the vibrations on his phone. He pulled it out of his jacket and ran a hand across his broad jawline.

"I can do this for you, mate." Ninety-Nine subtly reached under the car and carefully peeled the tape off the tracking device. He slid the transmitter into the cuff of his sleeve as he returned to full height. "Is your spare in the trunk?"

"Yes, thank you. Oh, thank you so much."

Ninety-Nine walked behind the car and opened his phone to send a text:

BAD LEAD. NOT HER.

"Mate, you're lucky we crossed paths."

Tom stepped back into the road and held his phone as a flashlight. Ninety-Nine removed the lug nuts and rolled the old tire to the back. He glanced back toward the direction of the bar and watched the sparkle of headlights approaching. His phone vibrated in his pocket.

"Best to not stand in the road, little guy. Got any flares?"

"Yes, in my emergency duffel in the back seat!"

Tom eagerly opened the driver's side door and leaned inside. He tugged at the bag but one of the straps was caught on the emergency brake. Ninety-Nine looked at the reply on his phone:

DELETE LEAD IF NEEDED

He ran his gloved hand over his face before reaching down to his boot holster. The glare of the oncoming headlights flared in his peripheral vision, interrupted by a dark shadow.

"Got it!"

Tom pulled the bag out of the car and stepped back into the lane with a triumphant smile. The oncoming car blasted its horn. Ninety-Nine lunged and grabbed Tom by the collar with one arm, swinging the diminutive man over the hood of the yellow car and onto the shoulder of the road. The blaring horn of the passing car faded as it sped past them into the darkness.

"Oh my God, thank you!" Tom exclaimed as he stood, brushing the sand and dirt off his pants. "I didn't even see that car. You're like my guardian angel tonight."

"First time for everything."

Ninety-Nine glanced at the tire iron and knelt next to the spare. He attached it quickly and rechecked the other tires for any leaks before placing the tools and jacks into the trunk. He closed the lid and examined the license plate.

"You're not from around here, you said?" Ninety-Nine raised his eyebrow at Tom.

"No, sir, just winding my way back. What a wild night I've had. At least wild for me!"

"Are you going to tell the missus about your 'guardian angel'?"

"Oh no, just my cats. I have four at home. And I'll be sure to tell them all about you."

Ninety-Nine felt the vibration of his phone again. He pulled up on the cuffs of his gloves and scanned the road in each direction. He imagined a small apartment that reeked of cat piss, littered with empty microwave dinner trays and esoteric hobby magazines, awaiting the return of Tom.

"Well, drive safe, mate. Get that tire patched."

"Thank you again, Sydney." Tom extended a hand for an appreciative shake. Ninety-Nine shoved his hands into his pockets.

"Safe travels. Good night."

Ninety-Nine sank into the driver's seat of his Dodge and waited for Tom to pull on to the road. He had had his fill of collateral damage years ago, despite the continuing body count he accumulated for Mr. Rhodes.

"*Sydney from Australia.* You're lucky he was an idiot, mate," he muttered to himself.

The red taillights faded on the straightaway. Ninety-Nine pulled out the tracking device and held it between his thumb and index finger against the light of the moon. He frowned as he set the blinking black box device into his cupholder and opened his phone.

UPDATE?

He started the ignition and let out a slow sigh as he texted his reply:

GET ME THE DRONES

0:00   3:13

Chapter 6

One Tree Hill – U2

The three windowless rooms on the fifth floor of the General Accountability Office in Washington, DC, lacked any indication of a department logo or name. Unofficially, they housed the Department of Contract Audits, a task force so thin on staff they failed annually for a budget to maintain an internal website. Joshua Green sat amongst piles of papers and moldy file boxes that contained the parameters of his current project. His official title was Junior Counsel for Special Contracts, which was shared by the three other members of his team who also reviewed black-book financing for covert operations. He relished serving his country through cost reports and paper cuts versus stalking insurgents in jungle humidity or the prospect of being buried overseas as *persona non grata* as his family received a folded American flag. He did not explain his job at cocktail parties in any capacity other than to say he was in "actuarial accounting," which provided an easy conversational exit.

Joshua gazed at the silver framed photo of his wife, her auburn waves perfectly matching the wisp of hair on the head his newborn son seated on her lap. He refocused on the photocopied check on his desk. The payment recipient was not in his classified file of approved vendors. He squared his jaw before grabbing the folder to show his boss down the hall.

"Director Jameson? I've got something . . . I think," he stammered as he knocked on the open door of her office. Carmen Jameson was old enough to be his mother, speaking often with the same maternal authority, but had served in classified espionage before his parents had even met. Her silver hair was styled like his own neat, tight-cut brown hair, and her tall slim build also mirrored his own. She put down her phone next to a black plastic case containing three Purple Heart medals and folded her hands on her blotter.

"You think? Or you know?" She winked. "Give me the rundown."

"I found a set of payments where we have a double entry on the books. It may be an error from when we began electronic routing." He ran his finger under a line item at the bottom the page. "Let me rephrase that." He cleared his throat.

"You read my mind. Good. Always break it down for a superior. You never know what they know."

"Here's a series of payments from an active account. A contractor labeled OHR. When I go back to the date of the first deposit, it was when we apparently were retiring the process of payments done by manual paper checks."

"Right, we finally went to electronic deposits. It took us long enough, but that's the government." She flashed a quick smile.

He pointed again to the page. "On this date, about five years ago, there was a double payment of the same amount. Once by electronic deposit to OHR, and then another manual paper check paid out to someone named Colin Rhodes."

Director Jameson stared at the numbers and glanced toward the hallway.

"Get the door, will you?"

Joshua secured the office and sat in the visitor's chair across from her desk. She typed into her laptop and turned it toward him when she finished her file query.

"Joshua, while we are privy to many top-level projects, there are some that are more, how should I put it, *obscured* than others."

On the screen was a long list of projects with titles both familiar and unfamiliar to him. He scrolled down the results and stopped at a file name written as a string of random characters and numbers. He clicked into the file and saw the entire text was in encryption characters and symbols.

Director Jameson drummed her fingers on her desk as she started to speak. "Colin Rhodes was part of an intense armament project that was canceled. However, after an early retirement he came back and levied that information to incorporate his PMC."

"PMC? Private military company?"

"Correct. One Hundred Roads—clever pun—OHR. His proposal was aggressive: he pitched a silent force that could aid rebels in areas where we had yet to formalize operations. Kind of like a trouble-spot speculator."

Joshua studied the folder in his hand and rested his chin on his thumb. "I'm not following."

"Let's say that a group of unlawful combatants are working in an area for an organization that we do not sponsor. Rhodes's team would do the legwork before our first reconnaissance and before diplomacy is established. In theory, he would find groups we aren't aware of before they gain momentum, and then if necessary, drop the hammer." She lowered her glasses and pressed her gaze at Joshua. "They are preemptive *assassins* as needed."

He blinked rapidly as he processed the information from his superior. "Were any of these false flags?"

"False flags? Some, yes."

Joshua understood the level of secrecy that the unfolding details required, going way beyond his daily routine of auditing parts invoices for experimental planes and the room service bill for a SEAL team at a luxury hotel in Mumbai.

He also recognized that his clearance was muddy for this type of information, despite the "Top Secret" designation on his file.

"Are you telling me that these payments are legitimate?"

"It would *appear* so," she replied. "Rhodes pitched the project and offered to levy his payments as escrow into OHR."

"Escrow?" His thoughts moved away from the audit and toward a Pandora's box that he knew he should leave closed. The last time he had accidentally stumbled across an issue that he regretted discovering was when he completed his graduate work on British feudal financial mismanagement. His dissertation research led to him finding an embarrassing historical bond payment with five hundred years of compounded interest by the English government, and a call from Director Jameson to join her department upon graduation.

"This type of operation needs discretionary funds. We need to obscure the layers to ensure confidentiality and operational independence," the director continued.

Plausible deniability, he thought to himself as he closed the folder. "Ah, I see. So, as long as the payouts and escrow match up, we're good?"

"If you're trying to figure out the origin of this one double-entry accounting error, then yes, we're good." Director Jameson removed her glasses, placed them neatly next to her nameplate, and leaned forward. "Forensic auditing is not unlike forensic detective work. The older the body, the more it stinks."

He nodded slowly, patting the closed folder on his lap. "Alrighty! Well thank you much. I'll stay in my lane as appropriate."

Joshua walked back to his office and put the folder on top of an archival box sitting on his visitor's chair. He sifted through a pile of copied checks, left for dead in storage before the slow-moving migration to electronic payments, and watched a small envelope drop from the stack. The flap was not sealed, and the name printed across the front was faded and illegible from minor water damage that had dissolved the ink. He pulled out the contents: a check for an identical amount as the manual one made to Rhodes but to a different recipient.

Samuel David Jefferson.

0:00

3:13

Chapter 7

I Really Like You – Carly Rae Jepsen

I figure Meyers Road is as good a place as any for this." Dana scanned the tops of the trees from the passenger seat of Nick's pickup truck. Blue skies and pines of congruent heights lined the road from end to end. "It all looks the same to me."

Nick pulled his truck over to the sandy shoulder just past the turnoff for Meyers. Dana's black backpack was tucked between her feet.

"You know," Nick said, "there's something soothing to me about the sameness. You can be in any spot in the woods, close your eyes, and not know if you opened them five feet or five miles away. It's all just," he said with a slow wave of his hand, "the same. I like it. It's kind of Zen . . ." He trailed off as he stared off down the road. "The trees never seem to grow past thirty or forty feet. It's the same as when I was a kid." He sniffed the air. "Some things are better when they don't change."

Dana whipped her finger in the air in a circle. "It's a little too blah for me. Not somewhere I'd want to put down roots." She opened the door, swung her legs out, and began to unlace her chukka boots. "So, here's the deal. You get to see the girls in action, but then you let me see those electric grid maps." She zipped open the bag for emphasis. "And you help me with a little electrical engineering, schoolboy."

Dana pulled out the first skate. In the daylight, the dark gunmetal shin guards reflected the strands of sunlight that breached the pine needles above them. Small boxy housings over each ankle connected the shin guards to the boots. Each skate was affixed with a set of four inline wheels, giving them the appearance of repurposed ski boots. Nick leaned in closer and studied each wheel, wrapped in neatly aligned wires. He extended his hand to touch one of the skates. Dana snatched it away and strapped it to her foot.

"So, each of these boots has a pedalboard inside. It's pretty much like a Segway scooter platform, but one for each boot." She snapped the shin guard with a clang, and then retrieved the second skate. "It took me a good six months to figure out how to skate in a straight line for more than twenty feet without falling over. It's not like they came with instructions or a quick-start guide. After that," she said, winking at Nick as she closed the second shin guard, "it was easy breezy."

Dana leapt out of the truck onto the cracked and tar-patched asphalt. Nick walked around to the liftgate and pulled out a long wooden board, eight inches wide, and propped it up as a ramp to the truck bed.

"So, the big mystery I have to ask: Where *did* you get the skates?" he inquired.

Dana rubbed the heel of her gloved hand across the toes of her boots to buff out a smudge. "My dad designed these back when old-school skates were the thing, so the wheels have an alternate mode like this," she said as she clicked the heels. The four inline rollers on each skate pivoted into two pairs, front and back, like a classic roller skate. She then clicked the heels again to return to them to rollerblade style. "I can switch the modes for speed or maneuvering. Big picture, I think he wanted to make an ATV or jeep that used this design. But he never did." She cut herself short, hoping Nick would take the hint to not ask more about her father.

"How fast can you go?" Nick lifted his Honda CRF dirt bike by the handlebars and rolled it down the ramp. Dana scanned the bike with a hint of conspiracy.

"You got a speedometer on your little Schwinn there? And a helmet with Bluetooth?"

"Yes, I just have to—hey!" he exclaimed as she grabbed the phone from his hand once he pulled it from his front pocket. She punched in a number. He heard the phone ringing from his helmet speaker.

"Now you have my number." From her chest pocket, she pulled out a pair of shooting goggles. She tapped them on each eye.

"Impact resistant. Very necessary," she declared. Next, she unrolled her coat from the bottom of the backpack and held it up for inspection before she slid each arm into the sleeves.

"This is my haute couture. You fall down too many times, you learn to pad the right bits. Kevlar inserts, courtesy of the gun shop, in the forearms and also in the jacket tails"—she smacked her bottom over the coat—"because I'm still young enough to care about *mon derriere.*"

Nick started his bike and revved it with a flip of the wrist as Dana started to push off on one skate. Her wheels growled with the same sound, like a tornado, as the first time they saw each other. The grinding intoned by the metal wires wrapped around each wheel echoed slightly in the open road.

"Keep up, and I'll show you all the fun moves," she bellowed into her earbud microphone. "A few years of skating lessons were the best thing Mom ever bought me."

Nick shot off behind her, still fumbling with his jacket zipper as she separated from him. The speedometer needle ricocheted from zero to thirty as he flicked his wrists on the shifters in rapid succession, trying to pull up beside her.

She pushed off one foot occasionally as with traditional roller skating.

When traveling in a straight line in daytime, the sparks from the skates were dim.

"This is called an arabesque," she said, her voice crackling over the headset, while extending her left leg straight behind her and balancing on her right leg. The tails of her coat streamed straight behind her, parallel to her outstretched leg and the road below. "I can push the toes in my forward foot to speed up, and let off or hit the heel to brake," she demonstrated in time with her words. As she transitioned from move to move, the wheels adjusted, shifting from inline to pairs and back. The pavement responded with a pitter-pat sound in rapid staccato bursts of one-two-three-four as each skate's wheels crossed the seams of a recently repaired patch of blacktop.

"So, what kind of power cell do those run on?"

"Not done yet, Curious George. Want to see a jump spin? Here's my single axel!"

Without taking a breath, she whipped her back leg around to her front, leapt into the air, and pulled her arms inward during her flight. She landed facing backward on one leg as her speed remained constant.

"Pretty cool, am I right?? That cost me a few co-pays at the urgent care clinic until I figured it out!" Still facing Nick, she laced her feet one in front of the other, skating backward, then spun around to face front without losing any degree of road speed. Nick pulled his bike up beside her as she smiled openmouthed with her cheeks tightly pulled under her eyes. She scowled and spit out a bug. Nick laughed and pointed over his shoulder.

"Let's loop back. There's a side road past the old lumberyard we can use for a speed test. Plus, I really don't want to get caught by any drivers out here and have to explain any of this."

Nick began to arc back across the road to turn around when Dana's hand suddenly clutched his shoulder. Her other arm wrapped momentarily around his waist to power through the turn. She rode on one leg with the other pulled up to her chest.

"In my brief roller derby career, they called this 'the DJ' because it was the only way I could corner at high speed. It wasn't meant to be a compliment."

"Are you retired from derby?" he shouted over the engine noise of the motorbike.

"Not really, just debating if I'm going to keep doing it." She hesitated as she searched for the next signpost. They turned off Meyers Road at a stripped and weathered sign for Hardwicke Lumber, above an arrow emblazoned with "TWO MILES" in flaking black reflective paint.

"Open up," he yelled, to which she nodded approval. An orchestra of sound exploded from the skates as Dana pushed her toes forward, arms folded across her chest. Even in the late morning light, the effusion was almost blinding from the pavement behind her, popping like the magnesium flashbulbs of a bygone-era paparazzi mob. Nick twisted the throttle furiously as the dirt bike roared forward, the front wheel almost lifting off the ground during the sprint. He looked down at the speedometer.

"You crossed forty . . . forty-five . . ."

"Go for sixty?"

"It's your funeral, and we've only just become friends."

"So, we're friends now?" Dana howled as she pressed her toes deep into the boots.

"You got fifty-five. We're running out of road fast. You're going to see a pretty big gate coming up."

The dead end loomed ahead of the racers. The road was blocked by a ten-foot-high chain-link fence with a double-wide gate, chained across the middle. Across the center, a wooden FOR SALE sign dangled by one corner from the diagonal crossbeam.

"Seventy coming up, Dana. Hit the brakes. Brakes! Brakes, Dana, brakes!"

Nick let go of the throttle to rapidly decelerate behind her. He clutched the brake an inch too far, locking the wheels and throwing the bike into a skid. Up ahead, Dana compressed into a ball, clutching her knees before flinging her entire body upright in front of the fence.

Her heart beat so loudly in her ears that she barely heard her co-conspirator's screams for restraint. As she soared into the air, she drew her legs up and to her side, twisting and arching her back as she vaulted over the fence. Her descent was the twisted nemesis of her ascent as she splayed her arms and legs out, leading with one foot until it contacted the road. A metal cacophony and blinding flare erupted as her skate made contact and bounced her back upward into a protective ball. She bounced again, rolling across the cracked pavement and spinning to a stop more than a dozen yards from the gate. She collapsed to the ground, facedown.

"DANA! DANA!" Nick leapt on the gate and hoisted himself over. She groaned as she turned to face him, pulling off her eyewear.

"Shatterproof. Did I hit seventy?"

"I didn't even see the final number. Are you hurt? What hurts?"

She coughed out her reply. "I'm good. I'm real good. That was a first for me and Laverne and Shirley. Sure, we've jumped a few traffic barrels, a raccoon family, but nothing that . . . high," she finished, looking at the gate. "Wow. It looked smaller from, you know, eye level." She stood up and leaned forward on the skates, almost falling face-first into Nick. "Batteries are drained. That's what I'm going to need your help with."

"After we look at the grid maps?"

"And you give me a ride back on that scooter of yours."

"Back to my house?" he pondered.

Dana pulled her eyewear up and smiled.

"I guess you should take me back to my place, you lucky young man. I think I need to change my pants."

Chapter 8

Midnight — Joe Satriani

N ick looked back at his truck in the driveway and then ahead at the industrial barn in which Dana rented the converted attic studio apartment. Tucked far into the woods, it was only visible once you made the final turn past the sign for Deacon Landscaping. Dana was already halfway up the stairs on the side of the barn that led to the door to her loft.

"I could throw some killer parties out here if I actually made friends," she shouted from the landing.

"I am in complete agreement with that statement, and the sentiment." He shoved his hands into his coat pockets and shrugged his shoulders. The barn was far enough from the main road that the trees created their own white noise as they silently swayed and their branches slowly rubbed against each other. Dana waved him up. "Nothing wrong with being a little selective when it comes to friends," he replied.

Inside, the apartment spanned the entire footprint of the barn. Except for the bathroom, it was one large room, with a small kitchenette and a bed separated by a movable partition, which Dana slipped behind. She pitched her jacket and shirt over it on to the floor. Nick saw her costume change as a good time to sit down and moved her toolbox that sat open on the couch.

"So, here's my rundown, Nicky. I moved out here about a year ago. I'm looking for something that basically amounts to a MacGuffin from my grandfather and father, who were both stationed out here in days of yore." Her torn pants arched over the partition screen. "Somewhere, out in the Pine Barrens, is . . . *something*. I have a safety deposit box from a trust but no key, so . . ."

She stepped out from the screen wearing soccer shorts and a white tank top. Nick could not help but trace the lines of her legs, noting the discolorations from repetitive road rash and a number of old and new bruises on her thighs. Her arms fared much better. He supposed she could squat press a pickup truck and arm wrestle a black bear based on the sinew and thickness of her limbs. Dana seemed to notice his investigative stare, crossing her arms with indignation, not modesty.

"I'm *assuming* that whenever I can find this place, the location that my grandfather and dad wouldn't tell me about, then I'll also have the key to open the box or whatever they left me."

"There are procedures for safety deposit boxes if you're the next of kin, or some other legal means, aren't there? Why this treasure hunt?"

Dana uncrossed her arms and sat on the floor in front of the couch. "My dad, my grandfather, my family . . . they may have been very bad people." Although she had thought this for over a decade since leaving her grandfather during the gloaming of his time on earth, she had never said these words or anything to their effect out loud, let alone to someone she had only just met. "I need to know. I need to know how bad, or if they were just caught in a bad place following orders, or if I'm supposed to be following in their footsteps . . . or skates." She feigned a smile as she stood up.

She grabbed a laptop festooned with worn stickers of cartoon animals and power tool brands and deposited herself on the couch beside Nick. Pulling up a navigation website, Dana changed the view to overhead satellite photos of the entire county.

"Here's what I've got. The old military base footprint was here"—she traced a finger down an imaginary line—"but they added fencing outward, expanding it to here and here."

"Okay, usually the base owns what they own," Nick mused. "They don't annex land. If anything, they give it to another federal agency like the Pinelands Commission or Park Service. Maybe it keeps their liability with the same lawyers on retainer. Or maybe it's just the easiest paperwork? I'm making this up as I go."

"Right." She elbowed him gently. "Are you a lawyer, too? Big brains on the boy from the Barrens. So, why would this area"—she traced a finger slowly around a zoomed-in section of road—"be separate from the rest?"

Nick didn't understand her question. He leaned closer to the screen and followed her finger to a small square structure, perhaps a barn or a shed, and a road that seemed to be unconnected to any of the roads in the area around it, like an unfinished street forgotten by a municipal planner.

"That's an airstrip, maybe? It's very tiny, but it could probably be for old prop planes or a helicopter loading area."

"Mm-hmm. So, how do I get there? When I've been rolling around, I keep seeing trees and fences, trees and fences, but no access. And that kind of open area should be visible from the road. It's not far in past the tree line. Unless it's not there anymore."

She reached under the couch and pulled out a zippered canvas portfolio bag. She handed Nick a piece of thick cardstock from inside.

"I think this is where they worked. My father and grandfather."

Turning the paper over, Nick saw a faded color photograph of six men, all wearing military dress pants, ties, and long beige coats that looked like a hybrid of a science teacher's lab coat and automotive coveralls. They stood in the middle of a concrete pad that looked to be wider than several car lengths. In the background were dense pine trees. On one side, the trees were mature. On the other side, the trees were adolescents and interspersed with charred husks of old growth the same size as the living trees.

Nick slowly cocked his head and looked over at Dana, who was staring at the photo. She was resting her palm on her cheek and smiling.

"That's my dad, second from the left. And that's my grandfather."

Nick studied the image of a pale man with light-brown hair and pale skin. He cut to Dana's peanut-colored shoulders and thick black hair. She intercepted his gaze.

"My mom is Black."

"Oh right, sure." He cleared his throat. She leaned forward and placed her finger in the center of the photo.

"And that 'guy' in the back? He's called the Atomic Juggernaut."

Nick turned his gaze back to the photograph, and the details began to gel in his mind of what he was seeing. Behind the men in the center of the photo was a large metal-plated six-foot orb, almost shaped like an egg, centered on two squat broad-footed legs. The arms were outstretched as if to embrace the men on each end of the photo. Each shiny and rivet-riddled upper appendage ended in a stout and stubby three-fingered fist, with each phalange as thick as a fire hydrant.

At the center of its chest resided a rounded and blackened window, like a portal or nose gun from a World War II bomber. At the top was a "head" canopy covered in a lattice of metal strips. Nick assumed a pilot and copilot would sit in each window. He pored over each detail, lost in a swarm of thoughts.

"That is a weapon my family helped to create. And it has a body count attributed to it. And the people who died weren't the bad guys." Nick snapped back to her gaze and put the photo down.

Dana bit her lip. "Apparently, a lot of people were killed in the development. On purpose." She reached under the couch again and retrieved a metal lockbox, large enough to hold two thick phone books. "This was a parting gift from my grandfather on his deathbed. He left me instructions on where to find this lockbox, which was filled with papers and a bank book. The bank book, that was for the trust he created for me. I'm not an heiress but it's a safety cushion, and he gave me some funds that I used to develop the blueprints from my dad. Laverne and Shirley were in there on paper, but he never made them. There were a few other papers and clippings, maps and other things that I still don't know what they are, but inside the bank book was this." She retrieved a photocopied paper with a string of numbers. "I had no idea what these were, but it turns out these are GPS locations. My dad had the old-school coordinates right here . . ." She paused for emphasis. "For what's right there." She tapped the laptop screen and flicked her eyebrows up.

"So, you know where to go—that's great!" Nick beamed.

"Yes and no. When I put the coordinates into the map, they pointed me to here, south a few miles, but when I used the satellite photos, I saw the road, or airstrip, here."

Nick put a finger to his chin. He looked at the photo and the satellite image again. "It's the trees. They don't match."

He shot up from the couch and out the door. She heard him running back up the stairs, and then he bounded gleefully into the apartment and threw several electrical grid maps on the kitchen table.

"The coordinates are right. It's that the photos don't match." He unfurled one of the paper maps and grabbed any kitchen items in arm's reach to hold down the corners.

"There. This line is where the old forest fire ran. You had a line of trees on one side, and the road kept the flames from leaping over to the other side. That photo shows the old trees and new growth, so it would be somewhere along this line."

Dana brought the laptop to the table and leaned over Nick to slide it in front of him. He noticed that her sense of personal space was defined by a much thinner aura than his own, but he realized he didn't mind the intrusion.

"So, then, if we put in the coordinates, we show up here," she said, placing a large thumbprint on the screen, "but that's still in the middle of nothing. To be completely thorough, I went down that road a bunch of times, literally and figuratively, while snooping around."

Nick put his thumb right next to hers. Above each of their digits on screen was a tiny white triangle, almost indistinguishable until they both leaned in, almost touching foreheads. Dana took a quick breath.

"Is it me, or did they just cut a square of the satellite photo and paste it next to itself?"

"The government can do that. You can't get an aerial shot of the White House or Area 51 or, in this case, a slab of concrete in the woods."

Nick leaned back over the paper map. In the approximate area of the obscured satellite photo, he started to count a series of sequential circles.

"These markers indicate poles for power lines. Even the government a couple decades ago would have needed something to draw off. Solar panels back then would have been too big and inefficient. You can bury the line in the Barrens in the sandy soil if you're willing to pay for the insulation. Look here."

He tapped an imaginary spot between two circles. Dana observed, knotting her face as she focused.

"I thought X would mark the spot, clever boy." He smiled at her commentary. He impressed himself with how quick his logic was breaking down the solution to her enigma but also felt a surge of adrenaline from this secret hidden in the woods.

"Sort of. These indicate poles. Telephone poles, power line poles, but there isn't one here. This length from here to here is too long. Have you ever seen a power line sagging between the posts? That's because it takes a very specific distance to accommodate for the weight of a length of cable. If you had a wire stretch all the way from here to here, it would break under its own weight."

Dana darted her eyes between the map, the laptop, and Nick's gaze locked on her face.

"You're smiling like a dog who just got a belly rub," she said with a smirk.

"Maybe just a little."

"So, we go where there's supposed to be a pole, where the map is digitally altered, which is right next to the coordinates on a piece of paper I got from the lockbox of the damned."

"Yes! You got it!" he exclaimed, overjoyed by the treasure hunt he was now part of. Nick removed the various improvised paperweights from the corners of the map and began to roll it back up. He pushed the laptop over to Dana but noticed she had maneuvered directly between him and the door. He put his hands in his pocket and spoke carefully.

"One question: You said you needed a key to the safety deposit box? But you said all of this came from your grandfather's box, so you've obviously opened it."

She glanced sideways at him.

"Dana, what *aren't* you telling me?"

Dana wasn't surprised by the suspicion in his words, but his stance wasn't aggressive, instead rather confrontational. Her energy mirrored his as tension trickled down her arms.

"I do need a key for the lockbox. For the *second* box . . ."

Her breath was long and deep. This entire day had been moments of revelations for her, each one a small crack, breaking apart her shell until a fissure finally appeared. Her eyes welled up, and she looked through Nick before refocusing and submitting to his sharp gaze.

". . . from my dad."

Dana reached into her waistband and handed a torn white envelope to

Nick. She watched him read the letter slowly and carefully, digesting everything in the context of what they had just shared and discovered. She sensed he was attempting to organize the words into something actionable as he read, pausing sporadically to look up at nothing in particular.

My Dearest Dana,

I am so sorry I am not going to watch you grow up to become an amazing woman. This breaks my heart, knowing you are the output of everything that is perfect about your mother, and everything she makes me. As I write this, I am getting sicker and weaker, and I know this is going to be my time.

Your grandfather and I worked on many projects together for the United States government and its various armed branches. While I am most proud of the work that we did in what we call summit-level resolution photography, where we made lenses and cameras able to capture the most minute details, our folly is something you need to see with your own eyes.

We built a war engine, a mobile tank we called the Atomic Juggernaut. While we raced to work on the proper power supply—and I know I am close to a breakthrough—we powered this horrible machine with a subatomic power-plant battery, which we thought was shielded properly. As we ran through our tests, the pilots began to suffer from radiation due to leakage, and in my own stubborn thinking that I could make this work, I piloted the machine several times, infecting myself and risking my life.

Your mother was a beautiful and strong soul, as I know you will grow up to be someday. She blamed my father for what she deemed my death sentence, which is now coming true. Your grandfather and I did not see eye to eye on ending the program, even though we were responsible for the deaths of many fathers and sons. I suppose this would be an eye for an eye, as my own foolish pride also made me push for the program.

Dana, please know that what I did is not what I had hoped to do. I had hoped to engineer machines that could be used someday for civilian and peacekeeping missions. I had hoped to see you graduate from school and walk you down the aisle. The moment you were born I knew that the world needed to change, because my world did the moment you opened your eyes.

I am giving this letter to your grandfather to pass to you. Inside this envelope, there is a key that you will need to unlock something, which will be at my last assigned location.

I trust that my father, your grandfather, will do what is right. I also know that he may open this letter, so I have taken some precautions that I hope you will see. Use your head.

Please cherish the memories of your mother, and of me, every single day.

I love you, my dear Shooting Star,

Dad

Nick folded the paper and drew a deep breath. "My mom died when I was young," he said.

"Mine, too." Dana walked closer to Nick and put her hands in her waistband against her back. She looked down at the letter in his hands.

"When I turned eighteen, I opened the safety deposit box from my grandfather, and that letter was part of the pile of documents inside. The plans for the skates, papers, some photos, bank stuff, and that letter. The envelope was torn open already." She nodded at the envelope, then turned her gaze back to Nick.

"So, that's my baggage," she smiled sheepishly. "It's a little bit of kismet that I got to meet an electrical engineer, eh?"

"I'm studying to be one. I'm not certified. I mean, I do enough on the job and with my hobbies, but it's probably the same things you know. It's hard to earn money for school and work while trying to actually go to school. Takes a lot longer. I'm rambling, right?"

She held up her hand like a puppet and mimicked a mouth opening and closing. "That's okay. I think you have an honesty problem, and that's a good problem to have."

Dana walked across the room to a desk that was made from old two-byfours, which matched the bookshelf behind the couch. All her furniture was pieced together from discarded parts, some donated and assembled with Angela's help before their breakup. Nick fit well with the décor, and she appreciated not being judged by her lack of "stuff." She reached into a file organizer on the desk and splayed a set of blueprints across the table.

"Check this out. These were the plans for the skates. Well, it's one skate but I built the second one as a mirror of it." She turned the sheet over. The ink was visible as a faint stain that bled through to the other side. "There," she said, pointing to the inverse image of one of the circuit diagrams. Nick traced the lines with his finger as the diodes and lines were now visible on one circuit board as legible letters: D, A, N, and A in a row.

"Cute, right?"

"And pretty inefficient. Did you build them like that?" Nick scratched his head and reached across the desk for a pencil.

"I followed instructions like a good student."

Nick was oblivious to her reply. "I would guess the batteries last for an hour, maybe? Half hour? There's a terrible amount of resistance and burnout in this part alone," he said to no one in particular, but Dana assumed she was the audience. He drew some short lines in a few places on the sheet. "I'm thinking this should also be moved over here, and that's got to go." He put a dark slash through another part of the diagram. "You said you built these yourself off the plans?"

"Yes, professor." She gestured toward the makeshift bookshelf filled with old texts covered in plastic sleeves, some damaged where stickers and labels had been ripped off the spine. "I have about a dozen librarians who would arrest me for 'grand theft biblio.' And thank God for internet chat rooms. Not the ones you go to." He barely grimaced before she gave him an exaggerated wink. "You think you can clean it up?"

"I think I can do more than that." He flipped the blueprints over once and then a second time. "I think I can put Laverne and Shirley on steroids."

0:00   3:13

Chapter 9

LA Woman – Billy Idol

A gent Ninety-Nine sat on the trunk of his car, unbuttoning and rebuttoning the cuffs on his jacket, listening to the silence. He gave the appearance of casually relaxing on the side of the dirt utility road under the power lines, glancing intermittently at the tall towers that were beginning to blacken as the sun set behind them. The red sky at this time of day rebooted his memory to official missions in Qatar and unofficial missions in Queensland, Malaysia, and a few other locations even he would never mention in the corners of his own mind. He heard the faint whine of engines break the silence, approaching in a sound wave before he could see the thin dust clouds stirred up by thick off-road tires.

Two black Humvees and two large gray sport utility trucks drove in single file and parked in a fishbone formation when they reached his location, one of each type of vehicle on each side of the path with the Humvees in the back. The driver and passenger doors, emblazoned with flat black lettering reading OHR, immediately swung open.

"You guys are on time. But I'm always early, so I'm stilling counting it as late."

"Ninety-Nine, you missed your calling as a meter maid," said the young tanned driver of the first truck, pulling off his cap to reveal short dark hair segregated by a long surgery scar across the crown. "Just because your number is higher than mine," he said, tapping an embroidered 088 on his chest just above a dual ammo magazine pouch on his tactical suspenders, "doesn't mean I have to take your brand of manure without telling you to suck it from time to time."

"Eighty-Eight, you are my favorite. Or at least, of all the Eighty-Eights I've worked with, you're my favorite. You're also the only one alive."

Eighty-Eight smirked. He had first met Ninety-Nine during a black bag operation in the Outback, clearing out a local Aboriginal tribe on behalf of a land developer who was prospecting oil well locations. When the negotiations soured, the security detail was ambushed, and it was Eighty-Eight who piloted their Land Rover to an escape, adding a number of fatal pedestrian impacts to their collateral damage report. He became a reliable wheelman on later missions and was promoted when Ninety-Nine sold out the former Eighty-Eight to a Bedouin warlord in exchange for safe passage to the United States.

Two other men, marked as Thirty-Three and Forty-Four, approached with a matte black metal attaché case. Forty-Four, a small but athletic man with wiry tousled brown hair, opened it, expanded a small dish inside, and handed an encased phone to Ninety-Nine. Four other members of the team assembled at the back of the SUVs with a cooler and began to distribute sandwiches to each other.

"It's Mr. Rhodes, for you," Thirty-Three crooned with a slight French accent. His shoulder-length dirty blonde hair whipped across his pale face with the breeze. "S'il vous plaît." Ninety-Nine did not hide his derision to the fawning treatment. He had personally selected Thirty-Three from the French Foreign Legion for his demolition expertise, but he despised that the former Canadian walked about with the smug halo of the FFL training.

"Hello, Mr. Rhodes," Ninety-Nine bellowed into the secured phone. "Looks like the starting lineup is here, except for one truck, but we have the essential personnel. This should go right quick."

"Any further complications?" replied the firm elder voice on the other end of the line.

"None." He watched Thirty-Three walk into the grassy area beyond their cars, his light assault rifle at the ready as he walked the perimeter of the clearing.

"I should hope so. The ground team should be set with the drones. I told Forty-Four and Twenty-Two to use the commercial ones on the burner phone apps, and the other two drones you can use on the dedicated line so that I can monitor things. Based on your reporting, we should start them tonight on the watch." Mr. Rhodes punctuated his words with exacting emphasis on the hard consonants, which occasionally popped over the phone speaker.

"Affirmed. What is the window on our air ferry now that we have a defined hunting territory?"

"That's going to depend on the location of the facility, but I would assume we will use airport North 2 or South 2 with a two-hour land-and-load window."

"Washington Township or Cherry Hill airstrips," Forty-Four interrupted, directing his notation to Ninety-Nine, who sneered at the eavesdropping commentary. Forty-Four was the newest on the OHR payroll, and Ninety-Nine made a mental note that he should be the first lamb if there were any need of a sacrifice.

"Thank you, Mr. Rhodes," he said and then sighed. "Sir, if I may speak frankly, if this drags on much longer, this is going to be a real hump. And if our target doesn't cooperate—once we find her, that is—it's going to be a real mess."

"Noted. Remember we need her intact until otherwise dictated."

Thirty-Three emerged out of the tall foxtail grass as the sun slipped below the horizon, looking back at the deer trails that cut through the open area and disappeared into the woods. He gave a thumbs-up to Ninety-Nine. "Two deer stands. We don't want to sit here long," he announced. *He's a rookie, too*, Ninety-Nine thought, but Thirty-Three wouldn't hesitate on orders, even if he was signaling his disagreement or distaste. If there was one thing Legionnaires could be relied on for, it was their intensity when it came to subservience to a senior officer's commands when they were in a hot zone.

"I'm still waiting on the big bear and the dwarves," said Ninety-Nine as he did a quick headcount of the assembled agents. His biggest muscle and a set of twin brothers on the team were nowhere to be found. "Anything else, Mr. Rhodes?"

"Two items. One, get the drones up and in rotation in the next hour. Two, keep in mind that there is going to be a full-blown retirement by most of the team once we obtain compensation. It won't just be enough money to buy a little cabin in Turks and Caicos; it'll be enough to buy an island. Each of you. But that's only when the long game is done."

"Affirmative."

Mr. Rhodes hung up as Ninety-Nine finished his reply. The other agents went through the motions as if the mission was a milk run, but as the senior officer he understood that the beauty of their plan was not in the sale of the assets but the leverage of their "expertise" to the United States and other NATO allies once enemies of the state had built their own crude machinations. He did not believe in "false flag" conspiracies, yet he was now part of one, one that he believed was for the good of his adopted homeland. Eighty-Eight interrupted his musing. He was holding his phone high above his head.

"I've got the twins and the big guy. They got stuck in traffic getting off the Turnpike and are on the way. Should I send them to the next relay point?"

"Send them right to their lodging," Ninety-Nine replied. He glanced around the assembled team and popped the collar of his jacket. "Alright, you rats, get on with it. Thirty-Three, get an uplink to the server backdoors in the archives. We'll need to grab the tech specs. Forty-Four"—he pointed to his wheelman—"take my car to the wash and be sure to vacuum it out. And fill the tank, pup."

Chapter 10

What a Fool Believes – The Doobie Brothers

Nick stood in front of the door of his house for a moment, steadying himself to turn the knob. Dana poked him lightly in the shoulder to nudge him inside. He held the door open for her to enter first.

"Dad, this is my friend, Dana," he announced as they stepped inside. "Dana, this is my dad, Mitch. Mitch Andrews."

Nick's father spun around, a sock on one hand. His glasses rested just below the bridge of his nose and wiggled down to the tip as he smiled. On the table sat a shoebox of small spools of thread. Dana walked to the table and leaned over to peer into the box. She noticed the spools were organized by color and thread thickness, with duplicates of each underneath. She then looked at the sock before making eye contact with Mr. Andrews.

"Please don't tell me you're a clown who performs at birthday parties for kids," she teased as the elder Andrews stared quizzically at the young woman in a dirty leather jacket before him.

"I am not," he clarified. "Hello, Dana. I actually work for the electric company like Nick, or maybe he omitted that detail. You must be a new friend.

I don't recall hearing your name before." He rolled the sock slowly down his wrist and laid it on the table, then crossed his arms. He pursed his ruddy lips into an exaggerated pout. "I do moonlight as a tailor, but my other full-time job is protective father. You know how that is, I'm sure."

Nick felt the hair on his neck stand up. His father finally broke the silence, which was bordering on uncomfortable.

"Pretty girls always get the fifth degree!" he chortled while Nick blushed. "Please have a seat! If you plan to rob us, the good plasticware is in the top drawer, and the Tupperware *is* vintage." He broke into a broad smile and shuffled to the refrigerator. "Beverages, anyone?"

"No, thanks, Dad. Dana is a friend from . . . college. We're working on a couple projects together."

"Aha, good. Nothing better than girls getting into engineering. You know, Nick's mom had been studying that, even after he was born. I'm a big supporter of the 'Fem in STEM' movement."

Nick wiped a sweaty palm across his face. Mr. Andrews didn't seem to care that he was embarrassing his son.

"Honestly, I'm just glad she's not a paintball buddy. You need more friends who have bigger goals. You run with the wolves, you become a wolf. You run with the gazelles—"

"You live terrified of lions?" Dana interjected. The men stared at the words hanging in the air until they dissolved. "What, too grim?" She lifted an eyebrow as she searched for approval.

"I like you. You can date Nick if you want. Dad permission granted."

"Full disclosure: I'm only using him for his tools," she said, gently shrugging off her jacket. "Although once our project is done for class, he can ask me to prom."

"Dana, do you want anything to eat while we're here?" Nick interrupted, feeling the heat in his cheeks from his pending death by embarrassment. "We're not poor, just a bit spartan. We have a pretty stacked fridge, and Dad's learned my mom's cooking. He has it down pat."

"I'm good, but thank you," she replied. At the same time, Nick's dad slid an empty glass across the table before grabbing a pitcher of iced tea. "And thank you, wise elder." She winked and poured her own drink before Mr. Andrews could accommodate her. "I was wondering if the smarts might've skipped a generation."

Nick took the opportunity to get out of the kitchen. He walked to his room down the hall and kneeled down next to his bed. He rolled out a long and shallow storage tote from under it. Looking through the tiny tools and magnifying goggles inside it, he pulled out a variety of precision instruments and several notebooks filled with large formulas, the neon fringe of several bookmarks peeking out the tops. After placing everything in a knapsack and zipping the bag, he felt a droplet of sweat roll down his jawline, likely the result of his anxiety over Dana being in his house again, his father's loving but performance-heavy hosting style, and the increasing checklist of things he wanted to do to, and with, Dana's skates.

From his mostly barren desk he grabbed one last notebook and stopped to gaze at the family photo of him and his parents, set in a Popsicle stick frame he had made in first grade. He ran his finger across the top and looked back at the doorway of the bedroom, where Dana was now standing. He handed her the frame.

"I made that. All the other kids just made a basic frame for Mother's Day, but I added the little corners and made the easel for her after I brought it home from class."

"She's pretty." Dana looked deep into the image of Mrs. Andrews. She was naturally pretty, a prototype for Nick's angular features and sandy-blonde hair. Dana glided her finger over his mom's hair, mimicking the wind that blew through it when the photo was taken. She regretted not having more photographs of her own mother. Her memories were an amalgam of a handful of pictures, locking her mother's dark skin, soft facial features and cat eyes into specific angles framed by the same hairstyle of short black hair. She wasn't sure if she would even recognize her mother if she walked into the room right now.

"I was just a kid when she . . . I mean, early teens, but definitely a greenhorn to life," Nick continued. "It didn't mess me up too much, not any more than the usual teen angst. Dad steered me into electronics, which was a good 'left brain versus right brain' getaway. It helped me . . ." He paused. "To distract myself. I had to get a job as soon as I got my working papers. Anyway, sorry about Dad teasing about the dating stuff. I don't make the best choices in that department. Nothing to read into, but I should have prepped you for that."

"You don't have to prep me for anything. If you prep too much, you don't learn to think on your feet!" She kicked a leg up, her boot stopping at shoulder level, nearly hitting Nick in the face. "You flinched!"

"I did not!" he exclaimed, laughing. He handed her the knapsack as he grabbed the final notebook.

As they headed out the front door, Mr. Andrews nodded at the pair and winked at his son. Dana walked to the car while he stopped Nick with a firm hand on his shoulder. "Is this an all-nighter type of thing?"

"I'm not sure. I'll be back late tonight or tomorrow. I'll take a sick day if I have to."

"Okay. She's welcome here anytime, by the way. If you guys need the space, you can work on your project in the garage. I'll rearrange the bench. The only thing I have going on is that upgrade on your dang paintball guns." He leaned around Nick to look at Dana getting into the passenger side of the truck. "You have my permission to outgrow paintball, son."

Dana tossed their bags behind her into the cabin and then pointed to an imaginary watch while pretending to glower at Nick.

"I think we're winging it, Dad."

"And one more thing, Nick." He lowered his voice and avoided eye contact. "That's Photograph, right?"

Nick froze. "What?"

"The girl we saw a few weeks ago, the one I called Photograph, that's her, right? I'd never forget that face. I'm guessing you're not working on a school project." He gave his son a concerned glance followed by a warm smile. "Like I said, you're welcome to work here if you need to. I know discretion. Her secret is safe here."

Nick held up one finger to Dana to indicate he needed just one more moment with his father. "Dad," Nick said, lowering his voice, "just pretend she's not the girl we saw, for now. Unless she tells you, can you keep cool?"

"Nick, I get it. Her secret identity is safe with me. Now go do whatever you're off to do." As his son began to break away from their familial conspiracy, Mr. Andrews tapped him on the shoulder.

"Does Lindsey know you're hanging out with another girl?" His eyes stared over his glasses at Nick.

"No. And I think we both know it's probably a good thing for her not to know. I don't want to get my ears chewed off. But it's not a big deal. Just don't mention Dana if she stops by." He curled his lips and steeled his jaw. "We're on a break anyway." Mr. Andrews nodded once and waved to Dana. "Thanks, Dad."

As Nick got into the truck, he observed Dana's hands deep in her backpack, fiddling with her skates. She had already turned on the ignition and was humming along to the oldies station that she had located on the radio. As he backed out of the driveway, she gazed over at Nick's house, lingering for a moment on the faded mailbox sitting on a new cedar post.

"I like your dad. He seems nice. You're lucky you got a good one." Nick nodded with a blank stare. "You know where we're going tonight, right?" she asked.

Nick put his phone in the holder mounted on the dashboard and twisted it to face her. "Put in the coordinates. Let's see what we dig up."

The truck plodded down the county road and faded into the blackness and silence of the pines as Mr. Andrews watched from the stoop. When the taillights faded from red to maroon to nothing, he retreated indoors, still smiling.

0:00   3:13

Chapter 11

Undertow – Mr. Big

Dana and Nick plodded through the mix of sand, gravel, and pine needles adjacent to the paved road. He occasionally looked back over his shoulder to where his truck sat, about a quarter mile behind them where a break in the pines allowed him to park out of sight of any passing motorists. Traffic was nonexistent at this hour of the night, but he wanted to ensure they did not arouse any suspicion with their scheduled trespassing session. He held up his phone to affirm the GPS directions had pointed them toward the correct coordinates before returning it to his pocket next to his keys and a small penlight. Dana skipped ahead, humming, until they reached the next wooden pole supporting the faintly buzzing power lines that loomed over the road.

"Pole, pole, pole," Dana softly muttered each time they walked under another set of suspended cables. She stopped at the foot of the next support and adjusted her backpack as she looked up. She pointed to the dark cylindrical transformer suspended like a pirate ship's crow's nest and made a gesture back toward the woods. Sprouting from above the electrical line was a second heavy cable that ran perpendicular to the road and into the cluster of dense pines. Nick glanced at a photo of the electrical grid on his phone and inspected the cable's dark tentacle reaching into the woods.

"This is our missing pole. And that's a live power line going in." He squinted and then blinked as his eyes readjusted from the illuminated phone screen back to the darkness surrounding them. Running parallel to the line, across the sandy forest floor, he saw two partially overgrown tracks spaced about the width of a car. He knelt and ran his hand across the weathered and worn tread scars in the dirt. They looked to have been heavily used in their prime, but now they were remnants of a former road that led to mysteries suppressed in the trees.

"Dana, I think this is it," he whispered. "Do you want to come back in the daytime when we can see better, or at least bring something more useful than this?" he asked, retrieving the penlight and illuminating a small yellow circle to demonstrate the lack of lumens.

"We're here, let's keep going," she countered, strutting past him along the tire tread ruts. "I can smell the adventure! And a hint of pine."

After a short walk along the access road, they came to a tall chain-link metal fence topped with barbed wire, the gate chained shut. Nick smirked and pulled a wire-cutting tool from his back pocket. Dana glanced back at the road, which was surprisingly obscured despite the short distance they had traveled. By the time she turned back to the fence, Nick had already snipped a handful of chain-link connections and rolled back a section large enough for them to duck through.

The tiny crunching of pine needles under their feet was disproportionately loud in the peaceful night as they followed the coordinates and the phone's navigation. The sound of their footfalls abruptly changed as they crossed from soil to fractured concrete, laced with weeds and tiny wildflower hedges in every nook and cranny. They stopped together with a wordless acknowledgement of the vast opening in the woods before them, a retreat from the density of the trees. Ahead of them was a concourse that likely once served as a road or runway, now abandoned and left in a state beyond neglect. The moonlight that broke through the clouds added further incandescence free from the barrier of the elder tall boughs that fought to obstruct the sky.

"This is it," Dana said incredulously. "Nick, this is where my father worked. This is the place!" She broke away from the trailhead and jogged across the pavement, surveying the emptiness.

"THERE!" Dana cried and then bolted across the pavement. She pointed toward a squat concrete block on the other side of the manmade clearing. Beyond the far edge, a white and faded concrete trapezoid had been built partially in the ground. Nick ran to join her and studied the structure as he slowed his approach.

The building had a recessed entrance entombed in the earth. Under the edge of the overhanging concrete awning, Nick saw a large rusted hatch half embedded in the earth. There was no visible lock or other obstruction to restrict access, and an inspection by Nick's hands and tiny penlight revealed no latch or handle.

"HERE!" Dana boomed over his shoulder and directly into his ear. She leaned over Nick's back and pointed to a small circular recess that held a tiny metal access panel no bigger than a credit card. With a small application of muscle, she liberated it from its rusty hinge, revealing a clean and preserved keypad with a digital screen. The LED screen faintly pulsed with a yellow-and-orange glow as a formerly hibernating power source from beyond the door awakened.

"What's the code? Did you bring it?" Nick's excited voice felt too loud in contrast to the silence of the woods. The mystery ahead shook his senses and quickened his pulse.

"I don't know it. All I was left was a photocopy of a paper with GPS coordinates, remember?" She produced a crumbled paper from her jacket pocket and held it up to Nick. The clouds overhead swept in front of the moon and added a layer of darkness to their situation.

"Wow. Just wow." Nick grabbed the paper and sat down on the concrete, staring up at the night clouds.

"Scooch over." Dana adjusted the tails of her jacket as she sat down on the stone pad next to him.

"Why would he give you a location and no code?" he asked. "Unless the keypad was put in after he left?"

"If this a number I'm supposed to just somehow know, he should have left a clue." She watched her words transform into tiny wisps of breath as the temperature began to creep further down.

"Ok, so what numbers are important to you? What would your dad think you would never forget?"

"I don't know . . . birthdays, 867-5309, my locker combo for each of the three high schools I attended, which he wouldn't know. Damn. It's not *my* idea of a memorable number, it's *his*. It was always him and my grandfather who came here." She snatched the paper from Nick's hand and blew a long breath out from her lips, allowing them to rumble in a raspberry.

The clouds parted again, and she held the paper up against the moon. The torn piece of photocopy was nearly transparent. Suddenly, she smiled broadly and began to laugh.

"Oh my God, is it invisible ink? Or is it something hidden in the watermark?" Nick asked, leaning over to peer up at the paper with her.

"No, dummy. This is a photocopy of a piece of paper, and I tore it in half." She pointed to the rough edge on the bottom. Along the jagged bottom, her finger traced a pattern of stray marks, a few dashes and lines that formed the top of a scribbled word. "I didn't realize what it meant when I was going through the papers. It said 'Sparkles' on the bottom."

Nick squinted and saw that the lines and curves would have matched the top half of "SPARKLES" if written out in capital letters.

"That was my grandfather's dog's name. Stupid giant poodle." She lowered her voice and shook her head. "My grandpa loved that dog more than my dad, and I'm only half kidding."

She jumped to her feet and ran back to the keypad. Nick caught up to her as she stared at the numbers.

"So 'Sparkles' spelled on the keypad would be . . . checking my phone . . . ah-ha! 7-7-2-7-5-5-3-7," she muttered as she typed. She leapt back and made a gesture as if presenting a prize, but nothing happened. Nick stared in disbelief at the keypad and his coconspirator, who held a grin and a theatrical pose.

"Did you hit the Enter button?" he murmured.

"There is no Enter button! It's just a keypad with ten digits."

Suddenly, a sharp crack and a loud low whirring belched from beyond the entrance. Nick and Dana both pulled and pushed against the metal door without any knowledge of how it opened. The whirring continued to ascend in tone until the door at last jerked to the side, breaking free of the rust and warping caused by decades of neglect. The heavy panel landed in the recess with an echoing thud. Beyond the entrance maw, a set of tiny lights struggled to illuminate a short staircase descending out of view into the earth.

"Sparkles. He used his dog's name as a password to secure a people-murdering government project. Sparkles."

"He didn't mention any robot versions of Sparkles or, say, poison darts by chance?" Nick asked, peering into the dark opening.

Dana slid under his arm and leapt onto the first concrete step. "We're in it now, buddy. If there are any surprises ahead, your guess is as good as mine."

She reached over to a thin handrail and hit it three times with her fist. The pings echoed into a larger area beyond.

Nick swallowed. "Robot dogs that shoot poison darts would be *perfect* right now."

3:13

Chapter 12

Ice – Sarah McLachlan

The air did not smell as stale or feel as cold and wet as Dana imagined it should in an abandoned vaulted military facility. The slate-gray concrete walls were dry, evidence of a tightly sealed bunker, and there was little dust or decay. The short set of stairs at the entrance led down to a set of large, thick glass double doors with no handles or locks. They had been propped open by a pair of cinder blocks. Dana adjusted her backpack on her shoulders and touched the glass with her hand, imagining her father opening the doors with his back as he carried a lunch bag and a coffee on his way into work. Or perhaps an armed guard opened it with a greeting every day as her dad flashed an ID badge. She stepped through and onto the platform beyond.

"Holy crap on a stick, Nick. Look at this place," Dana gasped with wide wild eyes. "This is the bee's knees of secret spy shit."

Nick stepped forward and joined her in examining the room. They were on a terrace that ran the perimeter of the entire facility and was barely visible on the opposite side of the chasm in the dim emergency lighting. In front of them, a spiral staircase dug into the floor with blackened tendrils of polished metal that lead down into a large cavernous workshop. There was a large circle of tables, cabinets, computer terminals, and lockers, which were organized into stations, each bearing identification plates. Dana saw that each grouping of equipment was accented with a different color of paint on the furniture as well as demarcated on the floor in matching tape: red, orange, green, blue, yellow, and purple. Each station was aligned so that it faced into the center of the vast grotto, where a towering metallic sarcophagus appeared to be the focus for the long-departed scientists and soldiers who once worked on the premises.

The significance of this place was not lost on Dana. This room was part of her legacy revealed, a thin sliver of light on her family history. But she was not experiencing a moment of joy or resolution but rather confusion, as if hundreds of papers had been thrown into a document shredder and she was left with the task of piecing them all back together. She looked across the bunker, thumbs tucked under the straps of her backpack as if she was unsure whether to leave or stay. She jumped when Nick lightly tapped her elbow.

"Let's go down. Start somewhere," he suggested.

Once at the bottom of the spiral staircase, they approached the first workstation. "Let's see what we have here," Nick said as he ran his finger through a light coating of dust on the lip of an otherwise orderly desk. Each work area was similar in build but appeared different in function and accessories. The first area, outlined in blue, was home to circuit boards and processors, microbatteries, and a tiny army of magnification scopes. Nick pointed to each station in succession and announced the color accents.

"Yellow, green . . ."

"Tiny little college campuses," Dana joked.

Each space was like a mini technical school of varying engineering and scientific disciplines. The area outlined in yellow had plates of various materials cut to the same form and shape, as if dedicated to advanced blacksmithing or body work. The area outlined in green held a disproportionate number of books on chemistry and biology. That section was also distinct for the lack of physical tools offset by devices for measurement.

Nick inspected the desks for similarities, and at each one he found a journal accompanying a nameplate for whom he assumed had been the workstation's main technician.

"Jacobsen. Hardy. Geissler. And these two," he said, pointing at two adjacent areas where the desks had been pushed closer together. "Jefferson Jr. and Jefferson Sr." He waved Dana over. "Anyone besides you have a first name in your family?"

"Samuel. Sam," she said. "Colonel Samuel David Jefferson Sr. and Major Samuel David Jefferson Jr. Grandfather and father of Dana Janelle Jefferson." She put her hands in her pockets and took a deep breath. "My mother was Simone Florence Jefferson, her maiden name only revealed to my bank and boarding school principal." She faked a smile, seemingly treading carefully though her memories. She pulled the two nameplates for the Jeffersons off their desks and handed them to Nick. "I want to keep them."

"Just these two?"

She cocked her head and scrunched her face in imitation of deep thought. "Why not all of them? Might as well collect the whole team." She winked at him as he dug his nails into the adhesive backing on the nametag on the next desk.

"My dad is Mitchell Duncan Andrews. And I'm Nicholas Mitchell Andrews, in full," he said as he liberated the remaining tin nameplates off each desk and organized them in a tidy pile on the desk closest to the exit. "And my mom was Josephine, but everyone called her Josie, except Dad. He called her Mrs. Andrews. Even at the funeral." It was Nick's turn to fake a smile. She smiled back as a thank-you for sharing. She couldn't remember if her parents had even *had* funerals because she was either too young or too confused by each loss to sustain any memories. Her cold final conversation with her grandfather seemed to have painted over several happy murals of her childhood. It felt odd to be jealous of Nick's trauma, but she had no clarity to share with him, just a bunker full of enigmas. She snapped her attention back to the void around them.

"Let's check this out." Dana wheeled around to a locker and opened it. Hanging on the inside hooks were a flight suit coverall and a lab coat that looked like the ones they had seen in the photo of her dad from her lockbox. "Captain Hardy," she said, reading a name tag pinned to the chest. "I guess he was the pilot? Or maybe everyone was a pilot? That doesn't make sense."

Nick walked over to another locker and opened the door to reveal a similar flight suit, but much worse for wear. "This one says Captain Jacobsen." In unison, they both jogged toward her father and grandfather's desks and opened the lockers nearby.

"Senior's. Empty." He slammed the locker shut.

"Junior's. Empty." She gently closed the door partially and turned to Nick. "I guess not everyone was a pilot. Really, I was hoping for a key dangling on a rabbit's foot keychain or something."

"So would now be a good time to address the eight hundred-pound gorilla in the room?" Nick pointed at the metal sarcophagus in the center of the complex.

As her eyes became more accustomed to the dim lighting, Dana could now see the pattern of metal strips riveted together around the monument. Unlike most of the surfaces in the room, this one appeared to be dirty, heavily scratched, and scarred, especially along the widest seam that ran from top to bottom. Nick circled the massive structure, noting the height was at least twice his own. There were no apparent latches, hinges, keypads, or locks upon investigation. He ran his hands across the side at the same height as his eyeline until he felt a circular plate about three inches across, obscured by a thin layer of dust. It effortlessly spun open, revealing a dense piece of dark glass. His penlight faded and flickered as the battery drained. He pulled out his cell phone to use the light and shined it into the portal.

"It's a window, I think, but I can't see anything in there," he declared, then tapped the phone on the metallic mass. "It's empty, I think."

Dana sidled up to him, touched the glass, and then squatted. She tapped the floor with a notebook she had taken from her father's desk. Her fingers ran down the spine and around the front cover before she opened it. She leafed through the pages, taking in his sloppy handwriting in sentences and mathematical formulas scrawled on each sheet. She paused when she saw a page covered in red ink that matched her mother's penmanship. Another page of her corrections followed. Dana flipped ahead and read a page of her parents' banter discussing the strength versus conductivity of various alloys, and it was like she could hear their voices through their phrases and punctuation. In the margin of one page, she found a note from her father that said "birthday present for Nina" and a date close to her own birthday. She wondered if she ever met this "Nina" or if she was on the staff here once upon a time. Dana closed the book and glanced back at his desk, then at the sarcophagus.

"What the hell am I looking for?" she yelled, pausing for the echo to fade. "What the hell am I doing here? Who are these people?"

She felt the tears before she was aware she was crying. Ashamed of her lack of control, she put her head between her knees and sobbed, a mixture of frustration and sadness mixed with impatience and anger overflowing from inside her chest. The emotional release blindsided her. She was not prepared to feel this vulnerable, and a bit clueless, in the middle of a top-secret bunker in the heart of the Pine Barrens of New Jersey.

"And where's the big dumb robot thing from the picture?" She snorted as she wiped her nose.

Dana lifted her head and saw Nick standing over her with his face looking away. At first, she thought he was avoiding eye contact, until she saw the red beam hitting the top of the sarcophagus that held his attention. It was steady and only faintly visible, except for the line traced in the faint dust particles. They followed it back across the open room, up to the terrace, and through the double glass doors where they had entered. Nick placed a finger on his lips.

"Someone's up there."

Chapter 13

Lack of Communication – Ratt

Ninety-Nine approached the concrete bunker with his SIG516 rifle butt firmly planted on his shoulder. He preferred to avoid using night vision goggles when possible to keep his focus sharp and his other senses in play. He slid his index finger to the laser sight toggle and switched it on, aiming the red beam into the open circular doorway ahead of him. At first, the only sound was his breathing, but then muted echoes of a conversation rose faintly out of the darkness ahead. Suddenly, he picked up a barely audible whining hum in the distance behind him. He lowered the muzzle by five degrees and turned to see Eighty-Eight coming out of the woods, holding a drone control pad. The whining grew momentarily louder as the drone descended from above the pine trees to land on the cracked concrete between them.

"Two people went in, male and female. She looks like the girl from the aerial view," declared an ecstatic Eighty-Eight. "She's got a pretty distinct jacket." He gave a thumbs-up to his superior as he clipped the drone control pad to a carabiner on his web belt and unholstered his sidearm.

"Silent," mouthed Ninety-Nine. He crept closer and stooped down just in front of the entrance. Coming up on Ninety-Nine's left flank, his subordinate craned his neck to spy over his shoulder. Ninety-Nine stepped inside and took one stair at a time, pausing on each step to adjust the laser sight down until it hit the landing. He noted the area ahead was dimly lit and the voices were growing in volume.

Without warning, a female screamed, "WHAT THE HELL AM I LOOKING FOR?" The sudden wail did not shake Ninety-Nine's nerves but Eighty-Eight flinched, his foot slipping and kicking the back of Ninety-Nine's legs out. Ninety-Nine slid down the staircase, catching himself on the second to last step with his heel, instinctively locking his arms and the rifle at the ready, aimed into the cavern below. The laser sight had come to rest at the top of a large cylindrical object in the center of the room. The owners of the voices were just out of sight, under the visible edge of the balcony in front of him.

"Sorry," whispered Eighty-Eight.

Ninety-Nine strained to listen to the voices, one male, one female. He noticed a light begin to fill the stairwell. There was a brief flash of red then blue, repeating, beyond the mouth of the bunker behind them. He slowly turned his head to Eighty-Eight.

"We're going back up."

Ninety-Nine toggled off the laser sight and took a deep breath. Eighty-Eight glanced up toward the entrance. A voice crackled over a loudspeaker.

"Police! Come on out, kids! Let's go!"

Ninety-Nine furrowed his brow and pointed at his subordinate.

"Did you use the bolt cutters on the gate?"

"Yes."

"Did you hide the bolt cutters in the brush like I said?"

"Yes."

"Did you close the gate latch and thread the chain through the links when you were done?"

"I didn't think of that."

"It's a deterrent that slows down anyone in here from getting *out* as well as anyone outside from getting *in*." He stared at the red and blue flashes on the walls. "It might have kept the police from just driving on through. Lesson learned?"

"Lesson learned. I got this." Eighty-Eight tucked his gun back into the holster and rotated his belt around his waist to conceal the firearm behind his hip, leaving the remote for the drone now at the front. "I'll go first," he whispered to Ninety-Nine.

Stepping out of the tunnel, Eighty-Eight was immediately hit with a spotlight. Concealed by the shadow of Eighty-Eight's profile, Ninety-Nine crept up the stairs and into a defensive crouch just inside the doorway.

"Officer Sanchez, New Jersey State Police," the officer shouted while swinging the mirror-mounted spotlight to the drone sitting in the middle of the concrete. "This area is government property. Trespassing and flying drones at nighttime is a double no-no, kids. You can thank the good Samaritan that complained about your drones later." As he swung the light back, he caught a glint from the barrel of Ninety-Nine's rifle, tucked just above the cement berm.

"Put the gun down and stand up. Now!"

Eighty-Eight stepped toward the trooper and then to the side with his hands raised at waist height. Ninety-Nine slowly rose, not yielding his rifle.

"Sir, put that down now," commanded Officer Sanchez. His voice began to shake, clearly recognizing that the rifle was a fully automatic military issue.

"We're private contractors with One Hundred Roads, and this is official government business," barked Ninety-Nine. "Officer, we're going to need you to keep your piece holstered while we sort this out."

"I'll need to see some ID, sir, but you can grant me the mutual respect of our posts and lower that stick," replied the officer as he slowly lowered his hand on his holster. During the exchange, Officer Sanchez moved imperceptibly to standing behind the open door. The door was not fully armored against a military rifle, but it could slow down a bullet enough to prevent taking a lethal shot. He took in a full breath of air to relieve the tight feeling of his bulletproof vest under his uniform.

"Officer," yelled Ninety-Nine, "let us take care of this. *We* are in control here. Head back to HQ."

"Sir, lower the gun," countered Officer Sanchez.

"Officer, go back to your station." Ninety-Nine stared to the side of the glaring spotlight to adjust his vision.

"Sir, lower it! I have another unit inbound," the officer shouted.

"You haven't requested backup, or they'd be here already. Let's not waste anyone else's time and let us handle our jurisdiction." Ninety-Nine leaned into his lies, a control tactic he found most useful when dealing with militias. "We'll have our boss send a write-up to your boss in the morning. We'll even save you the paperwork. Now let us finish up here, please."

"I'm calling this in now." Officer Sanchez nudged his chin toward the walkie-talkie strapped to his shoulder and moved his hand to open the line to call in.

"Damn it, man," Ninety-Nine whispered. "I'm sorry."

Eighty-Eight reached his arm back and pulled his sidearm, whipping it toward the state trooper and firing. Office Sanchez dropped the walkie-talkie and unholstered his own piece to return fire from behind the SUV door. Ninety-Nine fired a pulse of bullets at the vehicle. The radio mic cackled with static as the clearing returned to calm.

Ninety-Nine paused and swept the perimeter before advancing to inspect the damage. The state trooper lay next to the SUV, which was riddled with bullets across the open driver's side door. He motioned to Eighty-Eight with a swirling gesture and pointed to the drone on the abandoned tarmac.

"We are in the shit sticks now. We can't be here when backup arrives. Evac."

"But he didn't call for backup!"

"Someone knows he's here on a call, and we're on a clock now for when they check back with him." Ninety-Nine straightened his arm and winced. "We were out of options."

Eighty-Eight nodded, grabbed the drone, and sprinted toward the path. Ninety-Nine outran him, passing him through the open gate.

"We're leaving them inside?" asked Eighty-Eight between breaths as he peered over his shoulder at the concrete block shrinking behind them as they ran.

"We just expended rounds we weren't expecting to use, and now they have the fortified position and whatever weaponry is in there. We don't even know how many entrances go in or out. We found them once. We found this place. We regroup and come back ready." He grit his teeth, visibly frustrated with the sideways turn of events. "Come on."

Beside his SUV, Officer Sanchez lay on his back, his chest slowing heaving as blood spattered out of his mouth with each cough. His breath floated up toward the moon, framed by the jagged peaks of the pine trees.

Chapter 14

Take Me Home Tonight – Eddie Money

After spotting the red laser, Dana and Nick had crept to the bottom of the spiral staircase, just in time to hear a verbal exchange unfold between three men, one of whom seemed to be a police officer. There was no other way in or out of the bunker that they knew of, so taking their chances on talking their way out of whatever was unfolding looked to be their only course of action, even if it was extremely risky.

Nick clutched Dana's arm and nodded to signal that they should make their way up the main staircase. At the top of the landing, they stopped when they saw two armed men step closer to a policeman outside.

Suddenly, a storm of bullets echoed above them, a few errant shells ricocheting down the steps, rattling in the stairway. Dana huddled into Nick until the barrage of semiautomatic-weapon fire fell into a silence that stretched into seconds and then minutes. She clutched Nick's hand as she adjusted her footing to run. Nick pulsed her hand and shook his head as he kept his focus on the mouth of the bunker.

Dana peered over the concrete lip of the doorway and listened to the fading roar of a car engine down the dirt path toward the main road. Once she heard the tires squeal beyond the trees, Dana assumed the men with the guns were gone. She leapt from the bunker entrance, at the same time throwing her backpack toward the closest tree at the edge of the concrete. She spotted a police officer on the ground next to an SUV. She slid to her knees next to the officer, reading the name Sanchez on his badge.

"Sanchez. Officer Sanchez. You with me? Hey, this is okay. We got you."

Officer Sanchez turned his head toward Dana and started to twitch, his eyes fluttering half open. The wispy clouds of his breath were short and small and disappeared quickly in the cool air. She believed he was looking at her with some conscious acknowledgement before his head dropped back and his eyes closed. She put her hands on his chest and felt stiff material underneath his shirt.

"Shit. I think he's got a vest on under here, but he still took a couple of hits."

Nick got to quick work, tearing off the officer's sleeve and making a tourniquet to wrap around a gunshot wound on the officer's leg. "He's losing blood."

Dana looked surprised at his fastidious bandaging. She watched him calmly apply his craft with a sense of order that reminded her of camping injuries with her mom but on a more critical scale. The worst open wound she had ever attended to was a fishhook through a thumb. "What? I took first aid training at work to be prepared for on-the-job accidents. But this won't help for long. He has another hole just outside his chest pad, upper outer pectoral. We have to get him to a hospital."

Dana grabbed the officer under the shoulders and started to attempt to move him. Nick held up his hands, motioning her to lay him back down.

"Wait, wait, wait! Let's think this through! We have his car," Nick said, pointing at the bullet-riddled SUV and trying to settle his rattled nerves and not hyperventilate. "Let's get him in the back. I think we'll be able to drive him to the hospital faster than an ambulance could get here. They might not even know how to find this place." He ran his hand over his forehead, smearing it with the officer's blood. "Damn it. We screwed this guy by coming out here."

Dana ran to the base of the tree and grabbed her backpack. Nick jumped into the police SUV and started the ignition. The bullets had made their way in, damaging the radio and rendering it inoperable. He backed around to the wounded trooper and Dana. She opened the liftgate, and she and Nick hoisted the officer into the back. *Panic is a potent steroid*, she thought.

Nick found a first aid kit in the SUV and used the remaining supplies inside to reinforce the crude tourniquet he had made for the leg and an extra layer of padding on the upper chest wound. "Give me your belt." He held out his hand to Dana.

"I don't have one for these pants. Where's yours?"

He pointed to the leg tourniquet.

"Shit."

"Bad news is we're at least twenty-five to thirty minutes from the Two Pines trauma center," Nick said, grunting as he cinched the last notch in the belt around the officer's leg. "Luckily, I've been there enough times to know where we're going. It's a straight shot down the highway. I'll call and tell them we're on the way."

He looked over at Dana to see she had pulled out her skates and was snapping the shin guards in place.

"I can get there faster." She looked up at Nick's worried face. His furrowed brow was smeared with blood and his hands were shaking.

"Nick." She rested her hand on his own. "I got this. Head to the road and point the car toward the hospital." She climbed in the back with Officer Sanchez to make sure he didn't move. "Stop when you get to the blacktop."

"What?"

"Trust me," she pleaded. "Stop at the blacktop when we're out of the woods."

Nick spun the SUV on the cracked concrete and aimed for the rutted path out to the road and through the open gate with Dana lying on top of the officer in the back to protect against bumps. Nick successfully navigated the truck through an awkward skid as he swung onto the empty pavement of the main road. As he pulled to a stop, Dana opened the liftgate and swung her roller-booted feet onto the road with a clank and thud. Nick ran around to the back, and together they carefully laid Officer Sanchez into a fireman's carry across Dana's shoulders.

"I need a jumpstart," Dana deadpanned.

Nick saw that the watery sheen on her eyes was quickly extinguished by the fire burning through her light brown irises. She read his face and tightened her gaze to acknowledge she was aware of everything at stake and how much tonight was the closing of the door between life "before" and life "after." She threaded her left arm over the officer's right bicep, and then her right arm over his akimbo leg. Her gloved hands gripped the open liftgate, her palms pulsing with hot adrenaline. Her forearms contracted into granite posts. The weight of the officer's body, possibly near death, and the gravity of the situation literally and figuratively on her shoulders were no match for her iron determination.

"I'm not fully charged. I have maybe a few minutes of battery. So, when you hit sixty miles per hour, pull the car to the right."

"We can get there in time if we drive—"

"He may not have time." Her voice shook just a moment as she monotoned. "But I do. When I pass you, call them and say we have a wounded officer incoming. And stay with me." She broke eye contact. "As best as you can."

Nick jumped back into the cabin, simultaneously throwing the truck into drive and smoothly but quickly pushing the gas pedal to the floor. The police SUV charged forward as every cylinder punched the engine block, roaring as it injected fuel into the pistons. Dana held tight as the SUV lurched and built speed, her back moist with the officer's warm blood and her hot sweat. The chill of the draft rolling over the truck's sides began to build on her face.

The skates began their whining metal song, notes grabbed from the air and pulled together into a metallic chord of fury. Sparks burst from under her heels as the wheels continued their angry chorus, and she felt the acceleration pulling her and her precious cargo faster and faster. As the speedometer hit fifty-five, Nick started to ease right.

She inhaled slowly as her fingers relaxed. She let go of the liftgate.

The tires of the truck crossed the reflective paint as it headed for the shoulder of the road. Nick heard the high-pitched grind of her skates and barely caught a glimpse of her in the side-view mirror as she soared past him. With the officer across her shoulders, she shot past the police SUV like a comet chased by the roar of wind.

Her toes pressed against the acceleration pads, and for the first time since she had built the skates, she was afraid and felt nothing of the happiness that their speed gave her. She had never carried more than a few pounds, but the full throttle of the rollers continued to accelerate through the dark of the two-lane road. She glanced down for a moment to watch the lens flare of Nick's headlights behind her diminish as her shadow ahead bled into the natural darkness.

Nick watched her steadily pull away as he continued to accelerate. "If you fall . . ." he whispered to himself in the dark, his heart racing as he willed her forward, as if that was even within his power. He could hear the grind of her roller skates fade and drop pitch, occasionally seeing a spark like a fallen star gasping for life in the darkness ahead, until she was gone. He fumbled with his phone and dialed 911. The minutes were short but eternally suspenseful as Nick raced toward Two Pines. He shut the headlights as he slowed to a stop about a half mile from the medical center's driveway, and he could see a faint spatter of sparks as he approached. Dana skated slowly toward him, relieved of the burden of the trooper but worn down by the frantic sprint.

"He's good. I left him at the ER doors." She panted heavily as the skates sputtered and choked, stopping just short of the truck. She leaned over the hood and knocked on the grill. "We have to leave this here obviously."

Nick leapt out of the driver's side towing his knapsack as well as Dana's worn canvas backpack on his shoulder. She greedily grabbed her bag and kicked off the skates.

"Laverne, Shirley, you done good, girls," she gasped as her stomach lurched.

Nick surveyed the road in both directions.

"We need to split—now," he noted.

"We're walking?" Dana put her hands on her knees and heaved.

"I ordered an Uber after I called 911. Let's just get back to my truck, and then figure out what's next. Breakfast, maybe, to start."

Dana, still crouching, looked up toward his face. She pulled her cheeks into a semismile, still foaming at the corners of her mouth. "Can we stop for toothpaste somewhere first?"

She vomited on the shoulder of the road, the oncoming headlights of a car illuminating the bile stream. Nick put a hand on her back and patted her jacket. Seeing the Uber sign in the window, Nick waved to the driver as the car slowed to a stop to pick up its late-night fare.

0:00   3:13

Chapter 15

Electric Avenue – Eddy Grant

B ecky. I think her name is Becky."
Dana lowered the laminated menu and squinted under the fluorescent lights, one hand raised to block the blinding early morning sun plowing through the windows of the diner. Nick sat across from her and mirrored her pose to prevent the dawn glare. To Dana, the reflection of the sun made it look like he had gold sparkles in his hair, a fitting halo for a Boy Scout who had done more than his share of good deeds. The young red-haired waitress plodded over to their table and pulled a green pen from her apron. She scribbled furiously on her order pad as she approached at the edge of the booth. She grunted as her pen ripped through the top sheet.

"Hi, my name is Becky, and I'll be your . . . dang it, this was my lucky pen and I'm almost out of ink. Sorry. I'll be your server today, so what can I get you?"

"Hi, Becky. I'm Dana. I read your name tag all the way across the dining room and now my good buddy Nick here owes me a dollar!" Dana beamed with a delirious smile. Her cheeks were smudged with dried blood, the shoulders of her jacket adorned with a mix of mud and blood. Becky leaned back and shot a sideways glance at Nick.

"Did you just come from some kind of haunted hayride or something?"

Nick brushed at the dirty sleeves of his coat with a napkin and wiped the remains of a blood stain from his forehead. "Sure. Something like that."

Becky tapped her pad with her pen. "We have a morning special this week of French toast and bacon. I call it the Paris Piggies, but we haven't made that nickname official yet. Can I get you some coffee?"

"Decaf," Nick offered.

"Same." Dana flashed a wide closed-mouth smile at Becky and blinked rapidly.

Becky looked each of them up and down as she scribbled. Nick removed his jacket hastily before turning it inside out, folding it, and placing it squarely on the bench beside him. He caught a quick whiff of his shirt underneath and tried to discern if it was dried sweat or bunker musk, or a mix of both.

Becky arched a single eyebrow. "I'll bring you guys some napkins and a pitcher of water too. Be right back."

As the waitress walked back to the kitchen, Nick snapped his fingers in front of Dana's still frozen smile. "Hey. Hey. You good?"

Dana dropped her smile and rolled her eyes toward Nick without moving her head. "I would say no in the most literal definition of the word, but in the current circumstances, knowing I'm about to dump two thousand calories and I can actually feel my quads and hamstrings now, yeah, I'm good."

Next to his paper placemat, Nick began to pile up the notebooks and metal tags he had stuffed into his knapsack during their escape from the bunker lab. He shifted in his seat and pursed his lips to draw a long breath. "Those guys would have killed us if that trooper hadn't shown up. Dana, holy cow, we could have been killed."

She blinked rapidly. "You're not much into cursing, are you?"

"And you're not much into realizing how serious this thing just got. I mean, Jesus," his voice cracked as his volume grew, "we just dropped off a state trooper full of bullets! That guy might die!"

"Sure, this is serious. But if you'll cut me a little slack, I'm still full of adrenaline from carrying him on my back at a billion miles an hour!" She shook out her hair and widened her eyes. "I feel like we're the Hardy Boys. Or Nancy Drew. Or Inspector Gadget." She cracked a smile to lighten the mood. "I'm obviously Inspector Gadget." That elicited a tiny grin from Nick, and she felt pleased with herself that she could push his buttons and reset him.

Nick drummed on the table with his fingers and slid his pile of bunker trinkets toward the center of the booth. "I don't know what's useful here, and what might help us figure stuff out. I grabbed some things that looked interesting from one of the engineer's desks."

Dana picked up her butter knife and pointed it at the pile. "That's a binder clip. I know that one," she deadpanned. "Binder. Clip." She tapped once with the utensil for each word. "It's a spring-loaded device for securing papers. Also known as a chip clip at my place."

Nick was scowling but trying to keep the corners of his mouth from turning up into a smile. The waitress came back and slid the coffees to each place setting, then set down a short stack of napkins and the pitcher in front of Dana.

"Um, you may want to freshen up. You have a little thing on your cheek," she said in a low voice as she pointed her pen toward Dana's grimace. "I'll be back in a bit to check on the food order, unless you're ready now?"

"Paris Piggies for me," Nick started and then abruptly turned to Dana. "I'm sorry, ladies first. I'm tired. I'm forgetting my manners."

"Big date not going well, or too well?" Becky winked at Nick. "What about you, miss?"

"I'm going to have a pancake stack, a cheese omelet with pepper jack, skip the hash browns, and can you bring me like a full plate of wheat toast? Like, make it a double or triple or something like that. And jelly. Grape, strawberry, a couple of each. Oh, and a chocolate milk." Nick opened his mouth to comment as Dana muttered, "I told you I need a lot of calories right now."

As Becky headed back to the kitchen, Nick opened the first notebook. "So, here's what I'm thinking. We need to figure out who the guys are in the photo from your dad. If anyone's still alive, we track them down, ask for more information. Once we get some idea of who knows what, we can go from there."

Dana pulled out the picture and put it on the table next to the notebooks. She leaned back to look around the diner at the only other patrons, a middle-aged couple, and counted the cars in the parking lot, including Nick's truck. She made a note of the staff she had seen and how many she guessed were back in the kitchen, matching them up with the visible cars as well. She chose the table by the door in case a quick exit was needed as well as for the view of the interior and restroom doors. Her grandfather and father had always done this same routine every time they had gone out to eat back home in New Mexico, even when her mom was still alive. For her, *home* was a relative term now. She noticed Nick was holding an open notebook over her placemat.

"Here we go." Nick pointed to the interior cover page. "Looks like this gives each guy's name and his specialty or side project. Your dad is listed as power plant engineering and routing. And then, hang on . . ." Nick put the book down and reached inside his jacket pocket and retrieved a stack of plastic tokens, each the size of a credit card but twice as thick. "These were in your grandfather's locker." He fanned the cards like a winning poker player. Each plastic square revealed a name and a photo, heavily worn, but the faces and last names were still discernable. "I got the idea to snag these when you told me to grab the nameplates."

"Son of a goose." She stared at the familiar faces on two of the tags, smiling as she studied the handsome photos of her father and grandfather. They were each smiling with their dimples she had inherited. "That's amazing. Oh! Idea! Hey, Becky!" Dana waved her arms with a frenzy that matched the decibel level of her voice in the almost empty diner. "Do you have any of those crayon packs for kids? I like to color with breakfast!"

Becky smiled halfheartedly and presented a pack of five well-worn crayons. As she laid them between the placemats, Dana clapped and emitted a gleeful yelp. She quickly flipped her paper mat to the blank side and chose a red crayon out of the spartan selection inside the box.

"Thank you! Your tip just went up!"

Once Becky walked away, Dana began to scribble a set of stick figures on the mat. Each one was holding what looked like either a fishing rod or a primitive gardening tool. Then she wrote "pew pew" over the objects, clearing things up. She nodded approvingly at her artwork.

"And these are the guys who probably would have killed us, as you said, because they sure had no problems putting holes in a state trooper." She folded the paper like a greeting card and set it upright next to the notebooks. Nick put the ID cards for Dana's father and grandfather in front of the crayon art.

At that moment, Becky returned with their plates and put a new placemat in front of Dana before setting down the pile of food on top. She then grabbed an extra placemat and put it facedown next to Dana, smiled, and pointed to the crayons before leaving.

"She's very nice. You really do need to leave her a good tip," Dana said while digging into her omelet.

"So, I'm paying?"

"Well, you drove," Dana retorted between her forkfuls of pancakes. "Oh my God, these are the best. This place has the thickest pancakes. Did you know New Jersey has the highest number of diners per capita? I think there's an island in the Pacific that *technically* does because it's also a naval station, but anyway. Hey, are you looking that up right now?" Nick was fiddling on his cell phone as she paused her exposé on diners.

"I'm putting these names into some obituary and people-finder websites," he mumbled between his own bites of food. "Anselm Geissler, not finding him. Jens Jacobsen, dead. Cannon Hardy, can't find him, but I'm getting a lot of hits for a place called Hardy Farms. Looks like it's about an hour south. It says here that it's a private supplier for the military." Nick took a long gulp of coffee and then looked at Dana. "You know what New Jersey also has a high number of per capita?"

"Pickup trucks with bad pun license plates? Fans of sports teams who play somewhere else?"

"Farms. It's the Garden State. We don't have big agribusiness like the Midwest, but we have lots and lots of tiny farms. There's not a very good reason I can see why a local farm would have an agriculture contract with the military. It's not like they can pump out enough chickens or wheat for the local military bases. Especially when it looks like this." He held up a satellite map image of Hardy Farms on his phone. "There are four barns and a house, all within the property lines, here and here." He pointed with a crayon at the tiny screen.

"Think we should try there first?" Dana squinted at the screen.

"No one else from the list is coming up as alive, and there's no other evidence. It's basically all we have. I'm betting we can't go back to the bunker anytime soon now that it's open, unless we have some kind of actual plan."

Dana shoveled a triple stack of toast and jelly into her mouth. She signaled for the check and pantomimed putting her remaining food into a to-go box. When Becky returned with the empty containers and the bill, Dana reached into her pants pocket and pulled out a money clip with several wrinkled and battered twenty-dollar notes.

"You don't have to pay, I got this. You're a good sport. And this is my mess." She peeled off three bills and put them under her saucer. "And by paying, I'm calling dibs on the first shower. I smell like a truck stop now." She pointed at the tip money. "And, again, you owe me a dollar. Her name is *not* Ducky."

Chapter 16

Bungle in the Jungle – Jethro Tull

H ey, Tommy, I need a favor," Joshua barked as he entered the records building. The three-block walk from his office to the warehouse elapsed in a few minutes, but the security protocol and sign-in took three times that long. Finally, he entered the vast rows of bureaucracy brought to life. A lone desk adorned with four large computer monitors sat up front; the guardian of the rows of file cabinets looked up from his computer at the intrusion. His oversized shirt hung over his wiry frame, his dark hair slicked back like a greasy helmet.

"Josh," he droned as he crossed his arms over a dingy badge lanyard, "did you sign the logbook?"

"Yes. And it's not a book, it's a registration screen." Joshua craned his neck to spy on the online poker game on Tommy's second monitor. "You should hold with that hand, you know."

Tommy maintained his posture. "Did you enter the time and work code authorization?"

"Yes. And you know I only need to put in my department number for clearance." He sighed. Dealing with Tommy involved a series of rituals that Joshua loathed.

"And did you bring me anything useful?" Tommy raised an eyebrow as he leaned back in his rolling chair.

"Yes. Her name is Linda, and she's an intern with the FDA. She's single, and I asked Gretchen to send her down for old farm reports. You're welcome."

Tommy smiled and uncrossed his arms, finally giving him his full attention as he minimized the window with the poker game. "What can I do for you?" he asked cheerfully. "I'm up a few bucks today. I'm feeling generous."

"I need rosters," Joshua said, looking at the rows of shelving stacked with a hodgepodge of plastic, metal, and cardboard filing boxes, purchased over the years from an assortment of government suppliers. Each box in this building was full of archival paperwork, mostly useless, but occasionally he had found just cause to retrieve a dossier on a pre-internet–era research project plagued by accounting fumbles. Some files were intentionally left unscanned and undigitized to ensure confidentiality, usually in the instance when an operative was not confirmed as officially deceased. His lungs filled with the musky scent of stale air, his mind with electricity, and his heart with joy. *This should be an easy day of detective work*, he mused.

"There are more efficient ways to request names, you know. You just walked into the Hall of Fame and asked me if there are any shortstops in here," Tommy snipped.

"Ok, I have two names, and I'm looking to connect them, maybe match them up to a project. Possibly. I'm not sure where to start. Any idea how I can do that?"

"Come around here." Tommy opened a database on one screen and a map of the warehouse floor on a second monitor. "If the names were ever in digital format, I can run a search here and look for any correlating points. Even if the papers themselves aren't digitized, we usually link one or two pieces of metadata to the magical boxes. Base of operations, transfers, location overlaps are easy catches. However, those may or may not relate to something in here," he said, circling the floor map with his finger. "The names?"

"These here," Joshua said, handing over an index card.

Tommy took the card and typed out the names. He cracked his knuckles as the results appeared on screen. "Which one do you need?" he asked.

"Come again?"

"Which person? There are two *Samuel Jeffersons* in the system. A junior and a senior. That's jamming up the search results. I'm getting white noise here. And this Colin Rhodes dude crosses with both names. What are the odds, right? Father and son super spy team, maybe?"

Joshua grabbed the monitor and turned the pivoting stand to view the results more closely.

"That *would* be really odd. What did they work on?"

"Nothing we've completely transferred over to the digital world so far, but there's a listing for PX accounts in New Jersey for both of them. The PX is the commissary." Joshua shrugged in response, so Tommy continued. "That's the general store used on bases by the soldiers and civilians. You want some noodles or a stapler or a stuffed teddy bear, you go to the PX. And here," he noted, scrolling down the results even further, "is an account for Colin Rhodes at the same commissary. That's the only link I have. You can start there, I guess."

"You guess?" Josh shifted his focus away from the monitor in the foreground to the stacks of cabinets in the background.

"Yep, Aisle 246, New Jersey. Middle shelf. Boxes 43A and 43B probably, but you may need to check 43C through 43F." He reached into his desk drawer and retrieved a bottle of store-brand cola. "Happy hunting. Doors close in five hours."

"Happy hunting," Joshua muttered with a smirk.

0:00   3:13

Chapter 17

Mr. Blackwell − Kiss

Ninety-Nine stared at his freshly shaved face in the motel bathroom mirror, a hand towel draped over his shoulder covering the constellation of scars on his left pectoral. His right was adorned with a recent tattoo of a mono-color American flag, which covered an Australian one. A knock on the door distracted his short moment of vanity.

"It's Forty-Four," came a voice from outside. "Call for you."

Ninety-Nine tossed the towel aside and placed his pistol in the waistband of his pants behind his back. He peered through the eyehole before letting his teammate enter.

"Telephone for you. Now," Forty-Four declared as he swallowed hard. He put on an air of authority despite being known as a glorified secretary on the team, albeit one that was rumored to have had the highest kill count before joining OHR.

Ninety-Nine left the door open, clearly expecting Forty-Four to follow inside. He gestured to the dresser, on which Forty-Four promptly placed the attaché and opened it, signaled by a tiny metal clinking noise. Ninety-Nine lifted the phone headset inside.

"Yes, Mr. Rhodes. We had an unexpected incident."

"I am not excited by this development," admonished the older voice on the other end of the line. "We have a considerable set of new agenda items now. One, we no longer have control of the site, which has been found by our target. I now need to call in a few favors to get the site secured. There will be a few payouts and chips to cash in to do that. Two . . ." He paused for dramatic effect. "We now have a witness."

"Come again, sir?"

"State Trooper Christopher Sanchez. Stationed out of the Red Lion Barracks. Former National Guard, one tour in Afghanistan, and I might note he overlapped your time there by one month. Apparently, he was dropped off at a trauma center—Twin Pines, Two Pines, something backwoods—and transferred to the intensive care at First United Care Hospital across the county. He's in critical condition and looks to be under guard due to the unknown nature of his assailant."

Ninety-Nine rubbed his chin and glanced over at Forty-Four, who was sitting on the bed browsing the menus of local pizzerias. Forty-Four held up one of the glossy sheets and pointed to a supreme pie as he pantomimed dialing a phone.

"You could not have obtained all of this information from my report. Did we have a contact inside the hospital?"

"No, it was in the local newspaper. And that is why we have a problem you need to 'tidy up.' Once you terminate him, I will call over to the State Police Credit Union and arrange a deposit. He is a former soldier, so he is family, and I will not leave his kin in dire straits because of your sloppy execution." The line went silent.

"Right, sir. I will take care of it tomorrow."

Mr. Rhodes hung up as Ninety-Nine finished his sentence.

"All good?" inquired Forty-Four. "What's up?"

Ninety-Nine put down the phone and closed the case. He walked over to the closet area to retrieve his black duffel and sat it on the bed next to Forty-Four. It landed with a thud and a rattle. He unzipped it, inspecting the guns inside, which settled on top of a pile of clothes.

"Forty-Four, gas up the Hummer in the morning. Meet me back here in the afternoon. I'll call with the exact time once I get my ducks in a row. And when you talk to Eighty-Eight, tell him . . ." He thought for a moment and looked down at the bag. "We're good. But if he stops over or calls me right now, I'm not going to be pleasant."

Forty-Four nodded and swung his feet off the bed. "Yes, Olsen." He picked up his cell and got ready to dial the pizza shanty down the road.

"*Ninety-Nine.* Let's maintain some decorum of order, mate. I don't need to reiterate the stakes here, do I?" Ninety-Nine shuffled through the bag and retrieved a cornflower-blue shirt and dark pants with a yellow stripe down each leg. "What we're doing is creating a necessary darkness; we turn off the light and leave out some crumbs so the roaches walk freely. Then we flick on the light switch and exterminate." His weathered fingers traced his chest scars.

Forty-Four looked skeptical. "You make this sound so noble. We're selling top secrets to the enemy so that we can get paid for our expertise. We're contractors. Profit is the goal, and we'll be paid in spades by both sides."

Ninety-Nine swooped down quickly and clamped his hand on his teammate's shoulder. He dug his nails into the cloth until the threads began to tear in his grip. "Peace is the goal. Peace through war is a duty and a calling," he barked, his eyes bulging. "Making an obscene amount of money is a perk, yes, but do not forget that we are taking the highest risk for the sake of world peace, and a starring role on the world stage." He loosened his grip and backed away from Forty-Four. "This isn't my homeland, but it's my *home*."

Ideology was often a source of contention between Ninety-Nine and Forty-Four. When Ninety-Nine—then Olsen—met the junior officer—then

Martinez—the latter had been freshly discharged with severance after some civilian casualties in South America that occurred during a raid gone wrong. Olsen recalled the joint recruitment meeting with OHR during which Martinez continued to bring up compensation even during the most technical portions of the interview. True, the junior officer excelled in electronic surveillance, which gave him an edge with Mr. Rhodes during the process, but Olsen doubted his allegiance. Anytime money was discussed, Martinez lodged himself between the parties to ensure his cut.

"Okay, 'Ninety-Nine,' I'm paying for pizza, but I'm going back to my room with my half. I trust you'll give me the per diem for the gas money after I get your 'chores' completed in the morning." Forty-Four hesitated in the doorway with the phone case. "Say, Olsen, what are you going to do with the money? I'm just asking since going back to Australia is out of the question for you. You got a special lady tucked away somewhere?"

Olsen winced at the words. He leaned against the wall and crossed his arms in thought. "I'll probably get my mum a place out here, maybe Rhode Island, maybe Oregon. Somewhere she can sit and watch the sea from a nice rocking chair."

"Seriously? We're going to be rich! And your plan is to get your mother a porch swing?"

"Priorities." Olsen stopped short of reminiscing about his mother, Australia, and a girl from long ago.

"Whatever. You can come visit my island whenever you want. Open bar for all of eternity." Martinez swung the case and paraded outside. "I'll call you when the pizza shows up."

Olsen looked out through the open door into the parking lot and counted the cars. He leaned through the portal and surveilled a young couple walking to their room for the night before closing his door and turning the locks.

He let out a long sigh and stretched his arms before grabbing the ironing board from the closet area and setting on it the shirt and pants of the police uniform from his bag on the bed. He hummed a tune as he placed the stitched New Jersey State Police badges on the shirt and searched for a needle and thread in his duffel bag.

0:00

3:13

Chapter 18

Cry to Me – Solomon Burke

N ick and his father set their tool belts on the backs of their respective chairs at the kitchen table. It had been a long day at work, but Nick had the fortune of being able to grab a nap during some downtime. He groaned as he took off his jacket, then sat his clipboard by his schoolbooks. Next to them he spied the pile of dusty notebooks hat he and Dana had grabbed from the bunker and the placemat from the diner. He glanced at his father to see if he noticed these pieces of possibly top secret government property next to the centerpiece.

"Are those for your school project?" Nick's dad asked, nodding to the stack while pulling out ingredients for dinner from the freezer.

"Oh, those are mine!" Dana interjected, emerging from the back patio door. "I forgot to take those out to the garage. I emptied out the kitchen garbage, by the way, so my chores are done!" She winked at Nick. He ignored her and used the distraction to fold and place the placemat with Dana's crayon art into his shirt pocket.

"Dana, you are welcome to stay for dinner. We have plenty of plates and plenty to throw on top of them." Mr. Andrews finally took off his work coat and also put it on the back of his chair. "Are you off to work tonight?"

"I got my schedule rearranged. School, school, school," she chimed, smiling at the elder Andrews. "But I may be staying over tonight, if that's okay? There are a few things Nick wants to work on before we wrap up." Nick blushed. This was the first discussion of where she would stay. He didn't mind; her staying over filled a void in the house, and she appeared, by his estimation, to enjoy it. It was easy to see his father had already taken a liking to her over Lindsey.

"Well, whatever you guys need to do, do it. And probably a good idea to stay here instead of driving late at night. Did you hear about that state trooper who was shot? What a mess." Mr. Andrews picked up the newspaper from the counter and tossed it toward Nick. "They say he's in a bad spot. I don't know who would just unload on a cop like that. I bet he came across some out-of-season hunters and they made a bad decision."

Nick's throat constricted as he swallowed and looked down at the headline. Next to the article was a photo of Sanchez in his dress uniform standing in front of an American flag. He scanned the text as his dad continued.

"It looks like he's in the ICU at First United. Hey, remember when Tony arced that wire in the bucket truck? He was laid up in the ICU, too. It was a good three weeks before he got out. I remember, he was on the fifth floor, and we had to take the stairs every time we visited because they had one elevator down and visitors couldn't clog the other one. Boy, I think my knees aged about ten years doing those steps to visit him!"

Nick felt the weight of the folded placemat in his shirt pocket. Dana stood unmoving at the other end of the table with crossed arms. They exchanged glances back and forth, Dana slowly raising one eyebrow.

"Nick, you know, I've got to put that thing back together in the garage. That thing, Nick? It's still on the charger." She gave Nick a not-so-subtle nod while Mr. Andrews was turned toward the microwave. "And, Nick, do you want to run out for those . . . connector thingies?"

"Yes, yes, I do," he stammered. "Dad, I'm going to the store. We're out of those sixteenth-inch connectors. If I'm not back in a few, that means I have to run to the big box by the old mall."

As his father searched in the cabinet next to the microwave, Nick folded his jacket around his tool belt and briskly walked out the front door. Dana had already jogged back out the patio door and was on her way to the garage when her cell phone started to ring, an incoming call from Nick.

"Nick, what are you thinking?" she pressed him.

"I'm going to the hospital. If that trooper's awake, he might have an idea who those guys were."

"Do you think he's in danger?"

"The guys who shot him were the type of people who would *shoot a state trooper.*"

"So should we go tell a state trooper?"

"That's what I'm going to do, tell the guards at the hospital." Nick was unsure of the rationale himself as he replied to her.

"But why don't we just phone the police, put on a phony voice and say, 'Hey, put an extra guard on Sanchez?' "

"Because if we tell them before we talk to him, we may not be able to get back to the bunker." He dropped the keys, his hands shaking with nerves. "I'm making this up as we go along." He sighed and rubbed his eyes. "I don't have a plan."

"Neither do I, Nicky. But your plans so far are better than mine. My plan is just *eat, skate, poke around.*"

Nick allowed himself to laugh. "Are the girls charged back up yet?"

"Laverne is at ninety, Shirley is at seventy. I need them both to be at least at eighty. Almost done. I'll be out in a few minutes."

"I don't know if we have time. I just looked up visiting hours, and they end in less than thirty minutes. I'm already in the truck. I'll go, see if I can get in to see him. Maybe I should ask the guards if they need to beef up security. At least if I ask, I plant the seed in their minds." He paused, the sounds of gunfire and the smell of spent casings still fresh in his memory, muskier and more vivid than what he had ever been exposed to during hunting season or backyard beer-fueled shooting galleries. He thought for a moment about the simple times before he met Dana. Any second thoughts about participating in her life disappeared when he thought about State Trooper Sanchez clinging to life, and how he felt it was partially his fault and hence his responsibility to make it right.

He put the hospital address into his GPS and then steered the pickup toward the highway. He looked in the rearview mirror and noticed the trace of a smile on his face.

"She called me *Nicky*," he said to his reflection.

Chapter 19

Jet City Woman – Queensrÿche

N ick adjusted his hard hat emblazoned with the electric company logo, pulling it down to his eyebrows as he walked through the reception doors of First United Care Hospital, the largest hospital in the geographically second largest county in the state. Many of his coworkers had been treated at this medical complex, as had he after a broken wrist during a savage paintball match in high school, so he knew the layout well. A brief cinematic sequence played in his mind of the last few times he saw his mother alive. He pushed the memory down.

He walked with quick steps past reception toward the elevator bank. The nurses and other staff were busy talking with a tall and well-built blond state trooper who appeared confused and slightly argumentative. Nick glanced down at his clipboard and tool belt—all part of his ruse—as he entered the elevator and hit the button next to a metal label for ICU. He admitted to himself that he had no specific plan except to see if Trooper Sanchez was awake, and to somehow recommend to him or someone else that a transfer to another location was a good idea, without giving away too many details of his wheeled sidekick and the trespassing charges they committed. He stared up at the backlit floor numbers and tried to remember how many times he had ridden this same elevator to visit his mother.

"Hold the lift!"

Nick looked up and froze. The state trooper from the desk, wearing impeccably clean tactical boots and a tight buzz cut, threw his hand between the closing doors. With a jolt, Nick recognized the man as the guy from the bar whom he and Dana thought was suspicious. Further, he thought he heard a pinch of an Australian accent—an accent he had also heard from the bunker doorway last night. Even so, Nick put his hand against the elevator door to prevent it from closing, or else risk suspicion from a potentially dangerous man he knew nothing about.

"Thank you," the trooper said politely as he entered and stood next to Nick. His sidearm was clipped on the webbing of his belt, and he wore black leather gloves. Nick flipped a page of his phony work order for the electric company, but out of the corner of his eye he noticed that the New Jersey State Police patch on the trooper's upper sleeve was lifting up just a bit from the bottom. He remembered that happening to his Boy Scout uniform after his mom got sick and he was left to apply his own badges with an iron.

"Sure thing, sir." The doors closed and they began their ascent. Nick slipped his phone out of his pocket and forced his shaking thumbs to punch each letter slowly in a text to Dana:

BAD GUYS AT HOSPITAL

The elevator crept up slowly, stopping on the third floor for a pair of nurses to board and then quickly get off on the fourth floor. As the doors for the fifth floor opened, Nick prioritized his own exit ahead of the imposter trooper and turned right toward the recovery room wing, a newly remodeled and expansive area that faced the top of the new parking garage. Nick glanced out the wall of windows and could see his truck parked on top on the fourth deck of the fresh white concrete partitions. He searched through the floors below for any sign of Dana's blue truck. In the glass, he caught the reflection of the man from the elevator behind him, walking with a theatrical casual stroll but slowing down to peer in each room.

As Nick reached the end of the hall and rounded the corner, he jogged toward the last door, outside of which a state trooper was seated in a metal chair. He swallowed and prayed this was not another imposter.

"Hi, sir," Nick said, panting between breaths and leaning in to read the state trooper's name on the metal plate pinned to his chest. "Um, I'm Nick An–Anderson—with the electric company."

"State Trooper Duckworth," replied the man without extending a handshake. "What can I do for you?"

"I have a work order for a blown GFCI on a subpanel in there"—he glanced at the number plate—"room 535. A little urgent. It's an unused outlet but they need it swapped before they bring in a defibrillator Cybertron monitor tonight." Nick bit his lip and prayed his gibberish was good enough to get himself inside. Lying was not a natural talent for him.

"Sure, one sec." The officer looked past Nick. He turned to see the fake trooper was approaching from the end of the hall, straightening his tie.

"Let me just let my relief know," said Trooper Duckworth, smiling at the imposter approaching. "Hey, thanks for getting here early. I can actually see my kids before bed tonight."

Nick pivoted and faced Trooper Duckworth so the imposter could not see his face. He mouthed the words, "He's not a cop. Not. A. Cop."

Trooper Duckworth looked over Nick's shoulder but returned an almost imperceptible nod. He placed his hands on his belt and squared his shoulders.

"So, where did they send you from? Red Lion or Netcong?"

"Netcong." The man smiled as he stopped and adjusted his gloves.

"Wow, that's a hike. Pretty long ride to get here. I guess you must have been on the OT list. I'm just going to keep an eye on this contractor while he fixes something in the room. It'll only take, what, five minutes?" He turned the door handle as he stared at Nick. He nodded once, and Nick returned the gesture. The imposter placed his hand on the door before Nick could step forward.

"No one in or out except police, medical staff, or family," he growled at Nick, "and he doesn't look like a cop, an MD, or a Sanchez." He tilted his head left and then right with a crack and glowered at Nick.

The three men stood for a moment in silence, frozen in place until the standoff was broken by a low grinding rumble, like the scratching of metal-wound guitar strings, coming from around the corner, toward the elevators. The grinding sharply increased in tone as Dana rounded the corner on Laverne and Shirley, skidding to a stop at the end of the hallway.

"There are a lot of pissed off people downstairs on their way up here," she deadpanned.

0:00   3:13

Chapter 20

Jessie's Girl 2 – Coheed and Cambria

Dana was calculating her next move when the state trooper closest to her whipped around to face her, at the same time reaching for his sidearm. In a split second, she recognized him from the Stroudsberg Inn and realized this was who Nick had texted her about. Before she could react, the other state trooper lunged forward and knocked the gun out of the other man's grip just as he pulled it from the leather holster. As she saw Nick fumble with the door handle of Sanchez's room until it finally swung open, Dana pushed off with her back foot and soared toward the fray with a flurry of sparks seeding her black curls and leather jacket tails.

Her heart pulsed in her temples, beating between each moment unfolding in front of her as she closed in. The imposter trooper grabbed the real trooper's wrist, snapping it one hundred and eighty degrees at the end of his forearm with an audible crack, leaving him howling in pain. He then connected his knee with the trooper's face, knocking him out cold. Dana saw Nick scramble into the room, slamming it shut behind him. He must have locked it because the fake trooper tried to open it unsuccessfully and pounded his fist on the door before turning to face Dana.

"Well, this is a surprise, *Dana Jefferson*. I've been ordered to retrieve you." He grabbed the chair next to the door and, with a heavy grunt, pitched it at Dana. She dropped into a feet-first baseball slide. Her boots hit him in the ankles as he swung, launching him over her and separating his hand from the chair.

"Naughty girl!" He snarled and slid on one knee to grab his gun from the floor.

Dana looked for a way out and spotted the large wall of windows overlooking the parking garage. "Shit, shit, shit!" she yelled as she pressed her toes into the front panels of the skates and accelerated toward the glass sheet framing the nighttime sky.

As Dana gained speed, she heard a gunshot behind her. She crouched down just as the bullet whizzed past her head, shattering the safety glass in front of her. Her blood pulsed again in her ears as the nanoseconds stretched before her. She pressed her knees and surged forward, crossing her arms over her face and goggles.

Crashing through what was left of the window, Dana immediately felt the cold night air across her face, the crackling of the shattered glass fragments drowned out by the whirring of her skates. She was airborne. She soared over the short gap between the window and the top deck of the parking garage, falling like a shooting star. She extended her front leg in a graceful posture, cocking her back leg, and landed with one hop, remaining upright and spinning to a stop on the top deck, which was mostly vacant.

She looked up to see her adversary staring down at her through the broken window before he disappeared back into the hall.

"Nick, what have I gotten us into?" she muttered as she brushed a few tiny fragments of safety glass off the front of her coat.

Nick cowered behind the door of Trooper Sanchez's room, having dragged every movable piece of furniture except for the bed against it. Someone began to pound against the door from the hallway. He flinched at each impact. When he heard a gunshot, he prayed it hadn't hit Dana. He refocused on the mission at hand. Nick had found when he entered the room that Trooper Sanchez was still in a comatose state, breathing shallowly through a tube attached to a lone machine. He wouldn't be talking to him tonight, it appeared.

A new commotion came from the hallway, this time in a swell of voices demanding explanations. Nick sighed with relief as he guessed security and staff had arrived. He slid the chairs and tables away from the door and opened it, a throng of doctors and staff swarming Trooper Sanchez. A guard paused to assess Nick.

"Who are you?"

"I'm the electrician. Sounded like some kind of fight out there!" He patted the guard on the shoulder and twisted around him through the doorway. "Keep up the good work! I left my truck running." Nick slipped around another attendant heading through the door and jogged back to the elevators. He stopped when he felt a cold breeze blow past him and turned to see the shattered windows.

"Dana, what the *hell* did you do?" he whispered. His phone vibrated. "Dana, what the hell did you *do*?" he asked of the person on the line.

"Nick, you good?"

"Yeah, are you? I heard a gunshot, and someone pounding on the door, and then a mob of people showed up, and . . . did you jump out the window?"

"There's a first time for everything, right? I'm good. I jumped onto the top of the parking garage."

"That makes *plenty* of sense," he said with a sardonic note in his voice.

"I'm near your truck now."

"Stay there, I'll be down in a bit."

"Nick, I don't think staying put is part of the plan right now."

Dana had wanted to wait for Nick, but she realized she was at the top of the garage with only one way out, and the imposter trooper knew she was there. She was a sitting duck. She spotted exit ramp arrows and pumped her feet for speed to begin her descent, winding down through each deck, following the yellow arrows on the ramps. Sparks sizzled as they hit the bumpers of the cars as Dana rounded each corner, gaining speed on the descent. As she turned the corner to the second floor, a compact car jerked out from behind a van, bumping her hip and knocking her off-balance. She flailed her arms but managed to hold her speed.

"Sorry!" she yelled at the driver. "Just looking for the booth!"

She regained her stability and planted her feet firmly in her skates as she rounded the last concrete pillar before the ground floor. The ramp transitioned to the ground floor of the garage, and she assumed a toe-heel technique, taking the opportunity to catch her breath before speeding up again as she approached the gate arm for the exit. Her brain ran through the egress possibilities: she could go over, under, or through the stripped wooden beam extending from the gatehouse.

She opted to drop to one leg in a crouched position, with her other leg extended in front, and glided beneath the gate arm and past the booth attendant, who smiled wide and scrambled to snap a photo on his phone as she stood upright and rolled into the parking lot. Her headset hummed.

"Dana, I'm on the first floor, heading toward the lobby. There are cops and security everywhere." Nick's voice crackled in her earpiece. "Where are you?"

"Listen, you're going to have to meet me," Dana shouted, as headlights doused her in illumination. "I'm on the run."

A black Hummer was heading right for her. She saw two men inside the cabin, one being her pursuer, the phony state trooper. His blue eyes burned into hers with a ravenous anger. He pointed at her and appeared to yell at the driver.

She extended her middle finger.

0:00   3:13

Chapter 21

Photograph – Santana and Chris Daughtry

The pounding of her heart filled Dana's ears, adding to the roaring of the Hummer's V8 diesel engine as it accelerated toward her on the hospital driveway. She was running for her life but at the same time she felt so alive—she was *enjoying* the chase. She reeled toward the road and dug her feet into her boots, beginning to sprint like a speed skater as she chopped her legs like muscular hatchets at the blacktop. With each step, she surged multiple stride lengths, the motors on the rollers churning and groaning as her footfalls contacted the pavement.

Dana glanced quickly over her shoulder as she entered the highway and just narrowly missed an oncoming car. She crossed over to the leftmost lane. The Hummer pulled onto the road behind her and nudged a compact car into the grassy median. She saw a sign for the entrance to the Franklinbridge Mall quickly approaching on the right.

"Nick, I'm going to take these guys off the highway. They're causing too much chaos. I'll try to shake them off at the mall."

"The what? The mall? It's after hours, the mall is closed," she heard Nick reply through her headset. "I just got to my truck in the parking garage. I saw a little fireworks show heading toward the highway, which I'm guessing was you, and a very big black Hummer right behind you."

"That would be us, me and the girls." She glanced down at her skates and recounted the minutes of racing in her head. "I don't know how much juice Laverne and Shirley have, so I think I'll try to outmaneuver them inside." She panted as her feet scorched the ground with each graceful stride. She hit her rhythm and pumped her arms in unison with her legs like an ice dancer on the asphalt. The corners of her mouth sharpened into a smile.

"Inside? Inside the mall? Dana, it's closed!" Nick buzzed in her ear.

"Improvising, Nicky. Try to catch up to me there."

Dana jumped the landscaping adorning the mall entrance ramp. She could hear the churning angry diesel roar behind her. Up ahead, she noted the desolate mall's layout from the outside. It was a three-sided structure with an anchor department store bisecting each side. At each apex, multiple full-length glass doors marked the main entrances. She realigned herself with the traffic paths looping around the parking lot and headed toward the furthest apex. She peered as best as she could through the glass entryways. The lights were still on in the interior, and she made out a metal shuttered storefront. Only a handful of cars were in the lot, by the loading docks. *Lots of open space*, she thought to herself. *If I can get inside.*

The Hummer rattled over curbs and chewed the decorative bushes and small potted plants as it closed in, sweeping through the mall's parking lots and travel lanes. With every check over her shoulder, the vehicle leapt closer. Another lap around the perimeter would close the gap completely between her and her pursuers, she guessed.

"Nick, where are you?"

"I'm driving to the mall. Where are you?"

"Between a truck and a hard place."

Dana leaned hard into a turn with a quick leg-over-leg crossing motion and barreled toward the set of entrance doors. She leaned to one side and grabbed a decorative flowerpot on the concrete curb leading up to the mall. Maintaining her speed, she threw the potted flowers into the glass doors. With her arms crossed over her face, she lunged behind the clay fragments and into the explosion of safety glass. Diving through the shattered doorframe with her eyes tightly closed under her goggles, she was ignorant to the tiny cuts on her cheeks as the fragments skipped across her skin. Her adrenaline mixed with endorphins, and she laughed as she checked her earpiece.

"Nick, I'm inside now!" Her skates clanged as they smacked against the smooth faux-marble flooring. Her wheels gained traction and shot her forward. A thunderous cacophony of twisting metal and glass erupted behind her as the Hummer plowed through the doors in her wake of glass and sparks. "And so are they!"

She pushed each leg feverishly through the long white and antiseptic atrium, thankfully devoid of any workers still in the mall. Her joy ebbed as a rising fear simmered in her legs and stomach. *This isn't a race, this is a hunt,* she thought. The Hummer maintained its distance behind her as it blasted through wooden benches and a kiosk for cell phone repair, its wheels spinning on the polished floor that favored Dana's skates.

"Dana, what was that?" buzzed Nick in her earpiece. "Where are you?"

"I'm passing the food court."

"That doesn't help me."

"I'm passing Boscov's, and these guys are right behind me."

"Inside the mall? The Hummer is inside the mall?"

"Yep! Inside the mall." She dropped down to one knee as she slid through the outside arc of the next corner to maintain speed. "I think I can do a couple laps to get some distance before shooting out."

As she rounded the turn past a novelty T-shirt store, she glanced over her shoulder to check on her pursuers. The tires of the giant vehicle began to spin out, but the driver held its speed as the truck slid around the corner. Dana couldn't imagine the skill needed to perform such a move and shook her head in disbelief as the Hummer maintained its following distance.

"Nick, they just drifted a Hummer," she yelled.

"I'm sorry, I didn't make that out?"

"They drifted a Hummer! I'm going to need to do something else here. I can't outrun them."

She glanced over her shoulder again and saw the fake trooper roll down his window and rest the barrel of a rifle on the sideview mirror's bracket. She charged toward the next turn and heard a pop behind her and a dull *thunk* of a projectile smacking into a trash can as she passed it. She dove into the next turn on the inside track, clipping her shoulder on a column.

Think, girl, think! This isn't a roller derby track! Her eyes widened and a smile returned to her face. *Exactly! This* isn't *a roller derby track! Turn around!*

Dana released her toes from the control pads inside the boots and drove her heels into the brakes. The Hummer's pistons and fans coughed and wheezed as the driver tried to slam on its brakes.

"Look out!" she heard one of them yell as the bumper closed to within several feet of her. As she heard the words through the din, Dana dropped to the floor onto her stomach. The Hummer's high ground clearance passed over her back, whipping her jacket's tails in its draft. As the vehicle slid ahead into a trash and recycle receptacle array, Dana rolled and kicked up onto her feet and began to race back toward the doors.

"Nick, I'm going to be coming back out the same entrance I came in. Meet me on the highway if you're here." She jumped over the shattered and mangled door frames as she exited the mall and laughed again into her headset. "I still hear these guys behind me. They're blasting out now." She swallowed and stared through the parking lot lampposts at the roadway ahead of her. She needed help—now. "Nick? Navigate me."

"Okay. Head out the mall exit, then right on the highway. Just ahead is the Parkway entrance ramp. Get on it heading southbound."

Dana shook her head as she pumped her legs and roared onto the highway.

"Time is not our *amigo*, and I'm running out of power for sure. I've been burning wheels nonstop."

"Once you're on the Parkway, you'll hit an overpass shortly. It's just a Parkway crossover, so there's no exit ramp." The earpiece buzzed with static. "When you see it, juke right down the embankment and I'll be underneath in the truck. I'll get you."

"Getting on the Parkway," she said as she roared through the entrance ramp past a rattling sign for the New Jersey Garden State Parkway. "And when I'm on the overpass and jump off to the right, you'll be on the underpass, right?"

"Right," he confirmed. "Trust the plan, Dana."

"Trust the plan," she replied. Dana took one more glance at the Hummer behind her and noticed it was now missing a fog light and had a broken headlight. The Parkway was fortunately thin on traffic this time of night. She scanned the road for vehicles ahead and rechecked the pack behind her. A silhouette ducked out from the passenger side window of the Hummer, backlit by the cars behind it.

She decelerated for a moment to let an eighteen-wheeler in the left lane catch up to her position, at the same time allowing the Hummer to crawl closer. The truck began to shift into her lane, oblivious to the woman on roller skates in its blind spot. She leaned right and zipped to the shoulder.

"Dana, small problem," Nick called into the headset.

"How small?"

"Well, I forgot that the overpass runs the other way," he sheepishly confessed.

"So, the Parkway doesn't pass *over the road*," she deadpanned while smacking her forehead.

"No, the road passes *over* the Parkway," Nick countered.

Dana knew she had to think fast. She sped up in the shoulder and attempted to pass the eighteen-wheeler. Just as she got ahead of the tractor trailer, she eased into the right lane, trying to stay in the front blind spot.

"Are you there now, on the overpass?" she yelled.

"Yeah, I'm parked in the middle. There's an eight-foot-high chain-link safety railing on each side of the road. You'll probably see a red pickup and a guy on a cell phone regretting a number of life choices and waving at you."

"Stay there. I'm coming."

Dana glanced back again at the Hummer and noted a faint pair of red and blue flashing lights far back in the distance. She looked at the side of the trailer, then back to the rear bumper. She dropped her speed to let the bumper of the trailer catch up with her and lifted herself onto it.

A second tractor trailer cruised parallel to their lane. Dana lunged from the bumper and grabbed the door latches on that trailer, hoisting herself up. She scaled the rear cargo doors, occasionally setting off a grinding burst of sparks as she dug each wheeled boot into the dull steel panels to create footholds. She steadily climbed toward the cargo hauler's roof. A pop followed by a *thunk* next to her waist startled her. A bulbous dart pierced the trailer door inches away from her body.

"They're shooting darts at me, Nick!" Dana clutched the top lip and swung her legs over the trailer container roofline. "Red rover, do you see me? Nick?" she coughed into her headset.

"I do now," he replied. "Dana, I'm trying to cut these chain-link fasteners but it's not going well."

Dana stood in a sprinter's block stance on the back of the trailer roof with her head up and aimed at the oncoming overpass, her gloved fingertips pressed into the steel. The dull red shape of Nick's truck came into focus on the other side of the chain-link safety railing. The outline of Nick frantically fiddling with a hand tool on the fencing came into focus. The wind and the draft rolling over the truck's hood and air deflectors clawed under her goggles and stung her eyes. She glanced back one more time at the Hummer roaring behind her, adorned with an angry man in a cornflower-blue shirt aiming a rifle at her from the passenger seat.

Her thighs exploded as she shot up and began to propel forward along the trailer box toward the front of the truck. Her toes screamed inside the boots as they pushed the accelerators. She fired her body between the chrome-plated smokestacks and jumped, kicking and leaping into the air. The truck cabin slipped underneath the overpass as she impacted the chain-link fence, which caught her momentarily before ripping from its remaining supports. She tumbled to a stop on the overpass, enmeshed in a coil of metal grating.

"DANA!" Nick ran over and ripped the fencing off her. He slid his arms under her torso, gently lifting her up as she surveyed the scene. She put her arm over his shoulder so he could help her to the truck bed.

"Nick, I think I got shot!" She tucked her chin to her chest and saw a large red vinyl tassel attached to the stump of a tranquilizer sticking into the side of her stomach. She fell back into the truck bed.

Nick pulled the needle out and stared at the large chunk of leather it had ripped from her jacket hem, which had prevented it from penetrating her skin. With an audible sigh of relief, he pushed her wheeled feet into the bed and closed the liftgate.

"Just go—anywhere," she muttered between gasps.

The red pickup sputtered as Nick threw the shifter into drive. They shot down the road into the darkness.

Olsen kicked the bumper of the Hummer pulled over on the shoulder on the overpass and scowled at the pieces of chain-link fencing splayed across the road. He ran his fingers over the skid marks left by a small truck and surveyed the hole in the safety railing overlooking the Parkway.

"That was quite a show. I'm almost impressed." He walked back to the Hummer and reloaded the empty clip in his tranquilizer dart rifle. "We need to rethink this."

Eighty-Eight sat in the driver's seat, clutching and releasing the steering wheel rhythmically as his eyes bored into Olsen. "I'm the best driver on the team and I couldn't catch a girl on roller skates," he fumed. "And yet you're as calm as a cat in a sunbeam."

"We're supposed to get her alive," Olsen stated in an authoritative monotone as he held the rifle aloft and tracked an imaginary target across the highway. He pulled the clip out and recounted the three tranquilizer rounds marked with a caution skull before resetting them into the rifle's body with a forceful click.

"What now?"

Olsen took off his gloves and felt for the keys to his sedan in his pocket. The Hummer was not made for agile pursuit. Her speed was not the issue; rather, her mobility gave her an edge they could not overcome in such a cumbersome vehicle. He knelt for a moment to examine the damage; the massive diesel engine was still running high despite some concrete fragments in the front grill. He lamented some of the minor armor removal choices they had made to keep the vehicle lighter for highway mode. *We need to even the playing field against a girl on goddamn roller skates*, he admitted to himself.

"I'll call Rhodes. We need some petty cash."

Chapter 22

Moon on the Water – Koyuki Tanaka & Maho Minami

Dana opened her eyes, the subtle jostling of the pickup truck gently waking her. She rested her chin on her chest and checked that her skates were still on.

The red Ford Ranger crept into the driveway of the Andrews family homestead and onto the gravel path to the rear garage. Nick gently stopped the truck under the burned-out floodlights over the shed doors. From her makeshift lounge in the truck bed, Dana leaned up gingerly and knocked on the glass, following it with a weak wave.

Nick got out and walked around to the liftgate. "We're home," he said. Dana was sitting up and leaning against the back window. She winced as she attempted to move again and decided to lay back down on the cool metal bed.

"Can we just take a minute . . . or seventy?" She grimaced as the pain began to override the fading adrenaline in her circulatory system.

Nick opened the lift gate and crawled next to her. Her jacket was unzipped, revealing underneath her T-shirt coated in sweat and dirt. Her chest labored with each deep breath.

"Do you need to go to the hospital? Anything feel broken?" Nick asked.

"Did I get shot?" she inquired as she gingerly touched her stomach and ribs.

Nick held up the tranquilizer dart. "Didn't go in. I think you got the wind knocked the hell out of you when you lost that fight with the chain-link fence."

He sat back against the cab and let out a frustrated exhale, which mutated into a raspberry.

"I have no idea what kind of mess we're in right now," he said, addressing the clouds floating above before turning back to Dana. "This is so messed up. These guys want to kill people—maybe us—for whatever it is you're chasing, and I don't even know what our endgame really is." He returned his gaze to the deep-blue night sky and the dark-gray masses that slowly drifted in front of the stars. "Are we trying to find the people in that photo, or stop these guys from doing something, or should we just go hide out for a decade and let this blow over?"

Dana pat the bed liner beside her. "Just take a breather. Lay down for a sec."

Nick slumped down next to her so they were shoulder to shoulder. They looked up together at the night sky, dotted by a flock of geese gliding silently against the tiny backlit clouds, breaking the silence occasionally with their honks as they migrated under the half moon. The air was cool, but not cool enough to see their breath. Dana rolled her head from side to side to work out a neck strain, wincing as she made it to each end of the motion.

"I need to think." She crossed and uncrossed her legs, each time making a loud clunk with her skates against the tailgate. "Tell me something completely unrelated to all of this. What was your favorite family vacation?"

"Really?"

"Really! I'll go first. I didn't have many since my parents died when I was so young, but one time my mom and I took my granddad's truck out to the Bottomless Lakes State Park. It's this, like, crater outside of Roswell in

New Mexico, where the water goes down so far that you can't see the bottom. And the water gets really, *really* cold the further down you dive."

"We have a couple here in the Pine Barrens. They're a badly contained secret tourist adventure."

"No kidding?" Dana placed her hands on her stomach and interlaced her fingers with a slight effort. "Anyway, my mom and I went camping there one night—car camping, that is. I saw shooting stars and thought they were the aliens. It was the first time I ever saw a full-blown meteor shower." She inhaled deeply through her nose as she closed her eyes and smiled. "I can almost smell the desert when I think of it."

"Well, I don't think I have anything like that," he countered, his hands also lying against his prone posture. "We did a lot of things before Mom died—beach trips, a lot of historic places like Gettysburg—but they always felt like a disappointment. Don't get me wrong, they were fun, but, I don't know, I think I watched too many movies and TV shows. You know, where the boy goes on vacation and meets some girl on the first day and they have this magical time together."

Nick turned his head to Dana, who lay motionless, inches from his face, staring at him with a smile.

"That is the corniest shit I've ever heard." She burst out laughing, and he joined her. "I mean, it's really sweet in a puppy-love twelve-year-old way, but man, that is some sappy stuff."

Still laughing to himself, he turned his face back toward the moon. A large cloud began to roll in front of it, submerging them in dark shadows except for the furthest reaches of the back porch light across the yard.

"I know I tease you, but think you're a nice boy, Nicky." She bit her lip. "I guess that's why you're helping me. I *know* that's why you're helping me. Thank you."

"Maybe I have some kind of nurturer complex or something," he admitted. "At first, I thought, 'I just want to see those skates,' but then, I don't know, it just seemed like something really important that you couldn't do by yourself."

"So, I'm a damsel in distress?" She elbowed him playfully.

"I would say you're Don Quixote and I'm Sancho Panza. I make a better sidekick than a hero."

"The *sidekick* saved my ass back there." She stared up at the moon again as it fought to come through the encroaching clouds. Her pain was dulling across her body. She cleared her throat. "I felt like I had to find out this big thing about my family, about my dad, and my granddad, and that there was going to be some sort of payoff, some answers at least. I didn't realize I was being set up for something. I mean, I don't know, I even wonder if they really loved me or not in the end. If they saw me as something useful to clear their names or make amends." She choked up for a moment. "Like my life is being lived to finish theirs."

Dana put her arm by her side, not realizing Nick had done the same. He laid his hand into her glove. She closed her fingers around his. He inhaled slowly and deeply.

"My dad told me, after Mom died, that sometimes *this*"—he gave her hand a squeeze—"means more than any words. That's why businessmen shake hands. I forget if it was a medieval or Roman custom, but it came from the arm grab to see if the person across from you was hiding something in their sleeve." He glanced over at Dana and then back up. "I got your back on this adventure."

"Thank you. Although I *do not* remember that history lesson in boarding school," she answered with a tinge of sarcasm. "But this *is* what I need right now." She squeezed his hand back. "Just this. And maybe a shower and a bottle of painkillers."

They continued gazing at the sky. A silhouette crossed overhead, an egret who was most likely traveling from one pond to another across the wooded expanse around them. Dana nudged her shoulder closer to Nick until it was touching his.

"Can we just stay here a little longer?"

"Sure."

She closed her eyes.

The woods surrounding the property sat dark and still for several minutes, with no wind to rake the branches of the pine and maple trees. The ringing in Dana's ears finally abated. She could now hear deer walking through the forest, their hooves stepping on the needles and leaves. The only manmade noise was the quiet click of the porch door unlatching. Dana lifted her head just far enough to spy Nick's dad peeking out from the back door. He nodded and smiled as he noticed the two pairs of feet extending out of the truck bed, one in work boots and the other in oversized roller skates. He soundlessly retreated inside.

After a few more minutes of silence, Nick sat up and pulled Dana gently to a sitting posture. They headed to the house without speaking, until Dana quietly swore as she tripped up the porch steps in her skates.

Chapter 23

Mind Playing Tricks on Me – Geto Boys

Joshua stared at the whiteboard on his office wall. The immense surface overshadowed the framed degrees on one side and a black-and-white photo of the Capitol building, dated 1861, on the other. The reproduction of the dome under construction was a gift from his in-laws upon his assignment to Washington, although they did not understand the nature of his occupation. He stared at the photo and daydreamed how he might project a budget for such a monumental undertaking if the government ever decided to return to building grand structures. He turned back to the whiteboard and the list of abbreviations he had used to encode his research.

Six names corresponded with a handful of files in the archives, and on his board he listed annotations he created for each name:

SDS

SJJ

CRD

ANS

JASON

POW

Respectively, the annotations stood for Samuel David Jefferson Sr., Samuel David Jefferson Jr., Colin Rhodes, Anselm Geissler, Jens Jacobsen, and Cannon Hardy.

The crude cypher was intended to not arouse suspicion from any observers who stumbled into the office before he could erase them. The six names overlapped on the joint military base PX records, but it was the first and final entries for each that piqued his interest.

He summarized that based on the commissary account entries on the base, the men all started there around the same time, followed by an early departure by Rhodes and then the younger Jefferson. The payment checks to Rhodes, however, were dated well after the end of the last commissary entries. Joshua had decided to dig even further and was able to find confirmed death certificates for both Jeffersons as well as Jacobsen and Hardy.

As he continued to stare at the board, an abrupt and firm knock shook his concentration.

"One moment," he replied as he clutched the eraser and wiped hastily at parts of the board. His teammate Jenna entered without waiting and studied his wild erasing of the whiteboard.

"Is that the invite list to my baby shower?" she asked, chuckling and cradling her stomach with one hand.

"Ha, no. I was just brainstorming something."

She dropped a file into the box on his desk. "Those are the pension check files you asked for, and I emailed the digitals. Anything I can help you with? We have the same clearance, you know." Even though Jenna was his senior teammate by three months, he treated her as either a senior advisor or junior intern depending on the project and his level of self-absorption in his work.

"Maybe. What would you do if you retired and got a pension? Like, a big pension?"

She absently twirled a lock of red hair as she looked beyond his desk to where an exterior office would have a window, but her pondering posture encountered a bookshelf of legal and accounting guides.

"Well, I'd keep working doing something I liked, and insist on an office with a window. I'm just that type, I think. But maybe I'd also get a nice beach house for the weekends."

"Fair enough. So, a beach?" He scratched his head with the dry eraser, marking his ear with black and blue marker ink.

"Yeah. Doesn't have to be a private island, but I'd definitely have my own plane so I wouldn't have to go through the TSA with all the peons of the working class!" She laughed at her joke and leaned on the open door. "Do you know you can buy a used surplus trainer prop plane?"

"You can just go out and buy a used plane from the air force?"

"Not *exactly*. I had to check the auctions once for an audit on nonpaying bidders and I fell down a rabbit hole of pricing planes. Dan—"

"Your fiancé."

"Yes. Dan, my *fiancé*, has his license so I thought it would be fun to browse. It's uncommon, but there are prop planes and tiny helicopters. I even saw a cargo plane once for sale!"

"How the hell would we auction off a cargo plane? That's really not a good idea to give it to a civilian."

"That's why I said not *exactly*." She raised an eyebrow and tapped her fingers on the sides of her protruding belly.

"Don't keep me in suspense; you know something."

"All right, all right. They go to contractors. We auctioned off a cargo plane in a sealed bid between two commando cowboys. Just like us, they don't want to fly commercial. The winning bid went to an active private military company."

Joshua dropped the eraser. "A PMC? What was the name? Do you remember?"

"Sure, One Hundred Roads. The owner is a guy named Colin Rhodes.

'Roads' and 'Rhodes' is the only reason I remember. The bid was *really low*. The other company barely bid up the value."

Joshua swallowed hard. He misjudged the distance between himself and white board as he went to lean back but missed. Straightening back up, he continued. "Do those guys pay cash at these auctions? I've never looked into the nuts and bolts before."

"Usually, yes, it's all locked briefcases or cashier's checks, but this guy I remember because he just had the money rolled from the company's escrow account. So, it was just a transfer, no actual bill. That's part of the fun of our job, I suppose."

Joshua rubbed his chin, unaware of the growing facial smears from the whiteboard marker ink on his hands.

"Wait, wait. So, we paid the contractor, at some point before the auction, for services rendered or services pending."

"Correct."

"Then they bid in an auction and win, and then use the money we paid them in a transfer back to us." He glanced back at the faint marks of his hasty erasure on the whiteboard. "So, technically, we paid them, and they used our own money to buy the plane back." He ran the eraser over a smudge very slowly. "Net result is we paid them with a plane. And it's all above level."

Jenna nodded, her smile slowly leveling into a straight line. She screwed her head slightly as she asked, "Josh, that's bad, isn't it?"

"Not quite. Not yet. But why wouldn't they just *ask* for the plane in a requisition? Or lease with their PMC? Then all the paperwork, fuel, flight plans, and logs, that would all get handled by us and cut the paperwork by a third for their missions." He caught the words as they fell from his mouth and echoed in the office. *"Unless they don't want us to know about their missions."*

"But PMCs do secret stuff."

"That's the point." Joshua questioned if he wanted to show all his cards yet, especially regarding Rhodes. He ran behind his desk and grabbed a legal pad and pen, scribbling furiously and then tearing off the page when he was done.

"Jenna, when you rent or buy a car, they usually give you a full tank of gas. I would guess we would do something similar with a goddamn plane unless they didn't want us to know how far or where it was flying." He froze and grabbed a thought from the air. "Airplane fuel is expensive, though. We might only give them enough to go from point A to point B. Here, take this— it's time for a big favor," he said as he folded the paper and forced it into her hand. "I'll buy you the best stroller on the market for your baby shower."

Jenna tucked her hair behind one ear before she unfolded the paper. Her eyes darted back and forth across the scrawled lines.

Joshua continued. "It's a list. Get me some info on that plane. Former call sign, current if available. Storage and transport locations until the final transfer of ownership. Any indication of fuel load and initial flight log. I bet they didn't file it."

She nodded and then looked down again, appearing to read the details slowly and more than once, before folding it back up and handing it back to him. "Got it all. Memory trick of mine. You can shred this now. Guess I helped after all?"

He shook his head and smiled. "Maybe. I think you might have dropped a giant bread crumb from the sky, but all the crumbs are yet to be revealed." He slung his jacket over his shoulder and grabbed his keys from the desk. "There's just one more thing."

"Sure," she drawled as she reached for the door.

"I think Director Jameson was a little spooked by something I brought up the other day about this. So, keep it close to the belt, as best you can in maternity wear." He winked. "If you need to know more, just ask, but I want you to know I'm keeping some details close so you don't have to worry about slipping up and saying something you shouldn't."

"Hey, I can keep a secret. You know that," she said a bit defensively.

"I know. I'm just trying to make sure you're insulated from the details. Just in case someone starts poking."

She swung the door open but stopped and turned to him before walking out. "BabyStyle Oyster Zero Gravity. The blue-and-orange trim package. I'll consider that a favor paid."

"Done. And thank you."

Chapter 24

Cotton Fields – Credence Clearwater Revival

D ana squinted in the mid-morning sun as she walked out of Nick's bedroom and headed down the hall. She rolled down the sleeves of his heather gray sweatshirt that she had found hanging in his closet and reminded herself that she needed to wash her battle-damaged clothes from last night as well as a large load of laundry at her place that had been left in a state of neglect. The fading scent of grilled bacon and toast lingered in the air. As she passed the living room, she observed that Nick had folded his sheet on the couch next to his pillow and a pair of sweatpants. His boots were missing.

"Good morning, *Photograph*," Mr. Andrews called out from the kitchen table.

Dana stood still, startled for a moment, biting her lip while decided how to respond. Finally, she smiled and nodded at Mr. Andrews. "Thank you, *Mitch*." She rubbed her eyes with her sleeves, her hands tucked inside like a child wearing their father's clothes. Of course, her father had never allowed her to do so with his uniforms.

"Nick left early to catch up on his backload and probably get chewed out by our supervisor. I, for a change, am playing hooky." Mr. Andrews had placed a pink coffee mug at the end of the kitchen table and indicated that Dana should sit and have breakfast. "And, yes, Nick has finally told me everything you kids have been up to." He raised an eyebrow above the wire frame of his glasses.

Dana froze with her mug to her lips and glanced down at the tabletop. The back of her neck felt hot, her forearms tight, and a rush of blood swelled in her chest. She brought her eyes up to meet the gaze of Mr. Andrews, who was smiling with his arm propping up his cheek.

"It's okay, Dana. If I didn't ask Nick to explain it all about three times, I wouldn't believe it. Even harder to believe is that I don't think you guys even know everything yet."

"So, he told you about the hospital, and the mall, and . . ." She made a gesture of her fingers walking while making a whip-poor-will whistling noise. "My skates?"

"I think you know, I was with him the first time he saw you speeding around at night. And, well, me and him, we have to trust each other. We've been a two-man band for a long time now."

Dana half smiled as she watched Mr. Andrews nervously twist his gold wedding ring on his calloused left hand. "Nick is a really nice guy. Smart, too, quick on his feet. Not as fast as me, but you catch my drift."

"Yeah," he said, laughing. "He's smart. Real smart. But here's something he won't tell you." Mr. Andrews leaned forward. "He had a partial scholarship to an engineering school out in Michigan, but he felt like he needed to be here for me. It was a big sacrifice he made not going." He stirred the spoon in his mug slowly. "I told him not to pass it up. I told him to go, but he just decided he couldn't leave me by myself. I think he'd be a little homesick, too, if I'm being honest."

Mr. Andrews took a sip of his coffee, and Dana responded in kind. She felt more at ease with him every time they interacted, but she reminded herself to keep some distance. She had never taken down her guard fully with anyone since she had been left on her own, not even Angela, who had done her best to tolerate Dana's walls when they dated. But with Nick, and now with his dad, she realized, something about them gave her the will to lower her defenses a bit more, or perhaps to at least put a window or two in her walls.

"Did Nick tell you how his mom died?" he asked. Dana shook her head in earnest. "I think I'll let him do that when he's ready. I'll just say, he wasn't there when she passed, and I know it eats him up." Mr. Andrews ran his hand over the thin gray-flecked stubble on his cheeks. "He's got some guilt over missing out on saying goodbye to her. He carries a lot of weight he doesn't need to bear."

Mr. Andrews reached into his pocket and pulled out what looked like a blue-and-gold coin. He rolled it across his knuckles and then slid it to the middle of the table. Dana leaned forward and pulled it toward her. A gold triangle was framed by the words Unity, Service, and Recovery on each side, and a Roman number five was in the center.

"I made it through, and he doesn't need to watch over me."

Dana smiled and then pushed it back across the table. Her eyes watered with thoughts of the missed heart-to-heart conversations with her own father, as well as mother, but also at the idea of Mr. Andrews's ability to carry so many burdens without showing the strain. She imagined her own father would have done the same with her in another timeline.

"Thank you for sharing that. All of that. It takes some big trust to share something like that." She wiped her sleeve under her eye.

"Well, I needed to show my cards to let you know I'm here for you, too, not just Nick. This definitely feels like big mess to figure out, what with the car chases, the robot . . . oh yeah, he showed me the picture. Like I said, I still don't believe it."

"Neither do I sometimes. But I got a head start on believing it's all real when I found the blueprints for these skates."

Dana was about to stand up and then realized that she wasn't wearing pants. The sweatshirt came halfway to her knees, thankfully. In the disorientation this morning, she had forgotten that someone else lived in the house when she woke.

"Mr. Andrews, you know Nick and I aren't . . . we didn't . . . we're not . . ."

He chuckled and made a zipping motion across his lips. "Just be whatever you're going to be. He's a good guy, almost to a fault. He's kind of got a need to help people. That drove his ex-girlfriend nuts."

Now that she was feeling fully awake, Dana pulled over to the plate of food on the table. She picked up the toast and folded it into a triangle. *Just like Mom used to,* she mused. Her curiosity was piqued, however, by the sliver of an opening into Nick's former love life, and she latched onto the word "ex-girlfriend."

"Okay, I've got to know what Nick's type is," she sputtered between mouthfuls of breakfast. "Blonde, freckles, no callouses?"

Mr. Andrews roared with laughter. "So, you've met Lindsey, it appears? 'Cause that is a perfect description. She's a doctor's daughter from the right side of the tracks, but it's just an act. She swears like a trucker, and she's never liked me. I am a bit too 'working class' for her." He made a gesture of quotation marks in the air.

Dana quickly surveyed the room: the simple clean modern furniture, the narrow color range of whites and tans and light browns, and the impeccably clean and organized kitchen. She shook her head. "Please! If you're too barbaric and low-class, then I'm a cavewoman! Screw Lindsey!"

They laughed and sat together comfortably as she finished her breakfast and accepted a refill of her coffee.

Mr. Andrews grabbed a folder of paper and a notebook from the chair between them, carefully organizing the contents including the picture of

Dana's father and grandfather with the giant robot. "As you can see, Nick showed me your pile of loot. Here's what I'm thinking: You can go take a trip down to this farm guy, the agricultural contractor or whatever he does. Let me and Nick fiddle around with your skates, and by me and Nick, I really mean him but in my workshop. Since I'm off today, I can drive you to your apartment to figure out if the coast is clear there, and if it is, you can pick up anything you need. And, if it's okay with you, let me see if I can dig up anything on the people whose names you found in that bunker. I can have my buddy in billing run their names against old accounts," Mr. Andrews said, tapping a finger against his temple.

"Mr. Andrews, you're alright," Dana responded, mirroring his gesture.

"Why thank you, *Ms. Jefferson*. Now, please excuse me while I leave the room so you can regain a little modesty and locate a pair of pants."

Dana blushed in spite of herself and, once sure she was alone, headed to collect her clothes from the floor of Nick's room and grab a towel from the linen closet. She located the laundry nook beyond the kitchen and quickly stripped down and then wrapped herself in the towel. After starting the washing machine, she started the shower and examined herself in the mirror while waiting for the water to get hot. She ran her fingers over the blue-and-yellow edges of a bruise the size of her hand, just below her rib cage. She ran her hand down to her hip, where an older bruise had almost disappeared but was now adjacent to a new one from last night. Indeed, the whole of her body was the patchwork of discolorations.

"Dana, you saved an officer's life, twice," she consoled herself. "That's something."

She stepped into the shower.

She closed her eyes.

The hot water mixed with the tears as they trickled down her cheeks.

Chapter 25

Perfect Strangers – Deep Purple

Olsen let the engine of his Dodge Charger idle, and it growled as he accidentally tapped the gas while in park. He sat in the front parking space of the roadside garage and store Atco Super Sound and Sports and studied the cashier inside. Finally, the last customer walked out and left in his customized neon-yellow Honda Civic. As he was checking his diving watch again and noting the twins were five minutes late, the swelling rattle of their Hummer at last saddling up next to his car elicited a small smile. Two short barrel-chested men with matching shaved heads and shirt-collar-length beards stepped out of the Hummer, identical not only genetics but in dress and facial expression. It was be impossible to tell them apart if not for the 036 and 037 embroidered on their black fatigue shirts, and the fact that Agent Thirty-Six walked with a barely noticeable limp. The rear passenger door opened, and a large bald man labeled 074 dropped to the ground. Olsen thought Seventy-Four most resembled a hippopotamus. With his rotund torso, wide mouth, and rounded features, people often underestimated his lethal aggressiveness.

"Tighten up your tardiness," Olsen set flatly as they walked toward the building. He pointed at Seventy-Four and then swirled his finger in the air, indicating to him to walk the perimeter of the building to keep watch.

Inside, the clean checkered tile floor and displays of chromed accessories and engine exhausts sparkled under the white LED ceiling fixtures. A sign for trim decals and custom logos displayed on the wall behind the counter contrasted with the dull forest outside the window. The entire auto parts store was like a candy shop to Olsen. A short young man with pockmarked cheeks and an elegantly manicured goatee smiled from behind the register as he shuffled bills into a bank deposit envelope. He slid another small stack into his pocket and raised a finger to Olsen.

"One sec, hombre." He peered back into the shop and tweeted a trilling whistle. "Herb, get me a two-two-two." He leaned back over the counter and set his sinewy forearms on the counter. "Okay, gentlemen, what can I do you for?"

Olsen picked up a business card from the clear plastic display. "Are you Tito 'Peaches' Domingo?"

"That's me, proprietor of pistons and king of the quarter mile." He pulled a stool close to the counter and sat down, raising his height to match Olsen's eyeline.

"Why 'Peaches'?"

"Because I get 'em by the bushel, know what I'm saying?" He extended a fist to Olsen, who reciprocated with an awkward bump.

"Ok, *Peaches*," said Olsen. Agent Thirty-Six meandered to one window and slowly shut the blinds.

"Ok, *Flattop*," Peaches replied as he inspected the twins. "We're closing in a bit. You looking for stereo upgrades, tuner parts, or . . . something else?"

Agent Thirty-Seven walked to another window and lowered those blinds.

"Turn off the security cameras and we can get down to brass tacks," Olsen responded, to which Peaches pulled out his phone and tapped a few buttons. "Since it only took me about two hours of observation to see that you're not just pedaling auto parts out of this shop, we know you're our type of guy. And no need to keep inching your hand toward that pistol or sawed-off shotgun strapped under the counter."

Peaches made no change in facial expression. "I don't know what you're talking about, Chief. You guys don't look like police, but I'm still not sure what you're implying about my business." He pulled a toothpick from his pocket and placed it between his front teeth. Olsen reached inside his coat, holding up his other hand to imply this wasn't a threat. He produced a pack of crisp one-hundred-dollar bills, still in the bank wrapper. Peaches slowly placed his palms on top of the counter, his eyes glowing as he lowered his gaze to the cash stack.

"Yo, Flattop, I don't have enough chalk for that kind of bankroll. But if you want, I can put in an order."

"No, we're not here for meth. Do you see that Charger outside? I need some performance enhancements, and I need them tomorrow." Olsen slid a piece of paper across the counter. "*Tomorrow.*"

Peaches snatched up the list and looked over at the twins, who were guarding each side of the front door after making sure every set of blinds was closed. Peaches traced the thin lines of his sideburns and moustache with his free hand and looked up at Olsen with a smile. He nodded and rocked back and forth as he finished examining the list.

"This is gonna be *sick*. But I think what you need is a multitank nitrous system, like a three-five-seven cylinder. Pop! Pop! Pop!" He pantomimed the cocking and firing of an imaginary gun. "That's how you get multiple injection shots clean as each one empties out. You don't want a single big tank. Plus, I can fit it better under the hood of that thing."

Thirty-Six approached the counter. He pulled a Glock 19 out a concealed pocket of his armpit, placing it on the counter while retaining his grasp of the handle. "We have a speed problem," he chimed in with a soft but scratchy voice. "We need to outrun someone and it's not a straight shot. And this," he said as he produced his own small roll of bills that he laid on the counter, "is for the security camera footage from today. Because we were never here." He nodded to the CCTV recorder on the top shelf behind Peaches. Olsen soured his face at Thirty-Six's unnecessary display of his weapon and tilted his head to imply holstering it.

Peaches hesitated. "I'll delete the video before the backup upload. But I gotta tell you guys, this job is going to take a little time. I'd have to work overnight, you know what I mean?" He put his palms together and rubbed them in a slow circular motion.

Thirty-Seven walked out of the shop toward the Hummer and disappeared momentarily. He returned with a box of coffee and a bag of donuts from the local café and placed them gently on the counter. Olsen allowed himself a short smile at their preparedness.

"Man, you guys came prepared! I like you!" Peaches clapped his hands and opened the box to inspect the donut flavor selection.

Olsen gently closed the lid. "If you have it ready by dawn, we have a bonus." He pulled another bill pack from his pocket and slapped it against the counter before putting it back.

Peaches nodded. "Time is going to be tight. It's just me and Herb tonight closing up." He whistled again to the back room. A skinny teenager with a sawed-off shotgun emerged from the breezeway. He was decorated in disjointed tattoos that appeared to have been finished in fifty-dollar increments and had a deep scar down his jawline.

"What's up. I'm Herb." He cocked the shotgun. "Peaches, you need the two-two-two now?"

Thirty-Six already had his Glock aimed at Peaches's chest. Thirty-Seven copied the move in unison. Olsen held his hands up.

"Everyone, we're in an agreement here, no need for menacing." He fluttered his hands as the twins lowered their pistols to their waist. "Let's talk about finishing the job. We're in business, yes?"

"I just need you to know this is a mutual thing," said Peaches, waving to Herb to lower the gun. "This is a serious amount of cash for a serious job, and it can draw attention to me if the shop is open overnight." He glanced down at the list again. "Now this last part," he said as he ran an ink-stained finger under the last lines, "I see you want a little bit of that *Spy Hunter* magic. I don't know if we can put that in."

"I thought about that, but I think you can mount a pair of grease guns next to each exhaust pipe with a remote trigger, or a cable release."

"Ah, I got you. I can do that. Once we're done, you're going to be able to outrun most anything that's not modified on the road, one way or another." Herb leaned over Peaches's shoulder to look at the plans and nodded.

"Excellent," Olsen said. "We'll be back at dawn. Any funny business, and the police will be here on a hot tip about a meth dealer. But do as you're asked, and we're happy to pay."

Peaches took the original bill stack and handed it to Herb, who quickly disappeared into the back. The sound of the rear garage door opening followed as well as several dissonant metallic clangs as tools were pulled and thrown onto the floor in preparation. Olsen placed the car keys on the counter.

"One more thing, Peaches: What's the 'two-two-two'?"

"Security code. Two more guys than me come in? Grab the double barrel, and two shots per guy. One to the head, and one more makes dead."

"Huh, clever." Olsen jutted out his chin, impressed with the protocol that slipped past him when they had entered. He felt confident that Peaches was indeed the correct choice for this task. Herb stepped back through the breezeway and picked up the keys from the counter.

"One more thing, buddy." Peaches leaned in. "Why are these guys named Thirty-Six and Thirty-Seven?"

Olsen leaned in close to Peaches's ear. "That's how many bodies they've each buried." A monstrous silhouette passed between the streetlight and front door. "Seventy-Four is outside."

Peaches looked to Herb for his reaction, who looked calm but had beads of sweat forming next to his ears. The twins checked through the blinds before leaving. Olsen meandered for a moment as he listened to Peaches and Herb mutter over the list of enhancements to the Charger.

Peaches cleared his throat and gave instructions to Herb. "Pull the car around back, lock everything up, and delete that security footage. And make sure they get the good air freshener. You like pine scent, Flattop?"

"I'm learning to like it."

0:00   3:13

Chapter 26

Bang Bang – Jessie J, Ariana Grande, and Nicki Minaj

Mr. Andrews and Dana rolled up the gravel drive to her apartment loft, not too far behind a sky-blue school bus parked toward the back of the building. Before he had barely put his truck into park, Dana leapt out and ran toward the outside staircase. At the top of the landing, they both noticed a stout woman, about six feet by Mr. Andrews's estimate, holding a blue baseball bat over her shoulder and wearing roughshod denim coveralls with a half shirt underneath. Her brown hair woven with gray strands was pulled back in a simple ponytail. As his hand hovered over the door lock, the woman lowered the bat and donned a large warm smile, adorned by two rings piercing her lower lip.

"Girl, you're in a whole mess of trouble!" she yelled.

"MARY BETH!" Dana raced up the steps and nearly tackled her with a gigantic warm hug and a kiss on the cheek. "What are you doing here?"

"Well, you're all over the news apparently," replied Mary Beth, "and when you missed practice last night, I figured something was up."

Mr. Andrews took his time as he walked up the staircase, stopping a few steps below the embracing duo.

"Hello, miss, I'm Mitch. Mitch Andrews." He extended a friendly hand to Mary Beth. "I take it you're someone Dana knows." He adjusted his posture to bring his shoulders up and sucked in his gut slowly.

"Hey. Mary Beth Kowalski. MB for short, but most of the girls on the team call me Mama."

Dana separated from the embrace, still beaming with an ear-to-ear grin. "Mr. Andrews, MB is the captain of our roller derby team. The Angels. Asbury Angels. Mama, what's going on? I'm on the news?"

"Well, someone who looks like you was. This morning they were showing footage from mall security cameras on all the local stations. The buzz was about a joyride, destruction of property, something like that involving a truck . . . and someone on roller skates." She put her bat down, holding it like a cane. "I recognized your hair, that dirty jacket of yours, and your moves, and when you didn't show up for our first practice of the season, I put two and two together." She poked Dana's feet with the bat. "You always had some sweet moves, sister."

Another woman suddenly opened the door from inside the apartment, also holding a bat. She was taller than Dana, and her golden hair ran down to her lower back, glowing as the sun's rays traced the edges. Her eyes were as blue as the Asbury Angel's logo on her shirt, and she nodded to Dana.

"Angela. Hey." Dana addressed the statuesque Amazon with a cagey tone.

"You didn't return our calls," replied Angela. Her large eyes were sewn into a squint, her manicured brows arcing high over each one. Mr. Andrews noticed Dana staring into Angela's eyes, blinking a few times to hold the watery sheen at bay.

"Ang, I'm sorry I didn't call back. Things are a bit . . . complicated."

Dana finally embraced Angela, a long lingering hug that appeared, by Mr. Andrew's estimation, to be an apology from someone who was more than a friend. He glanced at Mary Beth, who held up a silent hand to him. When Dana and Angela separated, he could see a tear fall down Angela's cheek.

"It's okay. When I saw you on the news, I told MB we needed to get here and see if you were okay," Angela said as she wiped her cheek with her long hand. "Your place looks like it's been ransacked. I just didn't know what happened to you."

Dana released a long breath and held Angela's hand for a moment. She turned to Mr. Andrews.

"This is Angela. AC on the roster. She's my—" Dana paused. "She's my ex. But she's also a good friend. Someone we can trust." She turned back to Angela. "We may not have been a perfect match, but she's special to me."

Angela put the bat back on her shoulder and then put two fingers in her mouth and blew a loud whistle. The back door of the blue bus in the parking lot below swung open and out jumped a small girl with olive skin, her jet-black hair styled in an intricate braid.

"Hey, hey, hey, are we clear?" She skipped up to the bottom of the staircase, a hammer tucked into her belt. She presented herself with a curtsy to Mr. Andrews. "Greetings. I'm Paula, but y'all can call me Puck. That's what's on the back of my jersey. And my headshots."

"Are there any more of you?" Mr. Andrews asked. "My gosh, you're like a pack of dirty Valkyries. I mean, you girls all look weathered," he stammered, looking over to Mary Beth. "Not that there's anything wrong with that."

"That's not too far off," replied Mary Beth with a broad smile and a wink. "Let's go on in, Dana. It looks like they cleaned your place out pretty good."

As they entered the doorway, Mr. Andrews could see the doorjamb was kicked in, and the deadbolt still attached to a piece of wood ripped from the frame. Dana's jaw slacked as she surveyed the ransacked belongings. Furniture, what little she had, was tossed on its side, and dishes, clothing, and papers were strewn across the floor. She immediately ran to a lockbox that had been pried open and left empty in the middle of the room.

"No, no, no, no, no, they got everything in here." She ran to a corner of the room and began to push the dresser away from the wall. Angela joined the effort. As they pushed, a corner of carpet that was frayed more than the others was exposed, appearing to conceal a noticeable flat rectangular lump. Dana pulled up the corner of carpet, revealing underneath a plastic portfolio emblazoned with the neon-green text "Trapper Keeper" across a picture of a Pegasus.

"Oh, thank God," she jubilantly cried as she opened the folio. "My bank stuff, my pictures of dad, and the photocopies." She held a stapled cluster of papers that appeared to be blueprints. A photo slipped out and fell to the floor, and Mr. Andrews bent over to pick it up.

"Oh, it's the team. There's you! And Puck," he laughed while pointing to the diminutive skater being held by four other women in the group photo. In the back row, Dana and Angela were side by side, not facing the camera, but looking at each other.

Mary Beth sauntered to his side and took the photo politely. She handed it back to Dana. "Well, girls," she declared, "we've got some work to do. Puck, you grab some of those garbage bags and round up her clothes. Dana, get your valuables. Angela, you pull the team bus to the bottom of the staircase and keep watch." She pulled a pack of cigarettes out of her coverall pocket and lit one with a match. "Since you're likely not getting your security deposit back, do please let me indulge myself."

"Mary Beth, if I may," interjected Mr. Andrews, "can I run something by you?" The two most senior people in the room walked over to the doorway as Dana and Puck scurried through piles, collecting an assortment of mismatched socks and trinkets.

"Dana's got a place to stay with me and my son, Nick. I think it's a good spot for her to lay low. There are some pretty bad people after her for some really bad things." He read the confusion on Mary Beth's face. "Things *they* want, not things *she* did." Mary Beth nodded. "I know you may not understand the full extent of Dana's predicament, but just trust me, it's complicated." He looked through the doorway down at Angela standing next to the bus. "And, well, I think my son has a little thing for her."

"I read you, Mitch. The thing between Angela and Dana, that's over now. But just a heads up that Angela . . . that girl is a warthog in a supermodel's body. That's why she's the best on the team. She stuns with her looks and her right hooks." Mary Beth chortled. "I like that one. I'll add that to her bio on the website!"

Dana broke up their conference by throwing two black plastic bags of clothes between them and down the stairs.

"I think we got everything here. Mr. Andrews, I'll meet you in the truck. Let me just talk to the girls for a moment." He saw through her words; she meant Angela, not the girls.

Mr. Andrews did as she asked. As he sat behind the steering wheel, he observed Angela and Dana standing close to each other, inches separating their faces while they talked at the bottom of the staircase. They were animated as each took a turn during their cantor, discussing something that he suspected was of high importance, with frequent head shaking and arm crossing. Puck stood between them, and by her body language and gesturing, Mr. Andrews could see that she was mediating. The girls ceased speaking, and Dana again hugged Angela. Her flushed cheeks and wet eyes were obvious as soon as she got in the truck. She slumped into her seat as they watched the baby-blue school bus drive away with the team members onboard.

"Everything okay, honey?" he asked once she was settled into the seat and buckled.

"Yeah, I'm good." She sniffled for a moment. "She's a good person, like Nick, you know?" She looked over her shoulder at the bags containing all her worldly possessions, and then back at the Trapper Keeper on her lap. "Yeah. I'm good." She exhaled a long purposeful breath to relax the tightness in her throat. "It may only be a couple trash bags back there, but I've got lots of other baggage, if you catch my drift."

"Miss Jefferson, everyone has baggage. You just need to find someone with a matching set."

She smiled and looked at her lap. "Thank you." The rasp in her voice told Mr. Andrews he should pivot to another subject.

"Roller derby—now there's a sport I haven't seen in a long time. I didn't realize they still had leagues around here."

"Yes, sir. It's more of a club. We swap teammates and practice together with the other teams. It's like a family." She lingered on the word *family*. "I want you to know, I appreciate the small talk to lighten the mood. I'm still stuck processing the latest car crash in my personal life."

"Everything takes time. You'll be okay." He remembered saying the same thing to Nick not long ago. Dana looked out the window as they passed the row of tall pines lining the path, casting afternoon shadows across the dirt and gravel. The sun flickered across their faces through the boughs, and Dana wiped her cheeks with the back of her hand a final time. Mr. Andrews smiled as they turned onto the county road, leaving the apartment behind them on the unfinished driveway.

Chapter 27

Work from Home – Fifth Harmony

Nick was already at the workbench in the garage, perched on a stool with his head bent over Dana's skates, when Dana and Mr. Andrews arrived home. Dana took her bags into the house and then came out to the garage to monitor the tinkering in progress.

"Hey, what's going on with Laverne and Shirley?" she asked.

Nick ignored the question as he opened one of the housings. He swung a finger like a magic wand over the exposed electronics and held the hot soldering iron in his other hand. Next to the skates lay Dana's blueprints with Nick's handwritten notes stuck to them in careful placements.

"Dana, these are amazing! I mean, you know that, but there's so much more here than I realized. Look at this." He pointed the soldering tool at one sheet of paper, almost igniting it from the heat. "This circuit board, where your dad hid your name in the circuits? Well, I borrowed a manual from work," he said, pulling an open binder out from under the table. "This is a power station diagram. Notice anything?"

She leaned over his shoulder, glancing back and forth between the diagram and her skates. "I'm not the engineer here. Talk dumb to me."

"But you built your own skates."

"I followed instructions. Putting a frozen burrito in a microwave doesn't make me a chef." She mimed sprinkling salt over the desk before tossing an imaginary fistful at Nick's face.

"You did a lot more than microwave a burrito," he said with a wave of his hand against her phantom spices. "Your father put a lot of inefficient resistance in the design. The electricity from the power cells gets burned off as it passes through. This is why your batteries wear down. Now if you look here," he said, pointing again to the power station diagram, "this is basically a giant version of what your father designed. But your father's design is not complete."

He grabbed a short piece of wire with a pair of pliers and held it over part of Laverne's circuit board. "If you connect this section here, the dynamos in the wheels loop back into the batteries. It's called regenerative braking. They use this on big modern electric trains and some concept cars, but not usually at this tiny scale."

"So, the skates will be able to recharge themselves if you connect those parts?" she questioned him as well as her own comprehension of the diatribe.

"Dana, it's not just that." Nick was breathless with excitement, leaping up and running to another counter. He pushed cans of nuts, bolts, and gardening supplies to the side, and grabbed a lumber pencil from one of the cans. He scribbled directly on the wooden countertop. Dana began to recognize the pattern, a replica of the circuit board she had crudely built herself from her father's original blueprints. Nick broke the pencil in his exuberance as he continued to draw.

"Pencil, where's another pencil?" Dana scanned the shelves and found a box of old driveway chalk. Nick grabbed a piece from her and began to overlay a sketch of the power station layout on top of the pencil drawing.

"What your father designed wasn't a set of skates; it was the prototype for a closed kinetic perpetual maintenance electrical—"

"DUMMY. TALK. TO. ME. LIKE. I'M. A. DUMMY." She jutted her jaw and bit her upper lip. "You're so smart but *so* dumb."

Nick looked down at the diagram and drew a line with a piece of yellow chalk through the system until it looped back to the origination point. "Dana, this is *free energy*. Or at least really close to it. Maybe ninety-five, ninety-eight percent efficient." He leaned back, admiring what he drew. "He wasn't designing weapons; he was trying to solve the energy crisis. If you had a nuclear power plant with this design, it could probably run ridiculously clean and safe on a tiny amount of uranium." He couldn't hide his excitement as he shook his hands in the air. "You wouldn't need those smokestacks or cooling modules; you'd just need like a speck of uranium or other radioactive material. Just a few electrons to jump start the system and then it would just . . . go . . ." He floated his hand in the air in a slow-motion wave.

"Are you sure?" Her eyes opened wide as she began to process and understand the diagrams with her very basic engineering knowledge. The volume of information she had gleaned from stolen library books and online tutorials crawled from the corners of her brain back to her processing centers. The diagram was starting to make more sense to her now, but the implications of it remained hazy. "Can you do this?"

"Me? No. I can get the circuit board cleaned up so your batteries last a hell of a lot longer. That will take a day or two after work. But this other stuff," he said, making a circular gesture over the diagrams with the chalk in his hand, "this is what those guys might actually be looking for. Besides the big giant robot."

Dana looked over at the disassembled skates, her hands clenched into fists. "Or they want to make the big robot run off this stuff. And that means a big bad walking tank that you just wind up and let loose against the other toys in the playground."

"Two scenarios, Dana. Either they know about this or they don't. I think if they do know, they want your skates and maybe want you dead."

The word "dead" fell into the silent gulf between them. Nick puffed out his cheeks, and Dana scratched her head in thought, twisted her face, and pulled at a knotted strand of hair.

"How am I still pulling bugs out of my hair?"

"Dana, stay with me here. This is *serious*."

She reached into her pocket and placed the photo of her dad, grandfather, and the other scientists posing with the Atomic Juggernaut next to the chalk and pencil diagram. She squinted and leaned in close enough that her nose almost touched the photo.

"Hey, Nick, get a magnifier."

He ran back to the workbench and grabbed a jeweler's loupe for fine soldering. He held it over the robot and noticed a circle, barely visible in the grainy details, surrounded by three triangular sections. He drew it out on the counter in chalk and stepped back. His transposed picture matched the markings on the chest and pauldrons of the robot; it was the tri-foil international symbol for radiation. He looked at Dana's face, which was lost in disbelief.

"Atomic Juggernaut," Nick muttered. "A battle robot that's essentially a walking A-bomb with no need to refuel."

"Do you want a beer? I could use a beer," she said with a shiver. She walked over to the mini fridge and retrieved two bottles stashed behind a row of store-brand cola cans. She twisted the caps off each one and looked back at the photo. She pointed at the only African American on the team and tapped his face with her finger.

"Hardy, Cannon Hardy, right? This guy? That's the name that led to Hardy Farms. Let's start there since he's the only lead we have. I'll go tomorrow and see if I can get anything." She looked back at the skates. "I don't like traveling without the girls, but it is what it is." She took a swig from her bottle and noticed Nick's quizzical expression, still staring at the photo.

"Take my truck. I'll carpool with my dad tomorrow." Nick tossed her his car keys. "And Dana, I don't need to tell you to be ridiculously careful."

"I will. I promise." She held the keys tightly in her hand for a moment before putting them into her jacket pocket. "You take the bedroom tonight. I'll take the couch. I'm going to need to get up early for the drive," she added with a smirk.

Nick started to pack up and organize the parts and pieces splayed over the garage. "Oh, why thank you," he retorted with heavy sarcasm. "It'll be nice to sleep in my own bed in my own house."

He shut off the lights and closed the garage, and they walked side by side back to the house. As Nick held the back door open for her, he heard the low rumbling of a car's turbo-equipped engine and the crunch of gravel, as if it was pulling into the driveway.

"Go inside, I'll check this out," he ordered. "I have a bad feeling right now."

Chapter 28

Selling the Drama – Live

N ick crept around the corner of the rancher and slid his back against the vinyl siding to peer around the downspout. In the driveway, a silver BMW coupe was sitting next to his truck. He stepped out from the corner into full view when he saw the young woman with a blond pixie haircut standing next to it, fiddling on her phone. As he approached, she kept her nose glued to her screen, eyes hidden behind oversized dark sunglasses.

"Hey, Lindsey."

"Hey, yourself," she shot back. "Where have you been?"

"Working." He firmed his footing but felt his spine start to curl and compress. "What's up?"

Lindsey ticked away on her phone for another moment before tossing it into her purse. "You didn't come to the party like I asked you to, that's what's up. I needed you to be there. My whole family was there." She finally took off her glasses and glared at him. "I was *so* embarrassed."

He looked back at the front windows and saw Dana's outline through the glass. He dipped his chin to nod to her that he was handling the situation before he replied to Lindsey's tirade.

"I thought we were on a break." He hated this feeling. Nothing he said ever came out right when she was involved, and nothing he felt registered with her and her priorities. She had entered his life when his mother got sick and she stood by him when she died, but the payback for her support was disproportionate; he could see that now. "You asked me to go, and then the following day you got mad at me for something else."

"Just because I got mad doesn't mean you get to stand me up," she said. "If you want to be my boyfriend, there are things you need to do for me. *With* me." She inspected the pine needles that had landed on the hood of her car and flicked each one individually with her pink pearl fingernails.

"Can we talk inside?" he asked, gesturing to the porch.

"Is your dad home?" She turned up her nose and rolled her eyes.

"No, let's go talk."

She followed him inside and surveyed the living room before wiping a chair and taking a seat at the kitchen table. She focused her attention briefly on the neatly folded sheets on the couch before opening her purse to pull out her phone.

"Lindsey, I'm just . . . I can't keep doing this. I never know where I stand with you. When it's convenient, you want to be with me. When I need someone to talk to, you're not there." He felt his hands shake for a moment in what was becoming his version of a no-holds-barred confrontation. He questioned why he had difficulty talking to her and decided to finally open the dam.

"I've been there for *you*. You're not there for *me*. This. Ever since high school. *This*. I thought you were this really amazing person," he said, hardly believing himself, "and I was lonely and a bit lost. And you were there, and I thought you wanted to date me because you liked me. Why did you go out with me at all?" His blood pressure increased. "I feel like you're embarrassed by me."

Lindsey froze with the phone in her hand. She remained silent.

"Lindsey."

"Nick, I have problems, too, you know. You're the nice guy. I needed a nice guy to treat me nicely and be with me. You think my life is perfect because my family is successful and has more money than you? Well, I have a lot of pressure and things going on you wouldn't understand."

He stared down at the table, again working through words and sentence fragments in his mind. "What does that even mean?"

"Oh, I don't know. Listen, Nick, you're fun, I guess. And you listen to me. And someday, maybe you could really be something and take care of a girl like me," she countered. "You have so much more potential than almost every other guy in the entire Pine Barrens. You can still get there, and we can be this *amazing* couple."

Over her shoulder, Nick saw Dana leaning out of his bedroom door. She winked at him and put two thumbs up before she retreated.

"No." He stood up, pushing his knuckles into the table. "I'm not your accessory, or some investment. You've always taken me for granted. You only come to me when you're lonely or need an elbow ornament for a family function. I've been too stupid and lonely to realize I don't need you to be validated. I'm good *as I am*. This is my life, and it's pretty dang ok." He felt his throat tighten up. "I never *lost* my potential. Life happened. And right now"—he glanced back at the doorway and met Dana's single eye looking back just past the frame—"there's a lot more that I want to do and want to be. And I'll be that person, whether you're with me or not." His cheeks flushed. "And-and-and if it's a choice between being with you and feeling like crap, or being without you and being happy, I'm better off without you."

Lindsey sat with her mouth agape and put her phone back into her purse. "You can't talk to me that way!"

"Maybe someone should. And maybe"—he choked a moment on his own spittle—"maybe I should have the first time you broke up with me. But I was so lonely after my mom died. I wanted to feel something, even if it was pretending to be in love with you. I know now, though, I'm finally my own person, not yours." He walked to the front door and opened it. "I'd like you to leave."

"But I was going to give you another chance," she pleaded. "I don't understand."

"You're right, you don't understand. You take people for granted. You don't give back. And I don't want to be with someone who doesn't appreciate me." Nick became aware that his eyes were watering but hers were dry and bewildered. "I'm not going to let you do this to me anymore."

Lindsey clutched her purse and stormed to the door. "You don't know anything. You're not special, you're just a dumb poor kid with an alcoholic father. I was going to save you from this! I was your ticket out, and you blew it!" She stomped out onto the porch and failed at swatting the door closed behind her. He heard the revving of her car and a spinout in the driveway. Nick watched her drive off as Dana emerged from his bedroom.

"So, that went *well*," she said with a chuckle, but then immediately regretted the joke when she saw Nick's face. "Oh, I'm sorry. I'm sorry."

"No, it's alright." He flexed his fist open and closed. He settled for open. "I needed to do that. Finally. Long overdue."

"Hey. You did good. That was big. I'm . . . proud of you?" Dana stepped behind him and attempted a hug, which mutated into an awkward pat on the back. Nick appreciated the gesture. Silence fell across the room as Nick's breathing slowed and his sniffling stopped. He felt her hand on his shoulder blade as she traced gentle rubbing circles with her palm.

"I was so lonely after my mom died," he whispered. "And I couldn't talk to my dad, at least not while he was in his own bad spot. She was just there. I think that was all I needed at the time."

"I know," she whispered, "I know. Come on, let's go get some junk food.

A mouthful of fries will keep you from saying something stupid. It will definitely keep my foot out of mine." Nick felt her arms wrap around his waist. He slumped as she tightened her hug and felt her face pressed into the side of his neck, a moment of affection he hadn't felt from Lindsey in a long time.

"Let's go."

0:00　　　　　　　　　　　　　　　　　　　　　　　3:13

Chapter 29

Family Man – Hall & Oates

J oshua stared at the pile of musky papers adorned in sticky notes covered with his chicken scratch. He rubbed the bridge of his nose with one hand, his other holding up his cell phone to his head. His wife's voice droned in his ear, and he nodded silently in response. He spoke when her tirade offered a chance to interrupt.

"Yes, I'll be home late. I'm waiting on a set of files to be dropped off by a courier and then I have to review the audit and have it stamped before midnight." Joshua paused to listen to the huff from his wife on the other side of the line. "I promise." He listened to the next words she spoke and covered his eyes with his hand. "No, Jenna went home already. She's not on this project."

The line clicked as she hung up.

Joshua slumped over this keyboard. He felt a wave of heat slowly rising up his neck to the base of his skull, clouding his brain and colliding with the cornucopia of facts stuffing his gray matter. He had spent the past several nights reviewing flight paths and fuel transactions, extrapolating the cost of airplane fuel to the average burn rate of a late model cargo plane traveling at the average airspeed for a light crew with minimum load. He pored over a series of transactions and found a fuel purchase that fit in his range of estimates and gave credence to his growing suspicions. He checked his number and reviewed the spreadsheet over and over, and the numbers kept adding up to the same handful of location probabilities: One Hundred Roads was taking their new plane to New Jersey.

"What are you guys up to, OHR?"

The contractors had prepaid and acquired enough fuel to fly empty to New Jersey and then take a hull loaded with maximum cargo weight down the Eastern Seaboard and into the Caribbean; a direct line would take them to the northern tip of South America, possibly Venezuela. From there, OHR could transfer whatever they were moving and then refuel and return deep into the dark shadows, free from government acknowledgment and consent.

Or they could fly directly to a point somewhere between Atlantic City and a dead zone in the Atlantic Ocean.

Or he could be chasing rainbows in the dark.

He dipped his hand into his thermal lunch sack in his desk drawer, forgetting that his sandwich and snacks were long gone. His late nights were adding a new weight to his marriage. His wife had stopped making his lunch before she left in the morning, first to drop the baby at daycare and then to her job. His new schedule had prevented them from physically seeing each other many nights, three in a row being the current streak. Joshua resolved, even so, that he was in the right and continued plowing into the files, searching for clues. *Something was buried and the body was being exhumed by nefarious gravediggers.* Whether armed with an M1 rifle, as in his previous life, or armed with a spreadsheet on his PC, as he was now, his mission was finding out what OJR was up to and preventing a threat to the country.

He reached behind his monitor and hit the power switch. He watched the indicator LED fade from soft green to empty black. He fiddled with his wedding ring, twisting the gold band around his finger, and stared at the dormant computer screen. His reflection peered back. He watched his mirror image pull the ring on and off his finger. In the dulled colors of the monitor, he could also see the frame behind him with his wife and child. An idea began to coagulate.

"It's worth a shot," he whispered.

Joshua powered the computer monitor back on and pulled up the web browser. What he was about to do was a slight abuse of his position, but by his calculations it was worth the risk for the potential information reward. He loaded an ancestry website and explored the list of names on the desk. He started with the two Jeffersons, thinking having two names in a family would be likely to get him some hits. With just a little information, the branches of their family tree began to fill in the leaves and roots before and after the names. One name caught his eye, someone who appeared to be still alive.

"Dana Jefferson, daughter of Samuel David Jefferson Jr., granddaughter of Jefferson Sr."

He decided to try one more name: Colin Rhodes. With a little more digging, he found a living relative for him as well: Nina Rhodes, daughter of Colin. Joshua snapped the folder shut, turned off the computer, and dashed home to have dinner with his wife.

0:00 3:13

Chapter 30

No Time – The Guess Who

Marcus Hardy sat in his home office of his family's farmhouse, commencing with the rituals of what was to be another slow morning. He waited for his computer to come to life and shuffled a pile of opened envelopes on his desk, holding up random pieces to read in the sunlight: the electric company, bank statements, an invitation from the Black Business Association to speak at the next local chapter meeting.

He took a stack of papers over to the rows of filing cabinets that sat under some government-issued certifications and family portraits, one of which showed him as a child sitting on the lap of his grandfather, family entrepreneur Cannon Hardy. In the background, the radio repeated commodity reports and financial news interspersed with commercials for day-trading websites and related tools.

After he finished filing, he headed to the kitchen for more coffee. As he walked past the front bay window, his attention was diverted by a red pickup truck parked outside the motorized gate at the end of the driveway, despite the large "NO TRESSPASSING" sign mounted clearly. He reached behind the coatrack and unsheathed a shotgun that was tucked inside an umbrella stand. He swung open the door and boldly marched toward the gate with the firearm at his side. An attractive young woman with flowing black hair and skin slightly lighter than his own smiled and waved from the driver's side window. The zipper hanging from the sleeve of her leather jacket sparkled in the sun.

"Girl, you got ten seconds to tell me something useful," he shouted. He made sure she could see the gun. It had been a couple days since his last uninvited visitor, and he was not above firing a warning shot if necessary.

"Hey, hi, I'm looking for Cannon Hardy," she said a bit unsteadily, both hands up as if in surrender. "Maybe that's your father? My name's Dana."

She kept a tight smile on her face. Marcus nodded his head to the house behind him.

"Cannon's my grandpa, and you can find him back by the barns in the family plot, next to my dad. The fact that you know his name," he said, bringing the rifle up to his shoulder, "means maybe you know something you shouldn't. Are you with One Hundred Roads?"

"No, no, no. I'm with Dana Jefferson Enterprises, sole proprietor and only employee," she said, laughing nervously. "That's supposed to be a joke. Well, see, it appears my dad knew your gramps. Or, I mean, my grandfather and my dad knew him."

Marcus lowered the rifle warily. "I'm Marcus. Marcus Stefan Hardy. President of Hardy Farms. So, you're not with One Hundred Roads?"

"I'll say it again, nope," she politely replied with a touch of humility. "Can I talk to you for a few minutes, maybe inside . . . and unarmed?"

"I don't do face-to-face business. We're not a roadside produce stand here, and you can't buy eggs or apple cider donuts." He relaxed his grip on the gun and pointed it casually toward the ground. "Who did you say your dad was?"

"I didn't. Sam Jefferson. Junior. My grandfather was Samuel Jefferson. Senior." She carefully opened the door and stepped out of the cab. She reached into her pocket and pulled out the rapidly weathering photograph of the crew of scientists. She held it up on her side of the gate. "Recognize anyone?"

Marcus stared at the photo, examining each face as well as the robotic colossus behind the team. He pointed the shotgun to the gate control pad and punched the entry button with the barrel. "Yeah, you can come in."

A faint humming announced the gate opening.

Dana stepped through. The driveway was freshly coated, flanked on each side by white decorative stone curbs. The two-story house sat at the top of a small rise in the land, skirted by a uniformly green well-manicured lawn and a large willow tree on each side of the drive. The immense girth and height of the trees established their provenance as the elders of the estate, and Dana inhaled deep as she passed under the boughs.

"This is, like, the first place in South Jersey I've been to that doesn't smell like pine trees."

"It's a nice place," Marcus replied. He led her up to the wooden porch and pointed to the Adirondack chairs off to the side. Dana recognized the tiny imperfections of what were obviously handmade chairs as opposed to the mass-produced or plastic copies she was used to seeing around the area. Her grandfather had made quite a fuss when he ordered a set for the ranch back in New Mexico, instructing her to not leave her toys or skateboard against the wood. Marcus sat down and laid the gun across his lap. *He's still making a show of force*, she deduced.

"I apologize for the gun. There were some guys here not long ago, and then at night I thought I saw someone on the property out back trying to go into one of the barns." He asked for the photo so he could take a closer look. "So, what's your game here?"

"I'm trying to track down some things from my father. I have that photo of him, and that's one of his projects he worked on," she said, pointing to the metallic monster. "Even with your poker face, I'm guessing you recognize something in the picture, or otherwise I'd be either back in my truck or lying on the ground with a hole in my chest."

Marcus nodded solemnly. He put a finger in the air to indicate that he needed a moment, then trotted inside with the gun. He returned quickly with a photo frame but, thankfully, no firearm.

"This is me and my grandpa," he announced, handing her the frame. She held it gingerly and pulled the photo closer so she could see the details. In it was a young boy who looked like Marcus seated on the lap of what she assumed was his grandfather, Cannon. Indeed, he looked like a slightly older version of one of the men who appeared in her photo of the project team. In the background of Marcus's picture, she saw a metallic arch; looking more closely, she realized with amazement it was the legs of the juggernaut behind them.

"My grandpa worked on that. I know what that is. You probably do, too. After the project was cancelled, he used his contacts to start the farm business. Hardy Farms basically made money off government purchasing, tax subsidies, and so on. But when I came on, me and my big brain started leveraging the markets to bid on commodity futures. Now, we make money off the speculation and the end sale, and the capital is from the federal government's pockets."

"Wait, can we go back a second. You said the project was cancelled? When was that?"

"After the body count was discovered." He stared off into the distance beyond the front gate. "My grandfather told me that they were working on making robotic exoframes. Mostly for military applications, but also civilian ones like hazardous rescue. Then things went sideways."

"Why are you telling this to a stranger? We *did* just meet, right? This is big stuff."

"So is the fact that you have that photo. There are only a handful of people who know that thing exists. And seeing as you didn't show up with an army behind you, I figured you didn't know what you had."

Dana looked back down at the photograph of young Marcus and then snapped her head up. "Wait. You said some men showed up. Why? Do you have . . . *it*?" Her jaw dropped at the thought. "Is *it* here?"

"It's in the barn out back."

She sat still, realizing her incredulous reaction probably helped prove to him she was not the enemy. "I was under the impression that it was locked up . . ." she started to say but, deciding quickly to keep one secret from being disclosed in their chat, continued, ". . . in some vault somewhere."

Marcus scoffed. "The second one, maybe, sure. But my grandpa made sure that the prototype was removed and hidden before the program was canned." He stood up and waved to her to get out of her chair. "Government people love paperwork and red tape. Grandpa made sure he buried the prototype's dismantling under a mountain of it before he brought it here."

Dana splayed her fingers on her chest.

"It's *here*?"

"Oh yeah." Marcus leaned forward with a crooked grin. "Do you want to see it?"

0:00   3:13

Chapter 31

Anybody Listening? – Queensrÿche

With Marcus leading the way, Dana and he walked until they reached the last barn on the property. Each structure they passed was identical, painted traditional barn red with white trim, except this one, a deeper shade of red with gray trim, secured with a heavier, thicker double door and metal frame. The opening looked to be about ten feet by ten feet. Below a security camera perched next to the right door was an electronic keypad. Marcus entered a sequence quickly, using his body to block Dana's view. A short buzz followed his keystrokes, and the motors of the doors groaned and hissed as they worked. Marcus gestured to Dana to go through first.

Dana stepped into the structure, her shadow leading the way as the morning sun broke into the darkness. A large sarcophagus, identical to the one she had seen in the bunker, stood silent in the middle of the room. The seasons hadn't been kind to it, as discoloration from pollen, rust, and dust had stained the surface plates. Dana turned quickly to Marcus, who nodded at the structure and smiled.

"Been locked up for almost ten years now, I think. After Gramps died, I couldn't open it anymore. And I'll be damned if anyone else tries to open it without my permission."

Dana slowly approached the massive monolith, holding her hand out in front her until it finally touched the shell. The surface was cool but not cold. She walked in a slow circle around it, without removing her hand from her legacy. Her palm wiped a clean line around the container, like an equator.

"It's the same," she whispered. "I mean, *is* it the same thing as in the photo?" Again, she reprimanded herself silently, knowing she should be more careful about her level of disclosure.

"Yep. When those guys were here—they had to be from One Hundred Roads—when they were poking around, questioning my business, how I'm doing financially, that kind of thing, they never asked about this," he said, "but I suppose they think I know where this is. They just didn't think I'd actually be in possession of it."

Dana traced her hand around a circular plate close to head height and dusted off a dark circle of dense inky glass. "What is, or who are, One Hundred Roads?"

Marcus stopped and crossed his arms. He looked to be about same age as her, maybe only a couple years older, she thought, but much more worn by the responsibilities of running a family-owned business and by his guardianship of the monstrosity.

"One Hundred Roads. OHR for short. Government security contractors for hire. Black ops guys who do the government's dirty work. You know, like when they need to kill bad guys with plausible deniability. As I said, getting around government red tape was my family's specialty originally. And OHR came to us for supplies for dealing with insurgents. In other words, they ordered crates of blueberries and corn through me and used it for physical commerce with the rebels and such. Bribes in wheat and seed are much less traceable than cash. And a warlord with the promise of food can buy the complacency and respect of the hungry masses."

Dana's hair on her neck stood up. This was an enormous amount of disclosure from someone she had just met, not to mention the implications of what she had just learned. *He did leave the shotgun back in the house, didn't he?*

"So, you think these guys, One Hundred Roads, are looking for our big boy here?" She knocked on the sarcophagus, eliciting a deep gong that echoed inside the barn.

"They can have him," Marcus said, laughing. "Last time that thing was opened I remember seeing he was broken. But it doesn't matter: no one steals from me and my family. All they have to do is ask the right price." He lowered his gaze. "And seeing as you found me and have that photo, I think maybe you have your checkbook with you?"

Dana froze and felt her toes clench inside her shoes unconsciously. There were no roller skates to get her the hell out of here. Instead, she would need to shift from selective disclosure to full-speed fibbing. He continued before she could respond.

"Before you think I'm some kind of war profiteer, you should know my endgame here. It might make you a little more receptive." He walked over to a folding chair by the wall and sat. "This thing, this program, was a cancer factory. They dealt with a lot of dangerous materials. Mostly everyone, including my grandpa, got cancer from the radiation exposure over time. Lots of men got big severance packages once the government saw how many people this thing was making sick and killing during development."

Dana reconciled these details with the last time she had spoken to her grandfather and nodded silently as Marcus continued.

"My grandpa took his money and started this business. But he wanted to stick it to the man and make those bloody war dollars mean something. Once the farm got really successful, he started a hospital and funneled a large chunk of our profits into cancer research. He also provided seed money for Black-owned businesses, since the opportunities for people like *us* after military service aren't as lucrative as for other people."

Dana nodded again. She stepped away from the sarcophagus and stared intently at Marcus. His story made sense to her, and she was intent on listening to every note he played until she figured out his entire song. He continued. "The older he got, the more my grandpa felt responsibility for victims of the project . . . and the survivors. He decided to research the affected families from the program and tried to figure out a way to divert funds to them. He was able to do some direct handouts; for others he set up trusts or charities. As a matter of fact, I think we paid a large chunk to the Jefferson estate when he died."

She bit her lip. Was it possible her boarding school and her meager trust payouts were from all of this? Could her father's legacy really be just a series of graves and guilt-driven handouts? What about his energy project?

"So, assuming you saw some of that inheritance, am I right to assume you wanna make me an offer so I can be rid of this? All the proceeds go to charity," he said, smiling widely. Dana did not return the expression. She turned back to the monolith.

"Well, I think you make a good point. But I'm not going to buy anything that I can't test drive." She knocked on the blackened window with her knuckles.

Marcus laughed at her proposal. "That's going to be a problem. That thing hasn't been opened in at least ten years, not since my grandpa died. The design team put a security feature on it. It only opens with an optical scan, and only the six members in that picture of yours could unlock it. Once my grandpa died, no more key. If you think about it, that's beyond cutting-edge for the time when it was made. And the entire thing is a big Faraday cage. You can't just shock it or send through a surge to burn or reset the lock circuitry."

"Well, if I can just look inside, I can see what kind of condition it's in."

Dana leaned her head against the portal, trying to discern anything in the inky darkness. As her brow touched the glass, a loud click startled her, and a flare of green light from inside illuminated her face. She lurched back, blinking at the blinding spots on her retina. A chiming of multiple gears and motors followed, and the dust on the outer shell sifted. The sarcophagus slowly began to split in half as the front panel doors began to groan open.

Dana took several steps back, and her mouth and eyes widened. She looked at Marcus, who mirrored her expression of awe and disbelief. The thick metal doors continued to fold outward, birthing the massive metal construct into the ambient light of the barn. Inside stood the robot, slumped forward, its arms loose and barely touching the ground with its massive knuckles. The cockpit windows, one in the chest and one in its head, were hazy and dusty. In the stomach portion, a large section was missing, cleanly disassembled and removed, revealing an empty chamber where most likely a motor and power source once breathed life into the beast. Next to the front canopy in stamped letters, she read "PROPERTY OF UNITED STATES GOVERNMENT" and "PROJECT ATOMIC JUGGERNAUT."

"Ok, now that is not something I expected," stammered Marcus. He looked at her, then back to the machine, then back and forth again. "You opened that thing. How did you do that?"

"I don't know, I just looked into the porthole."

"That's where the eye scanner is. How did you do that?"

"I don't know! I just looked into the porthole!"

"Did you know how to get inside?"

"I DON'T KNOW. I JUST LOOKED INTO THE PORTHOLE!" Dana was mystified. "My eyes. It scanned my eyes."

Marcus slowly approached the cavity where the robot's stomach would be. "I don't understand. There's no power source. Grandpa took it out before he brought it here." He pointed to a series of missing rivets. "At least we're not in danger of radiation or accidental activation." He looked the object up and down slowly. "I haven't seen that thing in at least a decade. I forgot how big it is."

Dana still could not tear her eyes away. "If you sell it, a bunch of people with cancer get money, and a lot of cancer research gets funded?"

"I didn't think of it that way, but that's what my grandpa wanted."

"And the guys, from One Hundred Roads, they don't know you have this?"

"No, I don't think so."

"But if they know it's here, they would just take it, save the buck or two. And you'd be a loose end." Marcus nodded quickly and put his thumb on his chin. Dana's eyes softened their focus. She remembered the gunshots at the bunker, the fight at the hospital, the man with the flattop and Australian accent. "So, I think it's pretty important we keep this between you and me, Marcus."

"Sure, sounds like it."

"Marcus, would anyone else know about this?" she pleaded.

"Only the people who helped my grandpa steal it and pretend to dispose of it. And they're all dead—well, except for Anselm."

Dana whirled toward him. "Who is Anselm?"

He retrieved the photograph of the science team from his shirt pocket, which Dana promptly snatched from his hand, irritated that she had been careless enough to forget where it was. "That guy," said Marcus, pointing to one of the men. "That's Anselm Geissler. I met him when I was a kid. I think he just took his money and holed up in a retirement village. Merriweather Gardens. I know that because we sent a lot of checks to him, and he's so close we would drop them off in his mailbox sometimes."

Dana stared at him, her mouth open wider than at any prior moment in their short time together. "WHAT?" she yelled, her voice hitting a high shrill note. "Oh my God. He's the only one we couldn't find any information on." Dana folded the photo and put it securely in her inside jacket pocket. "*He* lives in your neighborhood? I mean, not literally, but he lives around here?"

"Yeah, I mean, we still send the checks—well, direct deposit now to an account linked to his address, but I haven't seen him in person in . . . a few years? He might be dead, but his checks go through every time."

"Merriweather where?"

"Gardens. Merriweather Gardens. Country club attached to one of those age-restricted enclaves."

Dana felt for her car keys but then whipped back to the open sarcophagus. "Let's figure out how to close this guy up. I'll try the eye scanner again. Then you go ahead and board him up, bury him in horse poop, I don't know, but let's make sure no one can find him." She took one last look and noted the robot's posture was not unlike a sad marionette hanging in a closet, forgotten by the world.

"Anselm Geissler," she whispered to herself. "Marcus, thank you for everything. I've got a date with a really old man."

0:00 3:13

Chapter 32

Dreams – Fleetwood Mac

D ana bounded into the garage, skipping the last few steps up. Nick sat huddled over one of her skates, which was locked into a table vise. He failed to notice her even as he started to close containers and organize tools on the wall and into a drawer. When he discovered her rocking on her heels next to him, he was startled for a second and then turned back to the table. She clapped to regain his attention.

"Nick! I saw it! I saw the robot! And I have a name and I think an address for another scientist we can talk to! Aren't you excited?"

"Yeah. I mean yes. Yes." He was processing her words on a delay. "Wait, what? They had a robot at the farm?"

"Yes! It was amazing! And a little sad. It looks like he's been decommissioned and had his heart ripped out. Literally. No power plant. But then I looked inside the window and my eyes made it open! It opened!" She hopped onto a clear spot on the table. "And there's this guy, Anselm, he might still be alive. He's at Merriweather Gardens, so we can do some footwork there."

"Wait, wait, wait. There's a *second* Atomic Juggernaut?"

"Indeed." She placed her finger inside her cheek and made a popping noise. "Bingo."

Instead of the excited response she was expecting, Dana was surprised by the one of concern he flashed her.

Dana paused and leaned in to make eye contact with Nick. "What's wrong?"

"Dana, you have to . . ." He paused as he struggled for the right words. "We need to be covert here. You can't disclose too much to people that we don't know are good guys or bad guys. Did you tell him about the skates?" He gestured toward the vise with a long thin screwdriver.

"No, no, I didn't. I don't think I did. I was careful—at least I was trying to be," she said with her hands on her hips and a small sneer. "But we need to find stuff out, and this guy knew everything about the program and who people were. And it turns out, *by the way*, he's funneling profits from government contracts back into cancer research and survivors' families. So, that leads me to think he's a good guy. I'm pretty sure about that." She took a sip of Nick's drink and waited for his response.

"Well, my dad ran a couple things through his buddies in the billing department, and it turns out that there was an Anselm Geissler who died a few years ago." He met her expression of sudden disappointment. "However, there is a new billing party for the utilities. His house is still in his family's name. A corporate account under the name OHR."

Dana dropped her head and swung her legs back and forth as if she were a reprimanded child. "So, how do we know whose information is right? Didn't I actually get info we needed to know?"

"I don't know, but I do know that we need to keep things on the down low and not expose as much info about us. About you."

She nodded in reluctant agreement. She was still feeling some of the jubilation at seeing another juggernaut and knowing that her eyes could probably open the one at the bunker. This was *her* legacy she was trying to discover. She and Nick had put so much effort into getting answers, and now she knew at least *how* to open the juggernaut. Why wasn't Nick as excited?

"My dad said he met with the roller derby crew," Nick said to break the short but noticeably heavy silence. "They sounded pretty cool. Mary Beth, Puck, and . . . Angela? I think that's who he said was there."

She hopped off the table and put her hands on her jacket lapels. She now sensed where Nick was steering the conversation by the coolness in his overall tone.

"Yes. Angela. My ex-girlfriend. You know, I *have* dated people from time to time. And yes, boys and girls." She could feel her hands tightening on her jacket reflexively as she grew uncomfortable. "Something wrong with that?"

"Sure, sure. I mean, *no*, there's no problem. That's cool." He swallowed and looked up into the garage rafters. "So, are you guys still a thing?"

Dana allowed herself to laugh at her mistaking the intent of Nick's probe. "She and I are done. We're just . . . friends. But you know how feelings are. You can say things are done, and feel things are done, but it's not a switch you just turn off. You have to let it"—she flourished her words with her hands—"empty out."

"Lindsey was just . . . well, not that," he said. "It was like we were only good at standing next to each other and meeting her relatives. We're in the most densely populated state but it feels like I only see the same dozen people over and over. And she was one of them. Plus, she wasn't that bad looking."

"Oh my, the nice boy from the sticks only dated her because she was there, and she was pretty!" Dana teased. She took off her jacket and pulled up a chair next to the skates. "Truth? Sometimes I think it was the same for me and Angela." She paused and let her smile fade. "You get close to someone, you talk about things. You find out stuff. You help them out. Angela and I helped each other through . . . you know . . . stuff."

"What kind of stuff?"

"Things you only share with someone you're in love with. That kind of stuff." Dana's focus drifted away from the table toward the emptiness in the room. "Anyway, so that's *done*."

"Noted." Nick took the skate out of the vise and presented it to Dana. "Laverne is done. Shirley was finished earlier. All you should notice is a ton of extra battery life. I think they'll run for a few *days*," he said, lingering on the last word in triumph, "until they need a charge."

Dana ran her fingers up the skates to the shin guards, and then across the ankle joints, tracing the lines of the soft edges. She admired her original work on the exterior design and how Nick had seamlessly disassembled and reassembled them. She watched his grease-stained cheekbones rise as he smiled at his handiwork. His shifted his eyes to meet hers.

"Why are you helping me, Nick?" Dana asked as she tucked the skates into her backpack on the floor and then spun her chair to face him directly. "If you're going to lecture me on disclosing too much, you should of course recall our first time hanging out and that we wouldn't be friends if I kept to myself and didn't run my mouth."

Nick stood up and put the last tools away in silence. She thought he was ignoring her until he placed the last box of screws away and turned back to face her.

"When life is really boring, and every day you look at your dad and think you're going to end up the same way as him, you look for things that are different and new," he said.

"End up the same way as him? I don't think falling in love, getting married, raising a really smart and polite son, *and* being a person who is strong enough to beat addiction is such a terrible role model to follow."

"It's hard to see the peaks when you lived in the valleys. So, maybe that's why I'm helping you," he said, while kicking the knapsack at her feet. "You have a different perspective, you weren't born and bred here, and it just felt like good timing when I met you. I was ready to come up out of the valley."

"Well, I just want you to know, whatever your reason, I appreciate you . . . you stupid boy." She kicked the bag, imitating him. "There, I said it. Now what do *we* do?"

"*You* go to Merriweather Gardens and see if Anselm is really alive after all. If so, you play it cool. Say that you're looking for information on your dad's army buddies. That's it. That's the story, and it should be easy to stick to it because it's basically the truth, right?"

She saluted in a mocking gesture and gave him a smile. "I call dibs on the bedroom tonight! Couch for you!"

As she skipped out the door toward the house, Nick looked back at his laptop on the workbench. He opened the display and pulled up the photos he first took of Dana with the camera installed on the electric pole. He thought about the moment he first saw her and the skates, and how excited he was at the idea of hunting down the amazing devices, as well as meeting their owner. He cycled through the shots in the file folder.

"Photograph."

He tapped his fingers on the workbench before setting his mind to cleaning up the remaining disarray in the garage. As he tidied the pile of papers and blueprints, he paused on the drawing of the power plant and Dana's father's proposal for a high-efficiency energy supply. He held the sheet up to the light and studied the lines and pathways as he imagined the flow of electrons in and out of the gateways and junctions. His mind glowed with the potential of the power if it could be replicated on a tiny scale, such as a battery. Samuel Jefferson Jr. had one of the most intelligent minds that Nick had had the privilege of discovering, even through his decades-old drafts, and he recognized that the flame burned in Dana, waiting to be unleashed upon the world.

"I just don't know how to tell her that."

0:00   3:13

Chapter 33

I'm No Angel – Gregg Allman

Dana placed her coat on the back of her chair at the kitchen table and watched the clock. Nick was due home from work at any moment, and her feet danced lightly as he pulled into the driveway. She bounded through the door before he could turn off the engine.

"Hey Nicky, I have an idea!" she yelled. "Want to take Laverne and Shirley out?"

Nick haltingly closed the door to the truck and peered at her with a skeptical raised brow. "Like a date?"

"Sort of," she said, giggling. "We need to test the power cell enhancements, right? So, let's take 'em for a ride, put them through the paces." She paused to retrieve a small power meter from her flannel shirt pocket. "And then we can check the battery drain and extrapolate from there."

"I like the way you think," he admitted with a faint blush rising on his cheeks. "We could probably run an hour solid with them on the bench and see how they measure up."

Dana held up her left hand adorned with fresh adhesive bandages across four knuckles. "Yeah, I tried that while they were in the table vise in the garage by putting my hand inside to run the push pedals. It's pretty much impossible unless it's my feet on the controls."

Nick led Dana inside the house, his head lowered, as she had learned was his habit while in deep thought. "We can't really just go out on the open road. We'd need to have a secluded place, and one where I can track your speed to get the miles per hour. Then I'd have to calculate the speed's effect on the power draw so we can finalize the approximately battery life."

Dana opened and closed her hand to mock his technical speech as she puffed her cheeks and blew a raspberry at his face. "I already thought about that, chief. I don't have to go top speed, just be consistent. And there's a housing development being built one town over with lots of paved roads and empty lots that we can just cruise through. You can just follow me in the truck."

She handed him a brochure for a planned community named Maple Creek that promised "entry-level luxury homes in a gated community lifestyle."

"How did you find this gem?" he asked.

"I did a dry run to Merriweather Gardens, and this is the next town over. And there's a lovely little drive-up burger shack I want to check out." She blinked rapidly and smiled widely to request permission to commence her plan.

"Okay, fine." Nick rubbed the helmet marks out of his sandy hair as he peeled off his work shirt and replaced it with a dark Henley. "Are the skates already charged? I'm pretty hungry now that you've mentioned burgers and fries."

"I didn't say anything about fries," she said as she reached for her bag next to the front door. "Let's go!"

The red pickup cruised along through the development at a steady twenty-five miles per hour with Dana in pursuit, locked at a two-car-length following distance. Dana broke into a grapevine step along the corners, crossing leg over leg, then leg under leg, to add variety and avoid boredom. Nick's steady stream of speed checks and time checks droned in her earpiece as he buzzed numbers over the Bluetooth speaker.

"Are we there yet?" she whined as she dropped her shoulders and leaned her head as far back as she could, looking up into dull evening sky grays and blues.

"Realistically, sure," Nick replied. "We have fifty minutes logged, about twenty miles, so that's good, easy math. Hop in and let's go eat."

He slowed the pace car as she rolled to the passenger side. Her skates clanked against the running board as she flung herself inside the cabin. Dana respected the silence that encircled Nick as they drove to the burger stand and ran her own mental calculations of her skate numbers to bide her time.

"We're here," Nick announced as they pulled into a space in the rear of the lot at Scooter Burgers, a restaurant lost to time, as was the case for many businesses in the Pine Barrens. The outside seating consisted of red-painted cedar picnic tables and benches, not unlike ones that could be stolen from a local park. The sign's neon tubes were cracked, leaving only the word "Scooter" lit by orange gas in the waning light of the sunset. The gravel parking lot was partially paved in a skirt around the building's foundation, and Dana leapt from the cabin in her skates to the rocky mix before grabbing her backpack for her pedestrian boots. Nick readied his voltage meter and notepad for calculations, oblivious to the small shadow approaching.

"Excuse me," whispered a thin female voice from behind the truck. Dana whipped toward the sound and froze as she realized her skates were still on and in public view of the little girl between her and the restaurant. She was barely ten years old and adorned in dirt-covered denim overalls and a ladybug-patterned shirt.

"Hello," Dana intoned as she slowly stepped back into the cabin. Nick stood behind the truck, scanning for the girl's parents. "What's your name, kiddo?"

"Stephanie," the girl whispered. Her eyes grew in response to Dana's acknowledgment of her existence. Stephanie brushed aside a clump of greasy brown hair that clung to her forehead.

"Do you have someone with you?" Dana inquired as she attempted to change her skates stealthily inside the cabin. Shirley fell with a soft clang onto the gravel as the skate slipped from Dana's hand. Stephanie gasped and began to smile. She took one big step toward Dana.

"Are you a superhero?" she whispered, her eyes glued to the skate. "I think you were on the news." Dana's eyes darted to Nick, who was rubbing the back of his neck as he whipped his head back and forth in a scan of the patrons sitting at the benches.

"No, I'm not," Dana whispered with a wink. "But you know something? I could be, someday." She stepped out of the cabin, now in her regular boots and placed the skates into her backpack. "Do you want to be a superhero, Stephanie?"

The little girl nodded and looked back toward the tables. A man and woman at the furthest table were arguing, and Dana spotted a tiny cup and small burger on a third tray that sat next to their own. Stephanie returned her focus to Dana.

"I wish I was a superhero so I could beat up Daddy."

Nick stepped around to Dana and put his hand on her shoulder. "This isn't a good idea," he whispered. Dana shrugged.

"Stephanie, what does Daddy do?" Her smile was friendly, but Dana's eyes began to burn with intensity.

"He's just mean," she replied as she rolled up her sleeve of ladybugs. Dana looked at the darkened cuff around Stephanie's forearm and then knelt in front of her.

"Some people are mean. They may not change. But you don't have to be like that. Is he mean to your mom, too?"

"Dana," Nick cautioned, "her folks are coming."

The father was walking toward Dana and Nick, a large man with a paunch and dirty jeans. The mother sheepishly followed and kept her eyes to the ground. The man lunged at Stephanie and grabbed her wrist.

"Don't bother the nice lady," he shouted. "Sorry if she bugged you and your boyfriend." He glared at Dana.

Nick intercepted Dana as she took one step toward the man, shaking his head hard at her.

A combination of confusion and anger crossed Dana's face as she watched the man drag the little girl back to the table and then to their car. Nick kept his grip on Dana's shoulders as she struggled.

"What did you do that for? That guy's obviously beating her!" she yelled.

"Actually, we don't know that. It's implied, but we can't just jump to conclusions and beat him up."

"He's beating his kid! You know I can kick that redneck's ass!"

"And what happens after that? There's a time and a place, and a right way to do things." Dana scowled and relaxed her shoulders in his grip. "E23-J8J," Nick said matter-of-factly. "That's his license plate. Tonight, we call in an anonymous drunk driver tip, say there was a little girl in the car, and let the police do follow-up." He winked at her. "Any cop fresh out of the academy will ask the right questions and maybe she and her mom are in protective services by tonight."

Dana cocked her head. "You just didn't want to fight him, did you? I mean, he thought you were *my boyfriend,* so it would be your duty to kick his ass," she said with a chuckle.

"I just want to keep you out of a police report if we can do that," he replied. "I have to think two steps ahead with you, since you like to leap before you look."

The duo approached the service window of the restaurant, and Nick reached for a bag already on the counter with his name on it. Dana pointed at the order and raised her hand to ask a question. "How?"

"I ordered ahead online," he said, winking at her. "And I guessed bacon cheeseburger with fries, extra ketchup. Don't let the unkempt exterior deceive you. This place is solid."

"You do think ahead," she smiled. "And extra ketchup is a nice touch."

"And speaking of thinking ahead," he said as he unwrapped their meal at an empty table, "I got a little project for my dad to work on. Technically, it was his idea, but he didn't realize it at the time."

"What's that?" Dana shoved a fistful of fries into her mouth, smearing ketchup on her lips and chin.

"I still have that camera I used to take your picture after we first me, and my dad sure does want to help us out."

Dana raised an eyebrow at his cryptic idea as he began to scribble in his notepad, panning back and forth between his notes and the voltage meter.

"This is interesting," he said. "According to the math—and I've checked it three times—the new resistance in the skates and the decreased entropy mean that my tweaks have increased your battery life to . . ." He paused as he turned the notepad toward Dana. "About eight thousand hours at twenty-five miles per hour."

Dana spit a half-chewed french fry onto the paper. "That's ridiculous!" she gasped. "You did that?"

"No, your father did. And you did by following his instructions and teaching yourself how to make them. I just cleaned up the work a bit."

She smiled at Nick as she swiped his napkin and wiped her mouth. "You really deserve the credit. Buy me a milkshake."

Chapter 34

Forty or Fifty – Spin Doctors

Dana packed the leftovers from Scooter Burgers into the refrigerator as Nick unfolded the light-gray sheets to fix his bed on the couch. She closed the door and looked at the photographs symmetrically hung by tourist trap magnets on the fridge. She lingered on a photo of the family of three sitting on a stone bench in front of a harbor, tall sailing ships in the background, and Mr. and Mrs. Andrews and a young Nick in the foreground. She carefully removed the magnet to bring the photo over to him.

"Your mom was really pretty. Is pretty," she sighed. "Am I allowed to ask?"

"About how she died?" he said as he sat down on the fresh linens. "Sure." He gently took the picture from her hand and looked over the fine details for a moment. "This was in Boston. It was the last time we went on vacation before her illness surfaced. Basically, brain cancer. She was having, like, blackouts and memory lapses, some headaches, and then the diagnosis came. I was in high school, and things went downhill pretty quick." He handed the picture back to Dana and nodded toward a larger photo on the wall of his mom and dad on their wedding day. The happy couple in the picture stood arm in arm in a garden grotto filled with white and lavender flowers. "Mom was really smart, and she asked the doctors a lot of questions as things progressed. Eventually she had to be hospitalized. She never came back home after that."

Dana slid off her jacket and sat next to him on the couch. She ran her fingers across the hem of the top sheet, soft and smooth, and flattened out the corner of the sheet. She reclined on the armrest and then fired a loaded question. "Were you there when she died?"

"No," he said with a soft voice. "She was getting pretty bad at the end. Frail, thin, and her mind was misfiring. Sometimes she'd repeat a conversation, and other times she'd forget my dad's name. When they told us she was finally crashing, I couldn't go in. I just wanted to sit in the hallway outside her room and wait for them to tell me it was over, and that she wasn't suffering anymore. I didn't want to remember her that way." He leaned back on the armrest on the opposite side of the couch and looked to the wedding photo again. "I just needed to remember everything I could about who she was, *how* she was when she was healthy, and I thought that seeing her that way would pollute the rest of my memories of her."

Dana put her feet up on the couch and hugged her knees. "I wish I had had that choice when my mom died. She got sick really fast. It was so sudden, over the course of a month. My dad told me over the phone that it was cancer. He was away for work. Mom disappeared for a couple days at a time for some kind of treatment." She placed her feet, covered in dirty pink socks, on Nick's thigh. "And then, she was just gone. He called me to tell me. He just sounded so . . . confused? He didn't sound sad. I didn't have a chance to say goodbye."

Nick put his hand on her shin with a gentle pat. "That sounds horrible, Dana."

"When I got older, I met some girls in boarding school with some really bad stories. There had separated parents, broken families, were abused. Some of the girls prayed to never go home. I came to peace with the idea of losing my mom so fast and not seeing her in the end. Because at least it *was* an ending." She stood up and walked to the kitchen for a glass of water. She pointed to the pitcher and a plastic cup, but Nick shook his head to decline.

"I don't know if I would be able to make the right choice if it happened again," he said. "It wouldn't really change anything if I said goodbye. She'd still die, I'd still have the memories and photographs, but in the moment," he said, setting his open hands on his lap, "you don't get to see that far ahead. And yeah, I think that's why I do some of the things I do. You can only prepare and anticipate so much, only see so many outcomes and the repercussions. But at the end of the day, your brain can just give up."

He looked up from his hands, weathered and worn heavily for his age from his time on the line, climbing poles and hauling cables. Dana stood over him with her hands on her hips, head tilted, her curls dimly backlit by the fixture over the kitchen table. Crickets chirped slowly with the falling temperature outside, playing their last songs before the frost.

"So, what now?" she asked.

Nick lay back on the couch and pulled the top sheet to cover himself. He tucked the pillow under his head as Dana pulled the top sheet over his shoulders and up to his chin. He smiled as he closed his eyes. "We get my dad a camera and put him on a pole."

Chapter 35

You Make Me Feel Like Dancing – Leo Sayer

H i, this is Joshua Green. I work on the contract audit team. I'm wondering if you can run a few names for me. Beneficiary information. I sent over the request form this morning. And if you need a warrant order, I'll have my superior file it under the anti-money laundering statues."

Joshua tapped the pencil on his desk, flittering his attention between the phone tucked into his neck and Jenna seated across from him. She slipped a note as he sat on hold. He scanned it as the associate on the other end of the line came back on.

"Hey, Joshua, it's Alex," chimed a high female voice. "I got the request. I'm about to send it back over. Just to let you know, for Nina Rhodes, her *father* is listed as having POA."

"Come again? Power of attorney?" He shrugged at Jenna, who returned the gesture of bewilderment.

"Yes, her dad," Alex confirmed. "Looks like it was signed over to him after she received a diagnosis of some kind of bone and nerve tissue cancer.

Pretty tragic at such a young age. Anyway, while we do see his forms have her listed as beneficiary, if she passes, that would go into a trust and then be reverted to whomever held that. But we don't have that info here in Vet Affairs. That becomes private banking."

"Okay, I can dig that up," he replied. Jenna splayed her hands at his lack of empathy. "I mean, that's horrible news, terrible. And Dana Jefferson?"

"I'm sending you the information on the trust that was set up for her. It's mostly empty now. Looks like boarding school cannibalized the lion's share, but she's still drawing money off it. Her current bank is in New Jersey. I sent you the details."

Joshua mouthed the words *New Jersey*. Jenna scowled and flung her hands into the air.

"Joshua, one more thing, are you going to need to inspect the attaché on file?"

"Beg your pardon?" He blinked rapidly and curled his lips.

"Hold on, it's actually in locker registration."

"Wait, sorry, slow down. There's an attaché case in a locker? I'm lost."

"Right. Under the Jefferson beneficiary information, there's an assigned locker and the contents are listed as a locked attaché. Usually it's personal effects, such as service items that are allowed to go back to the family. The locker is a bit unorthodox, however. It's registered as being at the joint military complex in New Jersey. Since her father and grandfather are both deceased, Dana should be given access to it but I don't think there was a notification ever sent. If you can get an official order written up, I can release it to you as evidence. Then it would have to go to Dana as next of kin, assuming she's still alive."

"Please send that all over, Alex. Thanks again." After the handset hit the cradle, he hit the desk with annoyance. "New Jersey! Why is everything in New Jersey?"

"I don't know! But that was all very helpful, right?"

"I think so. I'm hoping Dana or Nina can give us some clue as what their fathers were up to. Based on what I discovered before today, I think OHR is stealing something and then moving it somewhere. My guess? They're planning on selling whatever it is. I have to be ready to follow the money trail on the transaction."

He leaned back in his chair and stared into the fluorescent ceiling lights. He closed his eyes, still seeing the hues burned temporarily into his retinas.

"This has to be something big. OHR has to be dipping into something bad. There's just too many threads." He glanced at his dirty whiteboard. "And the threads keep coming to New Jersey."

"So, what now?" Jenna asked. "You don't exactly have a case here. And I'm not even sure what the case would be."

"There is something, I *know* there is. I'm going to need a little time to think. Maybe see if I can get some other files pulled. Whatever it is, we need to get some real evidence because these guys are going to be tough to catch red-handed. But I'm not too worried yet," he said, crossing his arms and smiling confidently. "We have plenty of time."

Chapter 36

Edge of Seventeen – Stevie Nicks

M r. Andrews glanced down at the GPS screen, then back up at the road with increasing frequency as he approached the coordinates in the dawn light. He put in his earpiece as he rolled to a stop and then called Nick.

"Okay, Son, I'm here, three poles down from the dead spot." He unfolded a paper map and traced a line along a set of power lines, including one that seemed to be missing right where an almost invisible break appeared in the tree line. He walked to the back of the truck and opened the boxes for his climbing spikes and the small camera Nick had helped him retrieve late last night.

"Dad, do you have the paperwork in the truck?" Nick buzzed in his ear.

"Yes, Son, I grabbed the work orders you whipped up off the kitchen table."

"And the camera has the mounting bracket?"

"Yes, Son," he responded, grunting as he put on the spikes. "I have the dongle to spike the cable line so we can borrow that for the feed. You know that's illegal, right?"

"This whole thing is illegal, Dad. But that dongle is legal to purchase. The upgrade kit, too. They just couldn't be sold together. That's how this hack works."

Mr. Andrews chuckled. "Got it. This is going to be easy, just up and down. Any trouble and I can talk my way out of it."

There was a silence on the other end of the line.

"Nick, you still there?"

"Yeah, Dad. If the guys we've dealing this happen to find you, though . . . they don't strike me as the conversation type, so no stories or jokes, just all business if you suspect it's them. When you're done, drive back to the dispatch garage, wait an hour or so, and then switch trucks. Just in case they tail you."

"I got this, Son. Love you."

"Love you too, Dad."

Mr. Andrews clicked off the earpiece, put the phone into his shirt pocket next to his electric company name tag, and started to climb up the pole toward the crossbeam. It had been a few years since he had climbed a pole instead of using a bucket truck, and each step took a little more effort and was a little less comfortable than he remembered. Once at the top, he drove in the first screws to attach the camera mount and oriented it toward the direction of the road where any traffic coming in or out of the bunker could be seen easily. He pushed it tight under the crossbeam so that the camera would be invisible from the ground level. He pushed the dongle, a small, curved clip, into the cable line that ran parallel to the power lines and connected it to the camera.

"One, two, three, and four." He counted each clip as he snapped the camera into the bracket. He peeled a piece of black electrical tape off a roll on his belt and secured it over the unlit red bulb above the lens. As he gave his work a final inspection and swung his tool belt around to his back to prepare for the descent, a black Dodge Charger rolled out of the woods and turned in the direction of his truck.

He poked a finger into his pocket to hit Redial.

"Nick, I'm gonna leave this on. I have you on speaker. I'm on top of the pole and there's a big black Dodge that has now rolled up right underneath me."

He looked down at the driver, who was stepping out into the road. He was tall, had a crew cut, and wore fatigue pants. He looked up with his hand on his brow to block the sun that was breaking over the treetops.

"Any problems up there?" the man yelled up to Mr. Andrews, who thought he heard an Australian accent. "Storm damage, mate?"

"Nope, just a maintenance audit. Papers are in the truck if you need them." Mr. Andrews heard Nick sigh with exasperation over the phone.

"Dad! He doesn't need to see them. Don't volunteer it. Just climb down and get out of there!"

The Australian stranger looked up and down the road, then back up at Mr. Andrews.

"Seems like there would be a two-man job protocol. Shouldn't you have a spotter?"

Mr. Andrews prodded the pole with his spikes before resting on the first footing on the way down. "Well, we got only a few men for all these miles of line," he yelled down. With each step of his descent toward the bottom of the post, his breath became heavier from the effort and adrenaline. "And us veteran linemen don't need spotters."

The man nodded. He looked up and down the road again, noting the single car approaching from a half mile away.

"You having any power issues?" Mr. Andrews yelled down between labored huffs. "I can have dispatch send someone out."

The car rushed toward the pair and passed at full speed. The stranger seemed to be studying the license plate as the letters and numbers faded into a blur. He continued. "No, mate, no power issues. Just thought it was curious to see a lineman working by himself."

Mr. Andrews only heard silence on the other end of phone as his eyes worked back and forth between his steps and the observing man. He contacted the ground with a terse grunt and hobbled back to the truck on his spikes. As he took them off, the man stood next to his car, unmoving, his hands buried in his coat pockets.

"Well, buddy," declared Mr. Andrews, "my shift is done. You sure you don't need anything?"

The man glanced up at the pole and then returned his gaze to Mr. Andrews.

"No, mate, I'm good. Thank you." He headed back to his car.

Mr. Andrews smiled broadly and sighed with relief. "You have a good day. And that's a nice Dodge. You got a Hemi under there?"

The man paused as he opened the car door. "It's got a little kick for sure."

He slammed the door closed and made a squealing U-turn, heading back the way he came and leaving a large skid mark across both lanes.

0:00   3:13

Chapter 37

Hotel California – Eagles

Inside the gated community of Merriweather Gardens, the identical houses sat in a cloverleaf layout, with paved roads each bending back to the central clubhouses. Residents were required to be fifty-five and older, and many of them had bought the houses during the initial construction. With extraordinarily little turnover, even from migration and mortality, the neighbors knew each other intimately. Many socialized in the clubhouse for event nights or walked daily along the central paths. The guard gate at the entrance ensured that no solicitors entered, and only approved visitors were allowed in otherwise. Dana knew details from her internet search, but she had a plan. She parked her truck on the road leading to the entrance and walked toward it, bypassing the gate by slipping between the hedges that enclosed the development. She carried her backpack low to the ground so as not to snag it on the briars.

Once she emerged, she walked with her head down, her curls obscuring her face from any peering eyes. She went street by street, following the painted house numbers on the curbs until she stood in front of a mailbox labeled 204, the last known address of Anselm Geissler.

She jogged up the driveway and rapped her knuckles on the glass storm door, checking over her shoulder for any nosy neighbors. The exterior was maintained with the same vigor as the other homes in the complex. The curtains were drawn wide open, but she could not see inside beyond the glare of the glass. After a long pause, the interior door creaked open to reveal a short man of advanced age but surprisingly good posture and mobility. He wore modern frameless glasses over his lined face. He smoothed his palms down the front of his cardigan and smiled.

"Hello. Can I help you?" he asked in quiet voice, searching beyond the young woman on his doorstep for her vehicle or companions.

"I think you can. My name's Dana, and I think you served with my grandfather, Colonel Jefferson, or my father, Major Jefferson?"

He looked her up and down, still smiling, and opened the storm door. "*Dana*. Oh my goodness. *Dana Jefferson*. Yes, come in, come in! So nice to meet you! Here, come sit in the parlor." He gestured toward the alcove by the front bay window, where there was loveseat and a reading chair.

Dana surveyed the upscale furniture and coordinated decorations admiringly, wondering if Anselm had pointed to a page in a catalog and handed the stylist a blank check. As she sat down in the chair, she noticed one item that appeared out of place: an asymmetrically lensed photography camera with no markings of any brand that sat on the middle shelf next to a compact stereo. She was careful to remember Nick's idiom and remain reserved rather than bring attention to it.

"You're Mr. Geissler? I'm sorry, I don't know what rank you were."

"Major Anselm Geissler, PhD. And yes, I was good friends with your grandfather. I'm afraid I didn't make it to his funeral."

"Neither did I," she flippantly admitted, then gritted her teeth at her lack of restraint. "I was little and it didn't seem to be a good idea. Trauma and memory stuff." *Good recovery*, she praised herself.

"Your grandfather worked on some very important projects. I still have one of his prototypes." He pointed to the camera, to her surprise. "That camera was for aerial reconnaissance when drones were still black ops and off-the-books."

"Can I see it?"

"Yes, just please be careful." He handed it to her with precision and flipped a chrome toggle switch as it rested in her hands. "It was an early digital depth recorder. You could read a serial number off a gun barrel at one mile, or so your grandfather claimed."

Dana turned the camera gently, inspecting each side. It was surprisingly heavy, but the old man had wielded it without indicating its heft. She had seen this camera before in her grandfather's home when she still lived with him. It was an opaque memory, only illuminated in her mind when the device triggered the recollection.

"Why yes, I think I saw this before." She placed the camera carefully on the coffee table. "I really wanted him to get an instant camera so I could take pictures of cats and lizards."

Anselm seated himself on the loveseat across from her and crossed his legs. His pants rode up slightly, exposing black socks with silver striped threads that, to Dana, resembled circuit boards. She opened the backpack at her feet and pulled out the group photo of the scientists from its secure location tucked inside one of her skates.

"Anselm—I mean, Major Geissler, can you tell me anything about this?" She held the photo up and then paused before extending it to him.

He leaned in and took the photo, straightening his glasses for a deeper examination. "Why, yes. Yes, I can. One moment." He reached into his pocket and pulled out a phone, which was vibrating. She could see the screen light up with a text message but could not make out the words as he quickly typed and then set the phone facedown on the table.

"Just letting my wife know I have a visitor. She is on her way home." He flashed a smile again and set the photo down next to the phone. "That was our biggest project, the Atomic Juggernaut. It had a very sad legacy, Dana, which I'm sure you know about."

The Atomic Juggernaut, yes, I know a bit, Dana thought before reacting with a slight nod. She felt her face flush with the tinge of excitement rising inside her as she saw the breadcrumbs leading further into the woods of her past.

He continued. "There was a fatal flaw intrinsic in the design. Two flaws, really. One was the radiation leakage. Once we discovered it, we removed the original engineer and replaced him with this gentleman, Jens Jacobsen," he said as he pointed to a man next to her grandfather. "Then we encountered another issue with the piloting system. Your father . . . he died as the result of a horrendous test one day—"

Before Anselm could finish, his phone vibrated. He picked it up and then quickly put it back on the table facedown.

"I'm sorry about that. Anyhow, your grandfather was working on cutting-edge sensory equipment so that the pilot of the juggernaut could see an enhanced view. But the computing technology wasn't where we wanted to be. Your father proposed a shortcut. I worked out a compromise to save us time and money, as we were bleeding through both at a voracious pace. You see, such a complex machine needed a central processing unit so that the pilot could control the motions. But the unit would have been massive to account for all possibilities. Just think, for example, about the instructions and locomotion required to do this." He demonstrated by uncrossing and recrossing his legs.

"Then we had an idea. What if the navigator ran the basic controls, with a pilot wired into the main processor of the juggernaut? The pilot, and his central nervous system, made the juggernaut move. In other words, the navigator would push a control to go forward, and the *pilot's brain* would work out the details of how to move the juggernaut forward."

Dana blinked rapidly as his explanation of early cybernetics rushed through her brain. "Like jacking into the ole noggin? I'm trying to grasp this, and my only point of reference is bad science-fiction movies."

His phone vibrated again. He wrung his hands and glanced down, sighing deeply before returning to his dissertation.

"My wife is persistent," he said with a small smile. "Anyway, yes, directly wiring into the brain. But at the time, to utilize the human nervous system and to make sure the data was relayed to the juggernaut without delay, the pilot needed to be completely submissive to the machine. You see, Dana, the pilot needed to be . . . there's no easy way to say this . . . the pilot needed to be essentially dead."

His last word hung in the air for a moment. Dana sank into the chair. The implications were swarming around her like a hive of hornets.

"So, people died for the program," she said slowly, "accidentally and intentionally."

Anselm didn't seem phased by her thesis. "Once someone had been diagnosed with cancer, he could choose to become a pilot. It was an alternate to what might be a long, slow death. In return, the families and survivors would receive compensation upfront. Life insurance times one hundred."

The phone vibrated again on the table. Dana's head swirled with the information. Her eyes darted from the camera to the photo sitting next to his phone and down to her skates inside the open bag. Anselm removed his glasses and held them up to the light for inspection, holding each earpiece between his thumb and index finger. Dana was struck by his youthful-looking fingers, lightly tanned, and bare of any jewelry.

He's not wearing a wedding ring.

She took an inventory of the exits from where she sat. There was the front door she had come in, and down the hall she caught a glimpse of a storm door heading out back.

Anselm continued. "When the program was being shut down, one of our teammates approached your grandfather about selling him the design. You see, he thought the private sector could continue the project. Then the juggernaut could be made for other parties, other crusades far across the globe."

Dana stared straight into his eyes. She held her silence to prompt him to continue.

"Of course, we would have to keep the flaws close to the vest to do so. Then someone had the idea that we could make money consulting how to counter the device. That is, we would sell the juggernaut plans to another nation's insurgents, and then consult with their government on how to counter such a thing. We get paid by both sides," he paused, "to be a catalyst and resolve a conflict at the same time. It's really an ingenious way to make peace profitable."

The conversation had gone far beyond sharing of old memories, and her mind was coming to a quick conclusion about what was happening.

"It's an amazing machine," she said lightly, at the time slipping a hand into her backpack to pull out her goggles. "My family made some really amazing things. Did they tell you about the skates?"

Her Cheshire cat smile was met with a confused reaction by Anselm. For the first time during their exchange, he dropped the playacting.

"The what?" he sputtered.

She took advantage of his confusion, moving steadily. She pulled out Laverne and Shirley, shining from a post-tune-up buff and freshly oiled. His eyes opened wide and his lips slowly parted.

"Did your father make those?" he reached a hand toward them.

"Yes! Mobility enhancement for soldiers and rescue crews." She calmly but quickly snapped one of the shin guards in place. "They can match a car's speed pretty well."

The phone on the table began to vibrate again, this time from an incoming call. Anselm glanced down at the phone and then up at the front window, no longer trying to hide anything.

"Tell me more about them," he stammered, seemingly trying to buy time. "What are they made of? Is that polycarbonate or an alloy metal?"

Dana clicked on the other skate and stood up to full height. "Is that window safety glass?" She pointed to the front curtains.

"I beg your pardon?"

At that moment, a black Hummer screeched to a halt in front of the house, coming to a stop with two wheels on the curb. Immediately behind it, a Dodge Charger roared to a stop, the bumper tapping the Hummer.

"Never mind, I'm not doing the window thing again," she announced. She turned toward the hallway, first throwing her backpack on and then grabbing the photo off the coffee table.

Anselm stood up, only to meet the force of the coffee table as she kicked it into his kneecaps.

Dana glanced back over her shoulder and saw the tall Australian man from their encounter at the hospital running toward the house.

Anselm wheezed as he clutched his legs. "Dana, I'm sorry, they told me to keep you here if you ever showed up. And I needed the money," Anselm panted, doubled over in agony. "But I thought you deserved the courtesy of an explanation before I handed you over to them." He winced again as he looked through the window. "You had a right to know. And I am so sorry this has to be."

Chapter 38

I Can't Drive 55 – Sammy Hagar

Dana gave him a disappointed look and then shot through the hallway toward the back screen door, kicking it open midstride and bounding onto the concrete patio. Her skates moved a bit awkwardly over the lawn as she cut through the yard behind Anselm's house. She spotted the hedgerows near the gatehouse. Bounding in her skates to avoid the flowers until she hit pavement, she looked back to see the Hummer and Dodge turning onto the street. She charged toward the gatehouse and slid under the arm as the two pursuers skidded around the corner, barreling down on the guard shack.

I hate these guys. I really do. She rammed her earpiece in and furiously tapped the call button.

"Nick, don't be mad! I got set up," Dana yelled over a cacophony of sounds.

It all felt like a bad dream, one she'd had before. It had been hard enough the first time to keep ahead of the Hummer; now she had the Charger to outskate as well. They were keeping pace even as she accelerated, swerving and weaving through the scant traffic on the roadway. Laverne and Shirley's shrill squealing stabbed Dana's ears as she leaned deep into a tight turn on the county road. She had called Nick once she had finally gotten her earpiece in place.

"Dana, what did you do?"

"Nothing! Sort of. They set up a trap knowing I'd end up visiting Anselm at some point. I swear, I was being careful, but the old man is a creepy, greedy dirtbag."

"Listen, just *focus on the objective*. Where are you now?" Nick crackled back into her ear.

"On some county road. 541? 549? Can't they just name streets after presidents in this state?!"

"Dana, focus!"

"Sorry. I've got two on my tail this time: the Hummer and that Dodge Charger from the bar. There's some more cars up ahead, and it opens up into four lanes. Once I get into the pack, I think I can lose them."

Dana studied her pursuers over her shoulder, trying to gauge the distance between them. In disbelief, she watched as the engine of Dodge surged, easily halving the gap between them. She grit her teeth. "Nick, that is not your typical Charger. He's coming in fast. I don't know how, but I'm in trouble. Any and all ideas welcome!"

She pushed her toes further into the boots and pumped her legs for any incremental speed that she could produce. The wind ripped across her face, and the dense patches of exhaust clouds punched her lungs as she heaved. She closed in on the pack of cars ahead, making an inventory of their order: tractor trailer, van, compact car, another van, and a tiny Mazda convertible at the rear. Passing the convertible was her first goal. The thunder of the Dodge clawed at her ears as she could sense it getting closer, the headlights filling the edges of her periphery with white halos. *They're right behind me.* She pulled parallel to the Mazda and waved to the driver.

"Lady! Hey, Lady! I'm sorry!" she screamed as the woman driving the convertible finally acknowledged her, eyes wide at the girl keeping pace with her on a pair of skates. As the Dodge's engine howled a third time, Dana grabbed the Mazda's driver-side door handle and threw herself over the hood. The Charger had caught up to the convertible on its left and launched the tiny car off the road.

"Dana, what is going on?" Nick yelled into the earpiece.

"A whole lot," she panted. *I just got that woman seriously hurt.* "Nicky? Stay on the line, Nicky. Things are going bad. Just stay with me. Please!"

"I'm not going anywhere, just tell me what I can do."

"I don't know!" she yelled. "I just don't know."

The black sedan slid right next to her. A bald bearded man shuffled in the passenger seat and the blond square-jawed driver sneered as his eyes burned into hers. "Nick, our friend from the bar and hospital is driving the car. And he's got a friend with him." The passenger window opened, and the bearded man leaned out a clunky rifle with a large barrel.

Dana's heartbeat drummed inside her ears, drowning out the pounding of the Dodge's pistons that she felt inside her skull. She extended her arm toward the car, her leather sleeve rippling in the wind as her fingers reached for the rear passenger door handle. *Focus on the objective, Dana.* Her pulse slowed and a fresh blast of air filled her lungs as her fingers touched the door handle's surface. She clamped her fingers around it.

"Back off!" she screamed as she kicked one leg into the open front passenger window, dislodging the gun from the bearded man's grip. She swung her leg back and flung herself over the Charger's trunk so she was now behind the driver's side. The driver made eye contact through the sideview mirror. Dana felt the burning annoyance from his reflected eyes. Over his shoulder, she spied a large dial gauge surrounded by buttons mounted above the steering wheel.

"Nick, this car is full of tricks. What do I do?"

"Dana, hang on," his voiced cracked as the earpiece spit into her ear. "I'm looking up maps, car schematics, anything I can think of right now. Just don't hang up. *Don't hang up.*"

The driver slid his hands out of her eyeline, and Dana braced herself for whatever they were going to throw at her next. The Dodge suddenly spit a viscous fountain of gray liquid from under the rear bumper. It took her a second to recognize the cold and wet sensation on her legs: *lithium grease.* The same substance that made her skates run smoothly was now separating her from the road and any chance of traction. The wheels of Laverne and Shirley slid along the road, out of her control. Spatters of grease decorated her shin guards and legs. She realized in horror that the cascade of sparks from her skates were immediately extinguished from the coating of lubricant.

As her arms flipped wildly as she grasped the air and tried to regain control, a sharp pain exploded from her left thigh. She had forgotten all about the Hummer in her battle against the tricked-out Charger. She glanced down and saw a bulbous dart had pierced her leg and looked behind her to see a rifle hanging out of the Hummer passenger window.

"Dana, what's going on?" Nick buzzed.

"Shit shit shit! Nick, I got hit for real! A goddamn dart . . ." Her adrenaline fought against the tranquilizer formula entering her blood. She reached down and pulled out the dart. Her legs and arms tingled, her jaw slacked, and her shoulders slumped forward. "Nick, I think I got it out in tiff. If got a goof feels," she slurred. Her lips felt loose and lackadaisical against her nerve impulses.

"You're babbling," he shouted back in the earpiece. *"Dana, stay with me.* Don't hang up. Play dead if you have to. Please answer."

"Pancakes. Got ith."

The Hummer rolled to Dana's side and she felt a hand grab her arm. The Charger was pulled over ahead of them. As the Hummer stopped, the driver of the sedan stepped out and strode over to Dana with a smug smile.

"Hello, Dana," he said as she slumped to the ground next to the Hummer. "I'm being rude. Allow me to introduce myself. You can call me Agent Olsen."

"You, the guy," she mumbled. "Olsen. Like the actresses." The tranquilizer's effects were numbing her nerves, cresting like a muddy wave through her veins. "Actresseseses. Oh, you got some friends? One, two, three friends! Ah ah ah!" Even in her stupor, she hoped the earpiece would pick up her words for Nick. Her thoughts merged and separated as she fought the fog creeping through her brain.

Olsen gestured to the man in the Hummer with the rifle. "Thirty-Six, you can lower that. I think she's got enough in her. We need her somewhat coherent."

"Thirty-Six? That's a crappy name. Did your mom and dad hate you?" She glanced down at her grease-covered and dirt-stained pants. Her head rolled around on her loose neck as she tried to see how many men were actually around her. Suddenly, she felt a pair of rough hands pick her up and begin dragging her.

"Okay," she slurred. "I met four dudes today! These two got a Hummer," she said as she pointed three wiggling fingers at the Dodge, "and Mary Kate and Thirty-Something drive the family car." She flipped her head toward Olsen and smiled feebly.

She could hear Nick faintly over the earpiece. "Dana, I got four guys in a Hummer and a Charger. Dana, are you still there?"

She flopped into a ragdoll pose as she was thrown into the back seat of the Hummer. She squinted at the blurry image of a touch screen display on the dashboard and discerned that the GPS guide map was on.

"Hey, where we going?" She forced her words to make sense but it was getting harder to fight the sedative in her bloodstream. She blinked to keep her tired eyes open but saw white spots were fluttering in her field of vision. "Are we going to see the robot? Is that what we're doing? Guys?" Neither man replied as they started the truck and headed back out on the highway.

"Dana, are they taking you to the bunker? Can you figure out where they're taking you?" Nick whispered in her ear.

"I think this is going to end well," she proudly announced while drooling. "I got a good feeling. I want pancakes."

Dana drifted in and out of sleep, Nick's voice occasionally coming through as if in a dream. Her body jostled with every bump of the road. Her eyes flickered open as the Hummer began to slow.

Olsen drove the Charger deeper into the Pine Barrens, the Hummer close behind him, until he reached the same pole that the worker from the electric company had been servicing earlier that day. There, he turned the car onto a dirt road, followed by the Hummer, both pulling up a few minutes later in front of the bunker, the juggernaut patiently waiting for them all inside.

Chapter 39

Scared – The Tragically Hip

Hello, Anselm."

"Hello, Rhodes."

Colin Rhodes stood in the open doorway of Anselm's parlor wearing his favorite civilian uniform: a black knee-length coat, black slacks, and an olive-green button-down shirt with a gold tie. His hair was dyed black in an attempt to defy his age, and although his build was muscular from years of intense training, atrophy had set in. He wore rimless square glasses centered on his nose, despite the crookedness from more than a few past fractures. His jaw was broad, and he spoke with punctuated emphasis and baritone. "Don't get up on my account."

Anselm sat in an armchair across the room, two icepacks firmly on each knee. The condensation left large wet spots on each wool pant leg. He winced as he sat up straighter and nodded a hello. Rhodes slowly surveyed the room. "I see you're incapacitated. How long was she here?"

"Oh, several minutes. We were having an intense conversation when your boys tried to call."

"I'd like to remind you *as I do all my agents* that my calls are not to be ignored. It's possible that her escape could have been prevented."

"Aye-aye, right." Anselm sat his icepacks down next to him and rubbed his shins.

Rhodes pursed his lips and lifted his chin. "What does she know?"

"I told her everything. She *deserved* to know. The project, the plan, how we were going to sell the juggernaut and then double down by selling our knowledge on how to counter it. She's lost everything because of the program." He looked up at Rhodes and firmed his gaze. "We wouldn't be here if it weren't for her family. We owe her something, even if it's just closure."

Rhodes knew the Jefferson name had been attached to many successful, albeit dull, projects for several years before they became acquainted. The Atomic Juggernaut was a synergy of projects, dreams, and talents that had lived and died under Rhodes's eyes. His fortunes, and his taxes and debts, were because of and despite the Jefferson family. He loathed to say their name, and it stung every time Anselm said it.

"We owe her nothing." Rhodes took off his coat and placed it on the back of a chair. "But now she knows, *and* she got away. We *will* catch her, but we're still working with 'ifs' and 'maybes' and that's not how I like to operate."

"Well, I have an insurance plan," Anselm countered as he reached for the camera sitting on the now properly righted coffee table. "Do you remember what this is?"

"That's one of . . . *his* . . . cameras." He licked his teeth.

"Right. Now, you know, as I do, that when we shut down, Jefferson Sr. erased some of our electronic keys and put in a final protocol with the eye scanner, so that only the last of us could access it." He smiled. "That was of course after you left the program. Anyway, after his son died, he thought it was the best way to create a failsafe, or lock people out if we all died. But as you know, unbeknownst to us, he shut out those of us who wanted to keep working on it and sell it."

Rhodes shook his head in disagreement. "I wasn't shut out. I was removed from the program and replaced with another engineer. I became the overseer in the budget office, remember?"

Anselm ignored the last comment. He turned the camera on and flipped open a display screen. "See here? This is Dana. I remember her father took pictures of her with this prototype. Super digital. It was decades ahead of the digital resolution revolution. It works like an old tin type, a daguerreotype from the eighteen hundreds. It records the light image down to the electron level, which in turn is what a retinal scan uses." He tapped the screen and a photo of a surprised Dana glowed in his living room.

Rhodes studied her features, noting the blend of her mother's beauty with her father's handsomeness. He knew both her parents but had never met Dana. Her mother had kept her far from any of her father's coworkers, and as the boss, he was especially siloed from their private life. His own daughter, Nina, and Dana would have perhaps been friends in an alternate timeline. Anselm tapped the camera to retain Rhodes's attention.

"A retina, Rhodes, is like a fingerprint, so no matter what age, it keeps the same tagging points in the same layout. Think of a photo of a tree ten or twenty years before how it looks today. The branches and divides will all be in the same places. A photo of her when she was eight or ten is the same retina imprint as her at, well, whatever she is—twenty-something." He smiled with his crowning achievement. Rhodes reached for the camera, which was promptly withdrawn by Anselm.

"So, you're going to tell me that *this* is your insurance policy? That we have an eye scan of her as of today that we can convert and use for unlocking the juggernaut?" Rhodes absently straightened his tie and glanced toward the bay window facing the street.

"Yes. I always knew that if I didn't deliver her in person, we'd have an alternate key source. And now I get paid, old friend."

Rhodes chuckled and stood. He meandered his way across the room toward the bay window and looked out at the two SUVs parked at the curb waiting on his return. He walked back to his coat and retrieved a pistol with a silencer, then placed it on the table between him and Anselm. "I just want to make sure we're both showing our hand."

Anselm inhaled and stood up, grunting with the final effort. He lifted one pant leg, revealing his sock with the circuit-pattern design and then just above that a metallic prosthetic that connected to a stump below his knee.

"Both of them, Rhodes. I got two new partial legs thanks to our work."

"Silver's work, to be precise." Rhodes tapped the silencer on the table. "You always were a coattail-riding slacker."

"Yes, Silver. And I paid Silver handsomely for it because the government wouldn't. And you know there's more of Silver's work inside me. I was the test bed for your daughter, remember?"

Rhodes ignored him and looked back out the window.

"Colin, I never asked, how is your daughter?"

"She is . . . as she is." He shuffled his feet, uncomfortable with the topic. "When we stop fighting wars, we can prioritize peace and maybe find the cures for what has destroyed the things we have lost."

"I detect some sarcasm. I know you. I am sorry about her. For her."

"Anselm," Rhodes sighed, "we did amazing things. And those things were routed into the Atomic Juggernaut program. We stayed out of the way of corporate research and development. We followed the money. And world peace is more noble and kingmaking is more profitable than helping burn and cancer victims." He broke his eye contact with Anselm. "This is why we quicken the pace and drive the invading wolves out into the open, where they, not the lambs, will be slaughtered. Until we finish the battles and anoint the kings of men, we cannot truly change the world. Or the past."

"You make it sound so poetic, warmongering for profit."

The two men both looked out the window. A rabbit hopped across the lawn, avoiding the leaves and only landing on patches of green grass.

"Fall will finish soon," mused Rhodes. He flipped open his phone momentarily to monitor the slowly accruing list of messages.

"Soon enough, Colin."

Rhodes reached into his pocket and unfolded a sheet of paper. He held it in front of Anselm. "Do you know what this is? We retrieved it from a pile of items taken from Dana's apartment." He flicked the paper and watched Anselm's face twist into a confused mask, studying the lines and pathways, junction boxes noted with electrical symbols, and the advanced mathematical formulas scrawled along the edges. His eyes widened and he reached to snatch it as Rhodes pulled it back. "Dana had this all along."

"That's amazing! I only heard rumors that Junior was working on that. Do you know what that is, old friend? Energy. Perpetual energy." He leaned back with a sneer. "That is ransom for the world. Not only is that the answer to the juggernaut's power crisis, it's the answer to the world's power crisis." He placed two fingers on his temple in thought. "It's missing something. There's probably another print somewhere for the transformer and relay station, but I've failed enough times working on something similar to know exactly what this is! Do you know what you can do with this?"

"Anselm, are you telling the dealer how to play his hand?" Rhodes fanned his fingers.

"I'm telling you that the card you're holding is the ace in the hole, an ace up your sleeve, and counting cards against a blind man. You can shop those plans to any nation and name your price. If you wanted to sell the juggernaut to the rogues, you have the kill switch and the answer with extreme prejudice."

Rhodes adjusted his tie again and placed the folded photocopy back into this pocket. "What makes you think we haven't done that already? I have two interested parties in the Pacific, one in central Africa, and another in South America. I just need to decide who is paying us first. And by 'us,' I mean *me*."

"Surely, old friend, I'm included in this?" Anselm extended both hands.

Rhodes thought he looked like a frail beggar, thirsty and dying in the sun.

"Anselm, my agents have her now. Alive. We're going to be able to open the sarcophagus." He made sure the silencer was tightly screwed into the pistol's barrel.

"Now wait, Rhodes. I delivered her. I had a backup so if something happened, we'd still be able to get inside the juggernaut's casing. I did my part, and now, not only do you not want to pay me, but *this,*" he said, his lip quivering as he attempted to finish his plea, "after all I did. For our country. For us. *For your daughter.* For everything." Tears started to well in his yellowing eyes.

"Anselm. You told Dana too much. If you had just sat and had coffee, or talked about the weather, while you waited for us to show up, she wouldn't be a liability. But you gave in to your guilty conscience. And until we have the robotic beast open *and* she's dead, we're not in the clear." He held the gun out to Anselm. "Go ahead. You know what you have to do."

Hands shaking but a resigned look on his face, Anselm picked up the pistol and placed the tip of the barrel against his own temple. He breathed in sharply and exhaled loudly through his nose. He swung the gun level with Rhodes's face and pulled the trigger.

A short click was followed by Anselm gasping. Rhodes's lips pulled back into a thin smile. "You were never a company man, Anselm." Rhodes took the gun from his former teammate's outstretched and trembling hand. He picked up the camera and then his coat, and made his way to the front door. He looked back to see a wet spot slowly forming on the front of the old man's pants.

Rhodes stepped outside and nodded to agent sitting inside the first SUV. "Forty-Four, it's time."

Martinez stepped out of the cabin and sighed. Rhodes nodded. The junior agent reached into the bag in the truck and produced a short knife and a stun gun. He walked with his head lowered into Anselm Geissler's house.

Rhodes settled into the passenger seat and perused his growing list of text messages. Minutes eroded. He flipped opened his wallet and slid a photograph from the billfold: a younger version of Rhodes on the beach, shirtless and fit, holding a young girl no older than ten on his lap. Her blonde hair was caught in a wild whip from the ocean breeze, circling her high cheeks with golden lassos. Her hands were small, even against her atrophied limbs. Her toes grew together into a single paddle below each ankle. Her face wore a beaming smile under her crystal-blue eyes. He ran his thumb across the side of her face in the photo as his own tensed.

"I am sorry, Nina," he whispered to the photo. "I do this all for God and country. And your future."

He returned the photo to his wallet and silently watched the door until he saw Martinez finally emerge from Anselm's porch, walking slowly down the driveway and carrying a mass of wires and metal attached to two shoes. He stopped in front of Rhodes to show him the metallic lower legs covered in blood before placing them inside his bag with the instruments of torture and dissection. Rhodes nodded as the agent reseated himself in the car.

"Forty-Four, you will never have to do that again. By need or command."

0:00   3:13

Chapter 40

Ball of Confusion – The Temptations

O nly white noise and the occasional whirring of faint engine rumbling hummed over the signal inside Nick's earpiece. He stared at the laptop on the workbench, feeling every minute as another pound added to his shoulders. He stared at the live view from the camera his father had mounted, but it remained static and unchanging, save the occasional 4-by-4 or minivan that drove past the line of sight. He whispered "Dana" every few minutes to see if she responded over her Bluetooth, but the continued one-way communication confirmed that she was unconscious. His sole hope was that she was on her way to the bunker, alive, and he would catch a glimpse when her captors turned down the gravel road.

"What's the good word, son?" Mr. Andrew's entrance into the garage startled him. Nick took his earpiece out and switched the phone to speaker, the choking burden of helplessness starting to wash over him. He shook his head and Mr. Andrews responded in kind.

"Nick, is this the point where we call the police?"

"I don't know if we can," he admitted, running both hands through his hair. "I think we're in a 'trust no one' situation. We know these tough guys have no problem shooting police; heck, they might even *be* police, or at least they have posed as them." He walked across the garage and stared at his paintball guns.

"Those won't help, son."

Nick studied the guns, counting the multicolored rounds in neatly stacked plastic bottles. He ran a finger down the laser sight and scope on his favorite rifle, mounted at the top of the small shrine to South Jersey sports and hobbies of his past. With his fingernail, he scratched a bit of pink paint off the side of the ammo hopper and turned back to the computer screen. His father stood close and put a hand on his shoulder.

"If we still had any real guns, I'm not sure if I'd still be here. But we also don't want to be in any position to take a man's life."

"That's a little preachy, but thanks." Nick reconciled himself with the advice. He was no alpha, and he certainly was not a fighter or a killer. Despite the hesitation he had expressed to his father, he was still considering if a call to the police would be the right thing to do, albeit the coward's way, insurance to live another day.

Mr. Andrews walked over to the laptop screen and leaned in while adjusting his glasses. He sat, assuming a sentry role for the time being.

Nick leapt to his father's side and pointed at the screen. There appeared, at last, a black Hummer and a black sedan. They slowed down just past the camera's location and turned into the woods, kicking up a small cloud of sandy soil and gravel.

"That's them! The vehicles are just what Dana described. And she must be in there. Her and the four guys."

"Four guys make up a tiny army. We need a tiny army, too."

Nick and Mr. Andrews simultaneously turned to each other, each with a variation of surprise and excitement on their faces. Mr. Andrews pulled out his phone. "I think I have Mary Beth's number in here. I asked Dana for it because I was thinking I might ask her out."

"Dad, this isn't the time for jokes."

"Oh, I'm not joking," Mitch retorted. "I was also thinking we should see how many dirty Valkyries can fit into a school bus and if they're up for a class trip."

3:13

Chapter 41

Rocket Queen – Guns N' Roses

T he four agents entered the bunker in silence. Olsen led the group and turned on the lights as the bearded twins dragged Dana by the arms down the stairs, her skates clanging on each step until the bottom. Her eyes fluttered as she was jolted awake by the jarring movement. She looked over at the stitched numbers on their fatigue shirts, 036 and 037, and scoffed.

"You guys need better names," she gurgled, still feeling the fog wrapped around her head. Her feet banging on each step momentarily wiped away the numbness with a prick of pain in her ankles.

"Good thing she comes with her own dolly wheels," scoffed Thirty-Seven, "but she's still a thick one, eh? She certainly doesn't skip leg day at the gym." The fourth agent, plump but muscular and marked on his shirt as 074, stopped halfway down the staircase, glancing across the vast lab and locking his gaze on the sarcophagus in the center.

"That's about the size of the casket I'd need," he laughed, flexing his monstrous arms and posing in front of Dana. He nodded to the top of the stairs.

"I'll roost up by the cars to keep an eye out."

"Aye," replied Olsen. He nodded to the twins, who put Dana on the desk chair closest to the metallic container at the center of the room. "Keep her awake until we're done." He walked over to a desk, now adorned with a modern laptop and a small stack of decaying papers that Dana recognized from her apartment. She watched as he thumbed through the pages, holding them up to the light, inspecting the schematics and studying what appeared to be a diagram of a cockpit. She had studied them herself on long lonely nights when Angela wasn't around, and she could identify each one by the barest of blurry details she could make out from her chair. Olsen mimed a variety of motions with his right hand that she imagined were the workings of the Atomic Juggernaut's pilot in action. She closed her eyes and slumped her head to her chest.

"Wake her!" shouted Thirty-Seven. Thirty-Six flung back his arm and swept it to within an inch of Dana's cheek. He playfully flicked her nose with his fingers. "Rise and shine, gorgeous." He licked away the stray hairs from his beard that encroached on his mouth. "You got work to do." He flicked her nose again, and Dana bolted up in the chair, blinking and swallowing before gasping.

"Oh, we're in the bunker," she announced, hoping Nick was still listening. She was still feeling some of the sedative in her limbs, but her brain at last began to clear the fog. She scanned the room again, her vision still a bit blurry. "So, what's the plan? Chips and dip and soda?"

"You're going to sit up, and open that thing, and then we kill you." Thirty-Six spoke in a clear voice. "Business." He zipped a pair of cable ties to each of her wrists and the arms of the chair. He pulled out his pistol and leveled the barrel at her. Olsen held up a fist.

"No guns! This thing is carrying a nuclear power plant inside it. We don't even want to chance a stray shot." He glowered at Thirty-Six. "Safety on." He pulled his own piece out and set the safety in a mock demonstration. Thirty-

Seven pushed Dana in her chair toward the sarcophagus. He wiped off the eye scanner as Olsen and Thirty-Six walked over to assist. The three agents lifted the chair high enough to push Dana's head against the black panel. The same flashes and noises she experienced at Hardy Farms began, her retinas registering once again as a valid passkey.

The sarcophagus groaned, opening with greater ease than the one in the barn. Again, the monstrosity inside was leaning forward with its arms limp, but this version had a full abdomen where the other's had been empty, indicating that the power source and contents were intact. Olsen ran his fingers across the stomach, leaving a trail in the thin film of dust, toward a latch on the side of its metallic rib cage.

"Let's make sure we kick the tires." He pushed the button next to the latch, initiating a hiss and creak as the panel's dormant power started ticking and whining.

At first, the door barely moved; then suddenly it sprang open, forced by a weight pressed against it, the object falling to the ground in front of them. The agents jumped back. Dana, unable to, sat up with as much force as she could muster in her sluggish state.

It was a body, mummified in the airtight quarantine, still wearing its pilot suit, worn and graying from age. Dana coughed on the cloud of disintegrated canvas that rose up from the floor, adrenaline surging into her heart.

Thirty-Seven approached the body carefully and, using his foot, slowly rolled the body over onto its back. Dana gasped. She could clearly read the name tag pinned to the chest.

S. Jefferson Jr.

The fragments of her memory and shards of every conversation about her father stabbed her with a pain that she felt deep in her sternum. Her initial reaction to scream was choked by her constricted throat, the dryness suffocating her vocal cords even though her mouth opened wide. Her jaw tensed until she finally inhaled a mouthful of dusty air and gasped.

"It's your father!" announced Thirty-Seven. He jabbed a black boot into the shoulder, emitting a sickening crunching sound.

Dana's eyes burned. She turned her fists up and pulled against the plastic ties with all the strength she could muster, but she was too weak. Laverne and Shirley stared up at her, still attached to her feet. Her toes were still numb but she could swing her legs a bit as she tried to contact the interior foot pads. *Why aren't they turning on? If I could just feel my toes . . .* She pushed out a large breath in a futile effort to make tactile confirmation of the controls.

The agents were absorbed by the machine. Thirty-Six approached Olsen. "So that looks like the top hangar doors"—he nodded to an area above the juggernaut—"and the hydraulic pad should lift it up per these interior diagrams of the lab." He pointed to an imaginary set of lines around the top of the room. "Once we get the truck here and we load this up, we can be at the Robbinsville airstrip in an hour. We have a better chance there than Cherry Hill. There are a lot fewer flight plans logged through there for private planes."

"We can use the rockets with the props if needed to get extra boost on takeoff," added Olsen, "and I agree. Robbinsville has less air traffic. We can shut it down for our window and be out. Tell Forty-Four to schedule the truck. I'll give Mr. Rhodes an update."

Dana looked down at her father's corpse again and yielded to her tears. She still could not make sense of what she was seeing. Her mind began to form a revised timeline of the one she knew: her father in his waning health, a memory of a final vacation, pushing him in a wheelchair. If he had lived, she would never have gone to boarding school or lived under the roof of her grandfather. He would be there to tell her future children his fantastic stories, see his expression in their faces. But she had been denied such a world. And the final, brutal evidence of that lost world was lying at her feet in an old jumpsuit. His face was turned away, sparing her from the eternal scarring visage of his sunken cheeks and hollow eye sockets surrounding an unsmiling mouth of atrophied lips and blackened gums. She wept.

Dana coughed and snapped her attention back to the moment. She forced her mind to dissolve the despair and doubt; right now, she had to act. Spitting out a deposit of tears that had seeped into the corners of her mouth, she surveyed the room again. Agent Thirty-Seven was placing some notebooks from a shelf into a black duffel bag. Thirty-Six inspected the contents with approval. They appeared focused on their tasks at hand. She touched her numb toes again gently inside the skates but received no return response. She recounted the three agents in the room and one outside. *Three agents that were unable to use their firearms,* she thought to herself. Only one door out, she knew. She began pulling again at the cable ties on each arm. *Focus on the objective. Get out.* She spotted wire cutters on the desk nearest to her.

"I'll go tell Seventy-Four to start the Hummer, and we'll be up with some more inventory," she heard Thirty-Seven say just before several thuds clamored from the bunker entrance above. A loud clang pealed in the antechamber. Dana clamored to turn her chair around to view the action. A large woman in coveralls leapt from the tunnel, swinging a baseball bat. Seventy-Four sailed up and over the railing, then hit the bunker floor below, knocked completely unconscious.

"Mary Beth?" Dana whispered.

Mary Beth shouldered her bat proudly on the terrace. Behind her a dozen women sporting jeans and leather, tank tops and capris, flannel shirts and yoga pants, each wearing elbow and knee pads in baby blue, swarmed the top railing. As they poured down the staircase like a column of fire ants, Thirty-Six and Thirty-Seven aimed their guns, while Olsen pulled his sidearm and grabbed Dana's head. He pushed the barrel against her temple.

"Don't move! All of you stand down!" he barked.

A woman's booming voice countered him from the top of the stairs.

"Let. Her. Go."

Dana saw Angela step onto the landing. Her baby-blue satin bomber jacket unzipped, she strode down the stairs past the others, her footfalls creating thunderous stomps as her boots hit each metal plate. Against the concrete and steel of the inorganic bunker walls, her mane was alive, a flurry of golden lighting. Her eyes were as cold as the sarcophagus's metal shell. Dana winked at her and whispered to Olsen as he held his gun steady against her head.

"We broke up because she's crazy. Good luck, bro."

0:00   3:13

Chapter 42

With a Woman – The Darkness

Angela advanced on Olsen's position. Behind her, the members of the Asbury Angels roller derby team began an assault on Thirty-Six and Thirty-Seven. Olsen firmed his grip on the gun held against Dana's head.

"You won't shoot her or you would have done it already," Angela said assuredly as she let her jacket slip off, presenting her spectacular toned biceps and triceps. Olsen shrugged.

"You're right." He swung the gun to target Angela. As he pulled the trigger, it stopped prematurely. He glanced at the safety on the side of the gun, still engaged from his prior edict. Angela hacked with her forearm to counter the barrel, dislodging it from his hand. As the gun fell to the floor, she delivered a deep punch into his stomach. He doubled over and gasped for breath.

"We didn't recruit her for her skating," slurred Dana.

Olsen retaliated with full-force punches, each countered by Angela, who parried blow after blow with an outside block. She stepped into his uppercut punch, blocking his arm and headbutting him. He staggered back and regained his fighting stance to reengage.

Dana pushed her feet down in her skates and felt the wheels contact the floor. She twitched her toes and heard the buzzing of the wheels engaged against the tiles. She spun the chair around so it plowed into Olsen's side, knocking him into the open sarcophagus and against the feet of the giant robot. Angela and Dana turned their attention to the melee at the bottom of the stairs.

Thirty-Seven was facedown on the ground, two girls holding each leg, pulling them at an angle, as he yelled in agony. Paula sat on his back, a finger hooked in each corner of his mouth, holding his maw open. She looked up at Dana and gave a beaming smile before slamming his face into the ground.

A circle of women surrounded Thirty-Six. He grunted in a feral rage as he punched and kicked at the cluster with more success than his brother. As he fended off one roller derby warrior, another took her place in the circle. His ferocity held as he continued to fight.

One by one, each woman stepped back to nurse a landed punch or to catch their breath. He turned to check on Thirty-Seven only to have his view blocked by Mary Beth. She stomped into the gauntlet and swung her bat at his abdomen, knocking the wind out of him. The team seized the moment and swarmed to subdue him.

"TURN AROUND! TURN AROUND!" Dana screamed as the now revived Seventy-Four rose to his feet behind Mary Beth. He grabbed her from behind and began to arch his back to flip her into a piledriver wrestling maneuver. Angela sprinted and assailed him with a flying dropkick to the middle of his back, crippling the musclebound man.

"Dana!"

At the top of the stairs, Nick emerged. Dana stomped her skates to get his attention as he paused to study the small riot. His eyes locked on her, and he bounded down the stairs two at a time to reach her chair.

"Hey, I called the gang," he said, almost apologetically, while fiddling with the plastic tie straps on her wrist. "I'd say I called for backup but really I'm just the secretary for the glee club here."

Dana smiled with a little fuzziness still in her eyes. She squinted through the halos that ringed each light in the ceiling and the two images of Nick she saw momentarily before her focus realigned. She laughed as he flinched at every loud thud and yell while he examined her wrist bindings.

"Wire cutters on the table, Boy Scout." She nodded to the desk.

Behind her, Olsen righted himself and glared at Dana. He began to charge only to find himself intercepted by Angela. She whipped around and lunged at him. Her shoulders smashed into his torso with a force that launched their intertwined bodies next to Nick, his shaking hands holding the cutters. Dana's chair rocked backward to the verge of tipping until she leaned forward and planted her skates. She drilled her feet into the skate control pads and shot herself in reverse, directly into a table behind the mob. Angela stepped back and held her fists in a guard stance against Olsen.

"Nick, hurry up," Angela bellowed, commencing another round of blows and parries against the agent. Angela landed a heavy punch to his collar bone, knocking him to the floor. Nick steadied the cutters and cautiously freed Dana's arms. She fell over while attempting to stand, and one of the derby girls quickly propped her up.

"Hey, Barbie," beckoned Olsen to Angela. He sneered and flashed a grin of blood-lined teeth. "Are you ready?" As he crouched, Dana saw his hand slip down into his boot cuff and clutch the handle of a small tactical knife in its sheath.

"Angela!" Dana shrieked as Olsen charged at Angela and feigned a punch with the blade concealed. Angela twisted to parry the blow, but he fisted the knife into her side with a triumphant yell. The woman warrior fell back, stunned, staring in disbelief at the handle sticking out from her shirt, surrounded by a halo of growing crimson. Angela's jaw hung open as she stared at Dana.

"Dana?" she whispered. She collapsed to the floor as Dana began to scream.

"No!" Nick shouted as he threw the wire cutters directly at Olsen's temple. The agent rubbed his fresh head wound and pivoted toward him with a scowl.

"Stupid boy. This isn't your fight."

A thud startled the small group. Olsen froze, his eyes bulged, and his body flopped to the bunker floor. Standing in his place, Mary Beth stood holding her bat, frozen in midswing.

Chapter 43

Silence

D ana felt Nick's shoulder under her arm as he pulled her to the stairs behind some of the team member. She felt as if she was floating up the staircase, despite the sense of feeling that had finally returned to her feet. Her eyes flashed to the blood trail that led the way out, and then back to the agents on the floor and past the desks to the open sarcophagus. She saw the blue bomber jacket on the floor, and the mummified corpse beyond.

She twisted again in Nick's grasp and saw a swarm of team members engulf Angela. One young woman ripped off her own grimy shirt to cover the knife wound. Two other girls locked arms to hoist her up the stairs. They worked in mechanical efficiency as Paula directed the girls to guide Angela up. Throughout the procession, Angela winced and cursed, squeezing her eyes shut and grimacing in pain. As they all finally reached the top of the stairs, her face relaxed and her eyes opened, seemingly focused on an imaginary point beyond the ceiling. Paula clutched her hand as they hurried her into the blue bus outside, but to Dana's eyes, Angela did not return her grip.

As Nick pulled Dana into the tunnel, she glanced back one more time at the juggernaut slumped forward in its casket, and she felt nothing. She closed her eyes and let herself be gently rocked by the rumble of the bus beneath her. The shouts of her friends and teammates reached her ears, but the words were indiscernible, just tones traveling from one end of the bus to the other. Nick's words came to her in bursts, but she could only vaguely nod as she processed fragments and phrases. She felt his hand on her head and then the bus come to a stop. Her eyes opened, and she watched Nick run to the front of the bus. Out the window, she saw a sign for the emergency room. She only then realized that he must have removed her skates at some point and put them into her backpack.

The bus emptied out. Dana found herself being pulled along in the throng by a gentle hand. Mary Beth gingerly held her forearm and walked her into the hospital and seated her in the waiting room. She looked down, and she was holding a coffee. She stared at a painting of flowers on the wall. Four flowers in a vase. She looked down again. Her coffee was empty. It was dark outside now, and Paula and Nick were sitting next to her.

Her feet felt cold. She was only wearing thin socks, filthy from a mixture of soil, sand, and grease. A doctor emerged from beyond a set of doors and Mary Beth hurried to speak to him. The doctor put a hand on her shoulder. Dana stood up, still holding her empty coffee cup, and gingerly walked over.

He nodded at Dana. "Your friend is in bad shape, but we think we're in the clear now. She lost a lot of blood, to be sure, but luckily there is very minimal internal organ damage."

Dana looked back at Nick and then into her empty cup.

"Thank you, doctor."

Chapter 44

Don't Walk Away – Electric Light Orchestra

D ana began to shake her hands, trying to rid her body of the shock of the evening, literally and figuratively, as her haze continued to clear.

"They said they're going to take the juggernaut to Robbinsville. Is there an airport there?" Dana asked, first sitting down, and then standing up as a call to action. Nick looked at her with a confused reaction and raised an eyebrow as she continued.

"We can cut them off, block the bunker entrance. Or how about we make something like a firebomb with a gas tank?" She looked at Nick for some kind of response.

Nick put his head down and shook it slowly. "Dana, we can't. This has to stop."

"Why?"

"Your ex-girlfriend is the hospital, and a whole bunch of your friends are nursing broken or sprained wrists or arms." He spread his arms out and spun slowly around the room. "My God, Dana, all this was to rescue you. This is now bigger than you and your crusade."

"Nick, stopping them is important." She walked in a circle, trying to think of how to make her case. "This is because of *my* family. *My* family did this, and *I* can stop it all from going any further."

"Dana, I don't think you get it that your actions have consequences. If these guys are willing to kill just to get this thing, imagine what they'll do when they *actually have it*! We're way out of our league."

"Exactly!" She stormed up to him, stopping inches from his face. "If they're willing to kill to get it, that is why I have to stop them!" Her eyes flashed back and forth across his stony face.

"It doesn't have to be you, Dana."

"It *does* have to be me. This is why *I'm* here." She panted as she glared into his eyes. "I found my purpose, and this is it, right here, stopping these assholes."

"Dana, I can't. I can't do this. This isn't making sense anymore. Can you stop being Photograph for just a minute?"

"That's your stupid name," she snapped, "not mine. I'm a Jefferson, and this is what we do." She put the emphasis on each word as her volume continued to grow, even though she was having trouble believing them herself. She turned her back to him before striding across the room and back over to the window. She knocked on the glass of the waiting room with her fist, rapping it in a mechanical tempo.

"This is what I'm supposed to do. My grandfather told me that he created this monster, and my father was a part of it. And they're gone. This is my responsibility to clean up."

"Dana." Nick slowly crossed the room and stood behind her, watching her face in the reflected glass. Her expression swung from manic to emotionless. "This isn't your responsibility. This isn't your fault, what they did. Your family is your family, but that doesn't mean you are responsible for their decisions. But *it is* because of you that people are getting hurt. Severely hurt. You can't just keep flying off the handle and shoot off on a wing and prayer without thinking." He put his hand on her shoulder but she shrugged it off.

"Don't," she whispered. "Don't tell me what I'm supposed to do."

"You're not being reasonable," he pleaded.

She spun around and pointed a finger into his face, hitting his cheek once as she prodded. "Don't tell me what to do here! I can fix this! I can stop them! And I'll do it on my own if I have to." She paused, her eyes watering. "It would be nice to have help, but if you won't help me, I will do it by myself." Her volume swelled. "And if something happens to me, well, at least I tried. At least I tried. You don't even try." She was searching for words to insult him, something to counter his words as they stung her. "You do what's safe and just sit in your garage with your drunk dad."

Nick stepped back as if she had slapped him and his eyes began to swell. "I'm going home."

He stomped out of the hospital waiting room and flung open the doors to the parking lot. Dana remained leaning against the window with her arm up to block her face. She saw in the reflection Mary Beth walk up behind her, lean in for a hug, but then change her mind. Instead, she put her hand on Dana's back.

"I'm going to call a ride for you," she said gently.

Dana looked at her, tears in her eyes, and nodded. She looked back out at the leaves outside as they left the branches bare to the oncoming chill.

Chapter 45

This Woman's Work – Maxwell

T he car service pulled into the Andrews's driveway next to both pickup trucks. Dana handed the driver a wad of crumpled bills and stepped out without any expression of gratitude. She adjusted her backpack and walked across the gravel in her socks, then up the steps to the front porch. No lights were on inside as far as she could tell, and the garage windows stared back, soulless and black except for the reflection of the house exterior lights. The porch light, however, was still on. She extended her hand toward the door and slowly turned the knob, exhaling as the door yielded, unlocked.

The house interior sat still and dark, the only illumination coming from the front and back porch lights, through the partially open blinds. A trace of toast and tomato soup hung in the air, further evidenced by the empty bowl and plate on the drying rack next to the sink. The main room felt much smaller at night, the kitchen practically in the lap of the living room, and the bedroom doors decorating a hallway that seemed to appear no bigger than a walk-in closet.

Dana laid her knapsack on the kitchen table with care to prevent the buckles from scraping the finish and to muffle any noise from the contents inside knocking against themselves. She glanced at the couch and was surprised to see bare cushions. Gone were the pile of folded sheets and pillow that had become the norm over the past weeks. Her brain immediately made an inference about Nick's change in lodging which led her to prepare to gather her belongings.

Dana crept quietly toward Nick's door, then gently turned the handle, noting no resistance from a lock. As her eyes adjusted in the dark, she saw the garbage bags containing the few possessions retrieved from her apartment still sitting in a neat pile next to his closet door where she had first placed them, three bags in all. She knelt beside them and slipped off her jacket to prevent the zippers and buttons from clanging against any objects hiding in the inky shadows. She looked over her shoulder at Nick's bed where he lay facing the wall, his back toward the open room. She bit her lip, opened the first bag, and discovered a blanket, a pile of books, and miscellaneous kitchen items. The second one was full of more tchotchkes. A stale musk of sweat, road dirt, and other indiscernible grime and dust rose to meet her nose; it was coming from her. She opened the third bag and unearthed her clothing cache, pulling out the first T-shirt from the top. It was unwashed, but much cleaner than the one she wore.

She leaned back against the foot of the bed and pulled her shirt up over her head. In midpull, her elbows became entangled in her sleeves, the shirt stuck on her back. Grunting, she tried again to pull it over her head, but the angle was wrong. Tears of frustration began to well as she breathed out through her mouth before one more effort. Then, at last, success.

With a loud huff, she dropped her arms limply to her sides and let the weight of her head fall to her chest. Her lip began to quiver as she struggled to pull the shirt over her head. She gave up and let the shirt sit in her lap. She ran her fingers through her dirty hair, untangling the knots and clumps from the long day. A gentle rustling in the bed behind her startled her.

She turned and saw Nick sitting up in bed behind her, wearing only his bedtime sweatpants he slept in regularly. One tuft of his hair stood upright, charmingly disheveled, the short golden strands luminescent from the moonlight coming through the window. His hand was extended, holding his faded gray T-shirt. She revealed the shirt already in her hand and sniffled and she wiped her nose with the sleeve. Nick extended his top again to her, and she took it with a reluctant smile. She did not deserve his kindness for the things she had said, but he was here, like always.

Dana stood up and faced Nick. She took the shirt from his hand and pulled it over her head.

She opened her mouth, but no words escaped into the space between them. Her shoulders slumped from the weight of her life finally pulling her toward collapse. She undid the buckle on her jeans and slid them off, then sat wordlessly on the bed next to him. He put a hand on her back for a moment, and then moved it to her shoulder. They both lay down, facing each other, their faces resting on opposite ends of the same pillow. Hers was hidden in the arc of a shadow, but his was revealed in the moonlight. She could tell that he had been crying, and she traced a finger down his cheek.

She mouthed, "I'm sorry."

He nodded and repeated back to her the same wordless reply.

She tucked her head, burying her crown into his chest, and pulled her legs up, pressing her shins against his thighs. She focused on the wall behind him, on the shadows of amassing clouds gliding in front of the moon, until there were so many that total darkness spread across the wall.

Nick's hand searched across the warmth of the comforter to find hers, which was limp and shaking. He threaded his fingers through hers and pulsed her hand. The moonlight seeped through the blinds as the clouds dissolved and a white glow embraced the bed. She rubbed her thumb across his knuckles until she fell asleep.

0:00　　　　　　　　　　　　　　　　　　3:13

Chapter 46

Can't Stop – Red Hot Chili Peppers

J oshua lowered his head as he straightened his tie and adjusted his cuffs. He hoped he exuded some confidence as he stepped into Director Jameson's office, having heeded her summons but unsure whether to brace for an emergency or a reprimand. He paused before sitting in the chair. A blue unmarked folder occupied the seat, which Director Jameson gestured to him to pick up.

"Do you know what that is?" she deadpanned as they both took their seats across from each other.

"No idea."

"That is a flag file. The moment someone touches that, it goes up the chain. High up the chain." She took off her glasses and rubbed the bridge where two indentations had formed. "I've been on the phone all morning with the budget office because of that thing." She placed her cell phone on the desk and tapped it. "With people who shouldn't have my personal number."

Joshua held the file but dared not open it without being prompted. He understood the stakes if he had accidentally opened a flagged file during his audits, and he swallowed hard with the fear that he had gone too far in his accounting treasure hunt of OHR.

"Someone," she started, "pulled that last week. The problem is, I don't know who specifically. I was notified once the flag went live since it's an accounting file. Once you open that, you're in this, too. Am I making myself explicitly clear?"

"Yes, Director. I acknowledge my participation," he responded, reciting the proper consent from his training for such a scenario.

"Just open the damn file," she hissed.

He peeled back the blue cardstock and read out loud. "Project Atomic Juggernaut . . . requisition of real estate . . ." He relayed a summary as he ingested each section. "Laboratory location, New Jersey. A township by the joint facilities out at Fort Dix. A listing of raw materials and costs, and a requisition from the Department of Energy that looks like a material transfer. And here," flipping another page as he spoke, "is a salary page for engineers."

Director Jameson folded her hands and rested her forehead on her knuckles. "Read the names," she said quietly, "but not out loud."

He affirmed her command with a short nod and ran his thumb down the list of alphabetically organized names. Geissler, Hardy, Jacobsen, Jefferson Jr., Jefferson Sr., and Rhodes. His mouth hung open as he looked up and met her icy gaze.

"You didn't pull that file, right?" she said in a low voice.

"No, I did not. But I'm guessing this name," he said, spinning the report to face her and tapping Rhodes's entry, "is why you wanted me to see this?"

"Correct. Do you have any ideas who would want to pull this file, if it was not you?"

He swallowed hard but did his best not to avert her gaze as he spoke. "Jenna found that he bought a cargo plane for One Hundred Roads. It was a sealed auction bid. But to find that out she wouldn't have had to pull this."

Director Jameson nodded and bit her lip as she processed the information. She picked up her glasses but did not put them back on her face, instead studying the fine metal wire of the earpieces before glancing back at Joshua.

"I believe you. My apologies, but that was a test to see what you knew. Actually, I *know* who pulled the file. Rhodes did, using his former clearance." She exhaled as she finally rested the glasses back on the spots on her nose. "If you knew that, if you were party to that, you wouldn't have told me about him buying a cargo plane."

She waved her hand at the report to indicate permission to proceed. He continued reviewing the pages, which revealed blueprints for large metallic limbs, a bathysphere containing a nuclear battery, and a final schematic of an enormous metallic robot. He read the label for the schematic aloud.

"Project Atomic Juggernaut."

"That's one big cat out of one big bag," she replied.

Joshua closed the folder and shuffled his feet on the industrial carpeting. "So, what would you like me to do now, Director?"

"Run every name in that file. Every name. If they have a relative or next of kin, run those names, too. Anything linked to a bank account that Rhodes touched—I don't care if it's a single dollar—flag it and freeze it. I'll cosign any necessary warrants or subpoenas later, but just freeze it."

Working to keep his voice steady, Joshua spoke up. "Would you believe I *kind of* sort of did all of that already?" He swallowed hard. "Director?"

She pushed her glasses up the bridge of her nose and glared at him before smiling. Joshua stood up, folder in hand, and headed for the door, then turned back with a quizzical look on his face.

"Director, is there anything else important that I need to know?"

"No, but here." She pulled two unremarkable shiny metallic objects from her drawer. They looked like credit cards but Joshua could not make out the logo of the department or account numbers on the face of either one. She placed them in his hand. "Here are two burner cards. Use them as you need, go where you need to go, and do your job."

He slid the cards into his front pants pocket and closed the door. Joshua slumped against the wall as he pressed the blue folder against his chest.

"How do I explain to my wife that I'm heading to New Jersey?"

Chapter 47

Vagabond – Wolfmother

N ick's alarm clock hummed with a soft buzz as the digits changed to 7:00 A.M. He reached over and slapped at the snooze button but was short and instead smacked the pillow next to him.

He sat up with his eyes still closed. He opened one eye slowly. The morning sun flooding the room with a white-and-yellow blaze. He opened his other eye and saw the space next to him was empty and Dana's plastic bags were gone. He grabbed a flannel shirt from the floor and jogged into the living room.

As Nick emerged from the hallway, he saw his dad at the kitchen table. In his father's hands was a single sheet of paper. He looked up and he held it out to Nick, who was attempting to button his shirt and put on his boots at the same time. He reached for the letter and promptly fell over. His father helped him up and pulled out a chair from the kitchen table.

"It was just lying on the table. I didn't mean to read it." Mr. Andrews slid a hand onto his son's shoulder. Nick laid the letter flat before he read the neatly penned words.

Nick,

You're right. I can't endanger people anymore. I need to make better decisions, which is why I am going to do this by myself. I have the opportunity to prevent some bad people from doing more bad things, and if that gets me killed, I'm not taking anyone else with me. But I am going to at least try.

You are amazing. You let me into your home. You shared things with me. You ground me. It's been a long time since I felt grateful for someone, or felt like a part of a family.

If something happens to me, please destroy everything I left in the garage. Erase me and my family.

If I do come back, grab your wallet and we'll get a giant stack of pancakes, toast, and bacon.

Dana

"Photograph"

Nick put down the letter and clutched a fist to his mouth. His dad slid a coffee across the table. Nick picked up the hot mug, his head ablaze with questions about where she was, and what she was going to do, and how she could take down a tiny platoon of mercenary soldiers for hire. "You do not get to live in the moment that may be the last time you see someone," he thought to himself, and the memory of his mother's death bled into his emotions. He had chosen not to be with her when she died, not wanting to face her mortality or his own. He regretted not risking the emotional impact of being there, of just trying.

As he entered the garage, he saw the pile of black trash bags stacked neatly below his paintball equipment. He reran last night, every line and curve of Dana's face, each word and touch they shared, each apology and breath they exchanged. He wanted to suspend time, to rewind and replay the last day, but he understood that time was never his ally, either freezing or moving too fast when he desired the opposite motion to guide him out of a decision.

He began to open one of the bags but reconsidered, not sure what he was intending to find inside that would help. Instead, he sat down at the workbench and flipped open the laptop to watch the surveillance camera feed. He cupped the warm ceramic coffee mug and leaned closer to the screen.

The camera feed was still, the trees in view swaying gently with the light intermittent breeze. Every so often, tiny groupings of pine needles skittered across the blacktop guided by stronger gusts. The shadows of the early morning covered the road in an abstract pattern, creeping in obtuse angles as the sun continued its ascent. Nick sipped his coffee in tiny mouthfuls as he maintained his sentinel duty, staring most intently at the opening in the woods that led to the path to the bunker.

As the hours staggered by, activity in the feed picked up. First, an eighteen-wheeler rolled into the foreground and backed into the opening between the trees, only to then turn back onto the road and head back in the direction it had come from. Then a lull, and then a car or two driving down the desolate road on repeat. He counted every one: three Hummers, four SUVs, a tractor trailer, and six compact cars drove at varying speeds past the entrance. Mr. Andrews floated in and out of the garage, once refilling Nick's coffee, next leaving a sandwich, then later taking away the empty dishes as Nick silently watched the screen.

"Have you tried calling her?" Mr. Andrews asked, suddenly standing behind him. Nick jumped at his voice, the first he had in many hours.

"No." Nick kept his gaze locked on the screen. The trees and road remained unchanged as a new pattern of shadows creeped in from the western side of the woods. A squirrel ran across the blacktop.

"I think you should call her," Mr. Andrews said firmly while sliding Nick's phone across the countertop. "You've been in here all day, and there's no sign of her on that screen."

"I don't know what I'd say. She made it clear she doesn't want my help."

"Start with 'hello' and go from there."

Nick looked up at his father and saw he was not going to let him off the hook. He picked up his phone, staring at the screen as if it were a completely foreign technology. At last, he pressed Dana's name on the recent call list and waited.

Mr. Andrews held up a hand. "Nick, don't hang up."

At first, the buzz was beyond their audible range, but with each ring on Nick's phone, a faint hum came from the direction of the garbage bags across the garage. Mr. Andrews ran over to the pile and, after leaning his head against each one, finally dove into bag number three and yanked Dana's phone from a pile of socks and pants. He held it up and frowned.

But Nick was not paying attention to his father. "Dad. Look." On the laptop, a pair of sport utility vehicles pulled out of the opening slowly, each pulling off to one side just short of the road. Behind them, a tractor trailer trudged slowly out of the woods, onto the sandy shoulder, and then onto the highway. The two SUVs then pulled out behind it. "Where are they headed? Robbinsville Airport?"

Before Mr. Andrews could respond, a shifting movement in the tree line in the top right corner of the frame caught their attention. Out of the branches and down to the blacktop dropped a fuzzy figure. The blur shot across the screen, leaving a wake of sparks.

"Dad, I'm calling the police. I'm going to report the theft of federal property." He closed the laptop and studied the black plastic bags and the array of paintball guns and pellets hanging on the wall. "And then I'm going to do something pretty stupid. And you're not going to talk me out of it." Nick cleared his throat and grabbed a jar of paint pellets.

Mr. Andrews crossed his arms in reply and lowered his brow. "You're right, I'm not going to stop you. Get after her. I'll call the police."

0:00

3:13

Chapter 48

Cliffs of Rock City – Brad Paisley

As the last SUV in the convoy departed from the bunker's secluded entrance, Dana adjusted herself in the hunter's tree stand where she had been perched since early in the morning when she had snuck out of the Andrews's house. If there was one thing she had learned about South Jersey, it was that hunters had stands like this all over the Pine Barrens, like vulture nests made of plastic and steel. Her goggles slipped over her eyes as she pulled her improvised balaclava made from one of Nick's T-shirts down to her neck. She balanced her crouching posture and pulled a Pop-Tart out of her pocket for some sugar fuel before beginning to slide down the tree. She silently cursed the flecks of pine tar that now decorated her jacket's sleeves and coattails.

She hit the pavement with a clip-clop as the last taillights faded into the early evening haze. She fired one skate at a time, giving a push to first Laverne, then Shirley. Gliding more between each stride to cut down on the sparks, Dana monitored the second SUV ahead of her. She had reviewed the maps of the possible routes to Robbinsville Airport for hours while waiting in the tree stand, memorizing the shortest distances versus the least chance of being spotted by other cars. The current route of the convoy suggested she would be hitting the major highways shortly.

Up ahead, the trailer veered toward the entrance for the Parkway. After the initial caravan of two SUVs and the tractor trailer had left the bunker, one more SUV and three Hummers had stealthily slipped into the formation from various side roads. The swarm of One Hundred Roads vehicles locked in place, SUVs and Hummers alternating, three in front and three behind the trailer.

Dana instinctively hit the Call button on her headset, then remembered she had left her phone behind. Nick had been so reliable with his navigation and guidance, the calm he brought with his tenor over her earpiece. He was always levelheaded when she needed solid footing to stand on, a firm hand pulling her back when she reached too high. These were the reasons she missed him, but also why she had cut him off from her mission. Nothing he could say would convince her now to put him in harm's way, like she had with Angela, and the bittersweet silence over the headset reinforced her convictions. She was going to do this by herself. She was able to admit to herself now how much she cared about him, and she would do anything to keep him away from danger, even at the expense of her own feelings. Her mission was just as important as his safety.

Her toes pressed forward in her skates as she turned onto the entrance ramp. The evening rush hour was thinning as the sun began to set, but she knew she needed to be careful to avoid being seen by other cars. Her advantage was clear as she crouched with her front leg extended, holding a shoot-the-duck pose behind a large blue family-friendly minivan.

"Yo!"

She looked to her left and saw a fire-engine-red Ferrari next to her, matching her pace. The driver was a middle-aged man wearing a suit jacket over a T-shirt, a large toothy grin set on his face. "Hey lady, I got a passenger seat," he yelled above the traffic.

Not exactly low profile, Dana thought as she smirked and reassessed her position. Between her and the convoy ahead was the minivan, a pickup truck, a utility van, and another tractor hauling logs on its flatbed, the long wooden poles stacked in a pyramid formation and held by massive cable straps.

"Hey, buddy," she yelled back, "can you tow me and pass that truck with the logs on the right side?"

"Sure thing. You give me your number?"

"You get me up there and it's a date," she winked.

"You got it, roller girl!"

Dana stood up from her tucked position and rolled to his passenger side door. The window still rolled down, and she grabbed the doorframe and held tight. The driver cracked his knuckles and hit the paddle shifters. The car swerved into the left lane, almost crossing the double yellow line of the multilane highway. Dana kept her legs tucked to prevent being dragged underneath the car. The caravan drew closer.

"So where do you want to go for dinner?" the driver yelled as they pulled up next to the log-carrying trailer.

"I'll let you know! Give it some more gas!" she roared back.

Dana let go of the sports car and grabbed the side of the flatbed. She pulled herself up onto the bed. The noise was nearly deafening as the Ferrari fired all engine cylinders, emitting a high-pitched whine as it soared ahead. The caravan was right in front of her now, including the trailer she assumed was carrying the Atomic Juggernaut.

"Let's go, girls," she shouted toward her feet. She climbed up the log pile, straddled the top beam, and grabbed the closest strap like a harness for a bridle. Once she caught up to the truck, she reasoned, she had no idea what to do next. Her perch gave her time to catch her breath.

A burst of gunfire interrupted her moment of reflection. An SUV and a Hummer pulled alongside of the truck, each one sporting a man in fatigues leaning out of the passenger window with a pug-nosed assault rifle. Dana rolled over the crest of the wooden poles and tucked her head below the top beam. As the truck rumbled toward an exit ramp, the pile of poles rattled slightly. A quick glance confirmed that one of the straps had been severed, most likely by the gunfire.

Dana leapt back to the top of the log pile and drew another hail of bullets in her direction. A loud whip crack accompanied a heavy canvas strap whistling past her head, narrowly missing her. The poles behind her back began to shimmy and groan, freed from their restraints. She charged up the pile as it began to unload its tonnage across the lanes, smashing into the Hummer, forcing it into the SUV's side and into the median.

"Nick, I could sure use you right now," she muttered as her truck began to brake and swerve to the shoulder. She spied the exit ramp just beyond and leapt into the lane, shooting up the ramp as the convoy from One Hundred Roads continued full throttle down the main highway. She surveyed the small pileup behind her, mostly just rear-ended cars and a Ferrari on the shoulder. *Good, at least only the bad guys got hurt.*

She felt her hand inch toward her headset again. *Nick, what should I do? Focus on the objective. He would tell me to focus.* She scanned ahead and saw a road sign pointing to Allentown, one town over from Robbinsville, according to her map studies. She checked her zipper and cuffs and reset her goggles on her nose. She recognized the county road number on the next sign. If she turned here, she could take back roads to the airport, where she wouldn't be seen and could floor it. She might even beat them there.

Taking a moment to scarf down the last toaster pastry in her pocket, she pressed her toes deep into the wells of the skates. The glow of the highway lights faded behind her and the scent of charring metal and blueberry fields midharvest faded as she soared into the darkness.

Chapter 49

I Like It – Enrique Iglesias

A chain-link fence surrounded the perimeter of the airport, and two weathered hangars sat just beyond. Dana moved toward the fence, skating on manual power, not wanting to give herself away with her sparks. She peered through the high weeds woven through the wire and watched the activity through the gap between the buildings. The caravan's remains were already here, and the eighteen-wheeler, with its tail open and ramp extended, was now backed up to a small cargo plane. She counted cars; two sport utility vehicles and two Hummers lined up facing the end of the runway, but now a black sedan had joined them. A head count was impossible at this distance with the sun setting behind her, leaving only black forms to her imagination and estimation. No more than a dozen, no fewer than six people was her current conclusion based on the moving blobs. What she could clearly see, however, was an enormous metal object, lying on its back, being moved carefully down a motorized conveyor belt: the Atomic Juggernaut.

She crept slowly through the foxtail grass and wildflowers farther along the property line. There was an open gate ahead, most likely the one the caravan had come through. She bit her lip as she debated her next step. The muddling voices rose and faded, one man barking directions at another, with one specific voice separating from the dissonance. Her blood rose as Olsen commanded the men to their tasks as he strode through their clusters to point and shout at them. She breathed slowly through her mouth to calm the smoldering embers of anger building in her chest.

She glided slowly through the gate and over to the back corner of the closest hangar, wincing at each tap and clack of her skates. Thinking she had managed to avoid observation, she leaned her head against the cool metal shell to collect her thoughts. The throng of men separated, with three chatting and walking in her direction.

With a deep breath, Dana whipped herself around the corner, sprinting directly toward the men, who stood dumbfounded as she reached out her leather-clad arms and clotheslined them. She slid to a stop as the remaining cluster of agents reached for their firearms in their holsters.

"Hold your fire!" roared a voice. A man stepped out of the cargo plane's bay and onto the ramp that extended from it. "That thing has an *atomic* battery! If you miss and hit it, not only do we lose a payday worth several million dollars—we will most likely glow in the dark and all die!"

The man then stared directly at her; his impeccable attire fluttered gently in the light breeze. To her disbelief, he smiled. Almost instantly, she recognized him, the last man in the photo: Colin Rhodes.

"Hello, Dana. I'm sorry this has to be hello and goodbye." He flipped his hand in a grandiloquent wave and turned to walk back into the cargo hold. "I said 'hold your fire.' I didn't say let her go. Have at thee, gentlemen."

Dana felt each set of eyes glancing up and down at her, most likely underestimating the unarmed girl who stood in front of them on a pair of roller skates. She took a mental roll call as each agent assumed a fighting posture of varying skill level and training background. There was Olsen, Agent Ninety-Nine, facing her with hands up like a veteran boxer. The bearded twins from the bunker, Thirty-Six and Thirty-Seven, were there, too, grimacing like a pro-wrestling tag-team caricature, each sporting a nose bandage and heavy facial bruises. The meaty Seventy-Four, who sported a cast on his forearm, completed the faces she recognized. A slim agent with spidery arms and 056 on his lapel filled out of the gang. Another short but athletic man with 044 on his chest stood apart from the group behind the entrance of the plane and crept toward the juggernaut.

"They'll have to call you Jane Doe at the morgue after we're done defacing you," growled Seventy-Four. He rose to his full height, towering over all the other agents, and spat a meteor of chewing tobacco at her feet.

Dana reached one hand to her coat zipper and pulled it up to her neck. "No. They'll call me Photograph, because that's the only way you'll catch me."

Seventy-Four cocked his head. Thirty-Six turned to Thirty-Seven and the twins shrugged at each other.

"It sounded better in my head," she beamed. Dana pressed her toes into Laverne and Shirley. She felt the seconds slow around her, the electric impulses swimming from her brain to her muscles. As she unleashed her motors, she flew toward Seventy-Four, cocking her fist back and firing it forward into his stomach. He doubled over from the mechanically assisted impact. She fired herself backward to avoid the long-armed swing from Fifty-Six. The tarmac surface provided amazing traction, allowing her to glide as if on a sheet of ice at terrifying speed but then stop on a dime.

"Get her!" Olsen barked.

The scrum rotated around her. With every incoming punch or kick, she slid right or left, backward or forward, ducking and diving, countering the blows on occasion with the Kevlar padding in her forearms. With every juke and jump, another burst of fireworks from her skates left a memory of where she had stood a half second earlier. She wove through the assault like a technicolor ghost, slipping out from every attack and laughing at every jab she landed on one of their surprised faces.

Olsen growled and roared with every missed punch. The other agents did their best to counter her attacks. Thirty-Seven froze to allow Dana to come in close with a punch but then grabbed her arm, yanking her off balance and spinning her around until he could catch her in a bear hug from behind. But Dana not only saw, *she felt* what her assailants were going to do before their actions. As Thirty-Seven held her still, Seventy-Four swung at her stomach with his cast-covered hand. Dana lifted her legs up, driving her skates into his incoming punch with the wheels at full throttle, shattering the plaster of his cast. His pained howling rang in her ears.

Focus on the objective.

Dana swung her legs back and directly into Thirty-Seven's boots, her wheels tearing through the leather before smashing into his feet. He dropped her and fell backward with a high-pitched wail, his feet mangled and useless.

Olsen stepped into her line of sight, holding a large knife in each hand, blades down. His smile was filled with menace and malice. Another four men emerged from the cargo hold to fill the places of the agents she'd taken down.

"Time's up," Olsen glowered. "We've got a schedule to keep."

"Enough talk, shithead." Dana's eyes locked with his and her jaw tightened. For the first time, she felt fear, true fear, of this man who could kill her, but she extinguished the flame with her anger. She was not going to back down. She owed it to Angela, to Nick, to everyone who had stood by her side. She owed it to herself. Prepared to do whatever was necessary, Dana started to charge, only to see Olsen's expression change from rage to confusion, his eyes losing focus as a light source from behind Dana flooded his retinas.

"Who the hell?" he stammered.

A red Ford pickup truck, high beams ablaze, barreled through the open gate, skidding and squealing as it swiped three agents, sending them sprawling across the tarmac. The truck came to a stop just beyond the plane, and the driver's side door sprang open. Nick leaped out with his paintball rifle and a full hopper of rounds. Olsen, still frozen, squinted into the blinding lights.

"What the bloody—"

Before he could finish, Nick unloaded a tirade of pink and yellow ammo into Olsen's face. He doubled over in pain, clawing the welts and stinging residue filling his tear ducts. Dana flashed a thumbs-up to Nick and then dove at another agent with a double-fisted punch. She kicked him in the ribs and turned back toward Nick's truck.

Nick ducked behind the door, swinging out to fire at the other agents. As each one attempted to attack Dana, Nick countered with a head or neck shot to stun, providing Dana with another opening to kick, slide, or punch, whittling down the will of the agents and their reaction times as they were blinded by bullet or by blow.

"Nick! Where's Olsen?" Dana shouted as motion in her periphery distracted her. She spied Olsen crawling toward the truck and slipping his gun out of the holster.

"I got him," Nick yelled. As Nick popped up to set his target, Olsen had already pulled out his gun and pulled the trigger.

Dana heard the gunshot before seeing the impact. Nick fell back, his shoulders hitting the pavement before his head, and then his legs limply fell last.

She faced Olsen as time slowed in the bubble around her. Inside her skates, pain stabbed her arches as she pushed the throttle pads, a firestorm of sparks filling the air behind her. She leapt at Olsen full speed, pouncing upon him before he could raise his gun again.

Her heart beat. Her chest heaved.

She felt a searing pain in her throat. Her feet left the ground as her fingers dug into Olsen's shirt.

The two adversaries barreled into the side of the eighteen-wheeler, the agent's body acting like a battering ram.

She did not hear his back crack against the steel, or the ragged cough as he spit blood onto her chest.

She simply dropped Olsen's limp body and turned back to Nick.

Time moved again.

Chapter 50

Photograph – Def Leppard

Dana slid across the tarmac to the red pickup and fell next to Nick. She cradled his head in her hands and felt for a pulse on his neck. His shirt was soaked in so much blood that she could not discern where he had been shot, but she knew the blood loss was becoming critical.

"I'm sorry, I'm so sorry, I'm so sorry," she whispered, tears falling into her mouth. She did everything right—she had left him behind, but she couldn't make him listen. She couldn't make him not care. Reaching down, her hand greedily grabbed for his, squeezing it for a response. A seconds passed, and then a weak squeeze returned her gesture. Nick's eyes fluttered.

"Nick, don't speak, I'm gonna fix this. You stupid boy, I'm gonna fix this." She gently laid his head down and darted to the truck cabin, grabbed his jacket, and attempted to fold it into some kind of bandage. She gently felt around his torso until she felt a bullet hole by this shoulder. "Okay, this goes here," she directed herself, "and this can go here." She put her hand on top of the makeshift bandage. "Okay, okay, you stupid boy. We're going to make it."

"Keep him busy," Nick whispered with shallow breaths. "Keep fighting."

She nodded and placed his hand gently on top of the bandage. "Hold this here. I'll be back."

Mr. Rhodes descended from the cargo hold, stupefied by not only the defeat of so many handpicked agents from the world's most notorious fighting teams but by the defiant choice made by his best one in using a gun after he had ordered them not to. He stared at Olsen's slack body in disapproval, making no gesture of aid as he watched the blood sputter from his mouth. He turned to his last man standing, Agent Forty-Four, and frowned.

"Open the hatch," he commanded, removing his jacket to reveal his aged but formerly athletic frame under his green shirt and gold tie. "Man the front cockpit." He rolled up his sleeves and strode over to the conveyer belt where the juggernaut lay dormant.

"Yes, sir," replied Forty-Four. The compliant underling jogged to a control panel, and, with the pull of a handle and the flip of a switch, pivoted the belt to a forty-five-degree angle, allowing entry to the cockpits. Forty-Four forced open the clasps on the front door and paused before attempting to seat himself. He stared dumbfounded at the lack of instruments and pointed at a series of thin protruding rods and bars on the interior cavity.

"Mr. Rhodes, this doesn't look like the manuals you showed us. I don't see the pilot controls." He settled inside and twisted around to search for some hidden throttle lever or flight stick.

"The pilot doesn't sit in the front." Rhodes looked down his nose with a stoic expression as he slammed the door shut. Needles extended from tip of each rod into Forty-Four's arms and chest. A roll bar slammed down and crushed his throat before he could scream. Another rod extended inside the cabin from the back of the seat, piercing his brainstem. The nervous system of the juggernaut was now operational as Rhodes opened the top cockpit canopy and slid inside, his face frozen in an icy scowl.

Dana snapped to attention as the juggernaut pivoted fully upright with a loud clang. The monster emitted a low whirring, ascending in tone as it straightened its posture and stood at maximum erect height, nearly twelve feet tall. The slumped metallic corpse she saw on the farm and in the bunker was nothing compared to the robot fully alive. A savage groan accompanied its first steps as the joints liberated themselves from their slumbering memories. Each canopy glowed with a red interior light; the lower cockpit revealed the face of Forty-Four, mouth agape in a death mask, and the upper cockpit displayed the savagery of an old war hero who had ventured too far down the path of greed and ego. From inside, Rhodes bellowed through the interior microphone.

"You're a pain in my ass, just like your father and grandfather before you."

Dana adjusted her jacket as the beast began to stride faster toward her. She rechecked her cuffs and gave her eyewear a final adjustment.

"Catch me, asshole."

She leaned into her skates and soared at the metal beast. The juggernaut lunged like a silverback gorilla as she juked to the right, skating under a closed titanic fist that smashed her shadow on the concrete. Crossing foot over foot like a hockey player on a breakaway, she arced around the machine to shoot herself to the opposite side of the airport. It turned to respond and swung again, only to find more dead air filled with embers from her wake.

"Think, Dana, think," she yelled into the air. She continued another pass, taunting Rhodes to bring the monster farther from the trucks and closer to the hangars. She scanned the area for debris, a weapon, anything she could use to implement an offensive plan. Nick still lay flat on his back, his opposite hand weakly holding the makeshift bandage over his wound. As long as his hand remained on his chest, she knew he was still alive. She skidded to a sliding stop in front of an empty metal oil drum next to the closest hangar and attempted to pick it up.

The juggernaut charged at full speed in an apelike gallop. Dana lifted the barrel over her head and threw it, barely ducking as a massive arm swatted the drum back at her position, embedding it into the side of the aluminum hangar wall.

"Shit shit shit!"

Dana charged toward the second hangar, watching over her shoulder as the juggernaut continued to rage behind her. She tried to pull and pry open the large locked doors in vain, snapping off one of the handles. She cried out as her adrenaline faded, replaced by futility and fear, which began to envelop her brain. *Focus, Dana, focus!*

Rhodes swung the robotic arm back to swat at his prey. As it tore through the air, she dove, legs akimbo, to avoid the impact. The juggernaut's arm finished its arc and clipped her feet. A loud crack from Shirley's housing announced the impact. Dana spun across the pavement, landed on her chest, and rolled to a stop by the plane.

"No, no, no," she whispered, glancing from Nick back to her skate. As she began to stand, her right leg slipped out from underneath her. She glanced down and saw Shirley's housing was broken. The skate would not stay on her foot. The shin guard was split from the impact, and she could not utilize the toe controls with a loose boot. Blinking in disbelief, she turned her attention back to the juggernaut. It strode toward her with an almost swaggering stride, stomping each elephant-like foot in triumph, arms swinging from side to side like two furious wrecking balls directed by Rhodes.

"It's been an interesting battle, Dana," he bellowed over the loudspeaker, "but I've won. Thank you for wasting my time and money."

He swung again. Dana grabbed the broken skate and pushed her good boot forward, standing as if on a push scooter, holding a graceful arabesque. She streaked to the open cargo bay of the plane and slid up the ramp, collapsing inside under the dim illumination of the interior emergency lights.

Her throat tightened and her cheeks flushed. She stared helplessly at the skate in her hand and the single good skate on her foot. A fog started to set in. *Focus!* Shoving her hand into the broken skate, she made a fist inside and watched the wheels turn as her knuckles pushed the accelerator. Her mouth felt dry, her breath heaving. Glancing out the open cargo bay, she watched Rhodes maneuver the mechanical war machine outside. He stopped at the bottom of the ramp. Her predator had her trapped inside his flying lair.

Dana lay back for a moment, taking off her good skate and placing it on her free hand to make a matched pair of metallic mittens. She clutched them against her chest, her babies, dutifully created from her family's blueprints. She stared up at the roof of the cargo bay, allowing her gaze to lose focus and her breath to slow to a calm inhale and exhale pattern.

She pointed both arms up and flexed her fists gently, the sparks of the grinding wheels fluttering down into her hair and stinging her face. She thought of Nick. She thought of stars in the sky back home where she grew up. She thought of Mr. Andrews and his gentle, unselfish manner, his grace and graciousness. She thought of Angela, who showed that their friendship had survived a breakup. She thought of her father, and the fragmented memory of his smile. She thought of her mother, her embrace from long ago, and the lost time she would never have back.

A jostling of the plane snapped her attention back to the moment. The machine nudged the tail of the plane and crouched, seemingly attempting to crawl into the cargo bay. Dana stood up and stared into his canopy window until she locked hate-fueled eyes with Rhodes. His wrinkled face stared back at her. This was the man who had ruined everything she loved and killed her dreams before she even knew what they were.

Her heart began a slow drumbeat. She began to run at him with an unbreaking gaze, each one of her fists a whirling gauntlet of sparks and grinding metal.

The robot's metallic arms spread out to grasp her as she sprinted toward it. Dana dropped to her knees and slid down the cargo ramp, arms outstretched to each side, and glided through the legs of the giant as each of her gloved hands erupted against the juggernaut. The makeshift buzzsaws on each of her fists sliced into the robot's knees, spewing fluid and fractured scraps of metal. The robot attempted to turn around, but each leg collapsed in a clumsy jig. The robotic monstrosity fell onto its back as Dana tumbled to a stop beyond the foot of the cargo door ramp.

The Atomic Juggernaut was defeated.

She groaned as she sat up, then limped toward the crippled titan, still wielding a buzzsaw skate on each hand. She stepped deliberately, avoiding any scraps that would slice through her socks as she approached. When she arrived, Dana heaved her arms above her head and smashed the hinges with first Laverne, then Shirley. She stared down at the mangled frame and shattered glass and the old man lying just beyond.

"Loser," she whispered at Rhodes. She held a hand up over Rhodes, her skate still whirring and her arm trembling with the alchemy of anger and adrenaline.

"That's exactly what I called your father and mother when they failed me," Rhodes sneered.

Dana's mind raced. *My mother? What does she have to do with Rhodes?* She lowered the skate so it hovered just above Rhodes's cheek, the sparks burning his skin and the buzzing wheels threatening to tear it open.

"Say *his* name. Say *her* name."

Rhodes spit a bloody lob at her cheek. "An entire family of failures." He attempted to wriggle his shoulders out of his harness, but he was pinned by the protruding remains of the hatch that she had sheared free. "You're a failure, too."

"Say their names!" His lips were tight as he refused to acknowledge any defeat even as her truth was standing over him. She studied the deep wrinkles that ran across his forehead, the flecks of liver spots, and the short silvery roots of his dyed black coif. Her focus fluttered as the toll of the project revealed itself to her.

Nick.

A spotlight illuminated them from above.

"STAND DOWN. THIS IS AREA IS NOW UNDER MILITARY ORDER."

A helicopter announced its presence to the airfield over a booming loudspeaker. Dana stepped off the immobile hulk as the engine rumblings of multiple Hummers encircled the runway. She stepped off the dead juggernaut entombing Rhodes and began to jog toward Nick's truck; another spotlight blinded her and the cocking of weapons pierced the darkness from all directions. She spotted a team of men already at the truck putting Nick on a stretcher.

She mouthed his name, but nothing came out of her mouth. The sounds in her ears began to blend into a dullness without treble or bass. She turned and watched several men pull Rhodes out of the Atomic Juggernaut. He clutched his chest as blood trickled out of his mouth.

An arm grabbed her elbow and pinned it behind her back. An officer shouted at a soldier. Her arm was released.

She saw a troop carrier in front of her. She closed her eyes.

She was inside the carrier with a medic shining a light into each of her pupils.

She looked down and saw her socks were dirty and bloodstained. Next to them on the floor was a milk crate with Laverne and the remains of Shirley.

The rocking of the truck reminded her of swaying in a hammock with her mother.

She remembered camping and the smell of burnt marshmallows. She tasted the saltwater taffy her father would bring back on every return from New Jersey.

She closed her eyes.

She envisioned the stars above the pines as she lay in the back of Nick's pickup truck, holding his hand in hers.

She felt a gentle touch on her shoulder and an unfamiliar voice in her ear.

"It's over, Miss Jefferson. You did a good job."

0:00   3:13

Chapter 51

The Lighthouse's Tale – Nickel Creek

T he windowless walls of the room made Dana feel claustrophobic. A single metal door led in and out, and two chairs and a metal table were the only furnishings. She sat patiently in one of the chairs. There was no clock in the room, but she estimated she had been waiting for about ten minutes after singing three pop songs in her head. She gently touched the bandage on her cheek and winced. The smell of alcohol and iodine seeped through even hours after the army medic's rapid but thorough treatment. The knob turned, and the door opened.

A handsome thin young man in a blue suit walked in, fumbling with a folder under his arm and two briefcases; one large and apparently heavy, the other thin and evidently light by the way he easily flung it onto the table. He gently placed the larger case in front of Dana, turning it around so the latches faced her. On the top surface was a large black shiny circle, eerily similar to the portal eye scanner that opened each sarcophagus that held a juggernaut. The man extended his hand.

"Hello, thanks for waiting. My name is Joshua. I am a registered actuary, a CPA, and my current role is in accounting for the federal government."

She instinctively shook his hand but showed no emotion. He placed the folder between them and opened it ceremoniously. He retrieved a pen from his coat pocket and clicked it.

"Miss Jefferson, or can I just call you Dana? Pardon the paperwork, but you know the government loves red tape and spending money on photocopies." He smiled at his attempt to lighten the mood. She did not respond in kind. "I'm not the bad guy here. You're not in trouble. You're not being set up. This room is soundproof, and there are no recording devices. So, let's just talk. I know you were debriefed by other personnel, but I'm here to discuss appreciation and transfer of ownership of confidential material."

"Come again?"

"These papers," he said, sliding one small stack across the desk, a pen placed on top, "make up our contract with 'Dana Jefferson Technology Consulting.' It's predated and includes an itemized bill of services rendered but also deductions for property damage and other costs incurred during the operation of 'retrieving archival government property' that you undertook. The net amount, after payments and said damages, is one hundred thousand dollars to be deposited into your bank account. Per your business's contract with the government, payment of taxes is not required."

Dana looked down bewildered at the pages in front her.

Joshua continued, undeterred by her lack for understanding. "This one," he said, pushing another stack over, "is for the transfer of contents of one government lockbox case, curated by your father." He tapped on the larger case. "We don't know how to open it, but I think you do. We ran multiple scans, and, apparently, it is rigged to deliver an acid solution to destroy the contents if anyone other than the appropriate person tampers with it." She stared at the case, unmoved by his words. "Dana, whatever is inside is yours, but we keep the case, as per the thorough legal document that accompanied it and was left by your father before he passed. You may put its content into this one. I picked it out myself. It's synthetic leather. I'm a bit of a vegan. Sometimes." He opened the smaller briefcase to show it was empty. "I sometimes slip and have a bacon cheeseburger. It's more of a health thing than activism. Anyway, here you go."

His rambling put her at ease, and for the first time since she'd been brought to the base, she smiled, faint though it was. She pulled the large case toward her, knowing what she needed to do, and lowered her eyes to the black portal. Joshua jumped slightly as the case made a short whirring noise and the latches sprang open. Dana lifted the lid slowly and paused so she could fully take in the contents.

Joshua placed a hand on her wrist as she reached inside. "Dana, nothing inside is my business. If you would like, I can wait outside while you transfer the contents to the other briefcase."

She shook her head and smiled again. He was young, barely older than her, but his presence was reassuring.

"Are you married?" she inquired.

"Yes, I am." He reached into his wallet and pulled out a photo of himself and a young woman with auburn hair. On their lap was an infant; she guessed he was a boy from the sports-themed jumper.

"Cherish every day you have with them." She strained to recall a vacation with her parents in the New Mexico mountains. She studied the smiles on the faces of Joshua's family. "She's pretty. You're a lucky man. Okay. Let's dig in. *Joshua.*" She said his name with mock inflection and a wink.

Sitting on top of the rest of the contents was a small gold bar stamped with the weight of eight ounces. She sat it on the table and pulled out a folder underneath. Without opening it, she could see the edges of blueprints sliding out, at least twenty sheets. She placed this folder into the new briefcase and then turned to retrieve two notebooks. She flipped the pages and saw handwritten notes and diagrams. After transferring these, she saw the last object in the heavy case, a faded yellow envelope, her name handwritten across it.

"Do you need a letter opener? I'm not supposed to bring any blades or edged items in here, but I can get one," Joshua explained.

She slid a fingernail across and cut the envelope. "I'm good."

There were two papers inside. The first was a property deed marked with an address in New Mexico on ten acres. She wasn't familiar with the street or town. "It appears I'm a homeowner now."

The other paper appeared to be single sheet of loose leaf folded in half. When she opened it, she immediately recognized her father's strokes. She paused, looking up at the fluorescent light fixture for a moment before she read it to herself.

Dana,

If you are reading this, it means things have come to a conclusion. I am sorry we could not be there to see you on your way.

I write this now with regret and apologies. As you likely know by now, your mother and I were put in terrible danger by factors and parties related to the Atomic Juggernaut program I worked on. Your mother, Dana, she is alive as of the writing of this letter. Once we realized the true danger of the program and found we had no way to escape it, we faked her illness and subsequent passing so she could flee. We did this out of hope that she could be kept safe to take care of you when the time came, but, still, I am so sorry we had to do this. She was given a new identity under a government protection program, but before I could find out what this was, a fire in the records building, and some clerical errors leading up to that, ensured that her new identity was purged from any records. So, I have no name, no location to give you, but you know her face, and I know she'll recognize yours. If anyone can find her, it's you. And when you do find her, tell her I loved her to the end.

I love you too, always.

Dad

Dana stared at the letter for what felt like an eternity. When she finally looked up at Joshua, her cheeks were tearstained. He was ready, extending a pack of tissues to her. She smiled with gratitude.

This letter was her past, but also her future. *Mom may be alive. Dad truly loved us. I promise I will find her and bring our family back together.* She dabbed her eyes with a tissue and pursed her lips to breathe out.

"This is everything I needed to hear."

"I am also authorized to give you this," Joshua said as he retrieved a black unmarked credit card. There was only a number on the front, no bank or issuer name on either side. "Use this for any relocation charges if needed. It expires in sixty days after first use, at which time any further use will be denied and a team of commandos will swarm on the location." He paused, unsure if she got the joke. "I'm kidding about the commandos, but the account does close sixty days after first use."

She held the card between her index and middle finger and placed it on top of the contents in her new briefcase.

"You have the gratitude of your country, and an apology. Mr. Rhodes will be charged with several high crimes. If nothing else, we have plenty of avenues to pursue RICO. He will likely be locked up for the rest of his life."

"Who's Rico?"

"The Racketeer Influenced and Corrupt Organizations Act. He's slid enough contract money around that if we find one drop that went into anything outside of registered One Hundred Roads accounts, he goes to trial for that, too. As far as his employees, well, that's a little more challenging. One Hundred Roads is now *persona non grata* as far as we're concerned. The business has been officially terminated." He smiled and tapped his pen on the table, a habit she assumed he deferred to when he was nervous. "I'm really good with fine print stuff. I read the full terms of use on every website." She smiled and let out a short laugh.

"Joshua, just one more thing, maybe two, that I need to know," she asked as she closed the briefcase. "How did you guys find me?"

"Your associate, Nick Andrews, called the antiterrorism hotline to report a government property theft and immediate threat at the airport," he responded. "And yes, he's fine. Before I came in to see you, I was informed that he was stable, and all vitals are good. A full recovery is expected." He tapped his pen again and squinted his eyes. "Is he more than just an associate?"

"He's my best friend. The best kind of friend."

"Ah." He slipped a finger into his collar to adjust it. "We are also covering his medical expenses, by the way."

"Really? Well, if you're in the mood to give away money then, big shot, I want an addendum to this contract," she stated as she slid the papers back to him. "Nick gets a stipend as my 'associate,' enough to pay for college classes plus extra."

Joshua opened his folder and retrieved a form paper dotted with empty boxes between paragraphs. He scribbled into a few of the sections.

"Okay, so four years of college . . . adjusted for five-year inflation . . . let's round that to two hundred . . . thousand." He clicked the pen and slid the paper back. "This is a strict nondisclosure agreement we are already drawing up for him, and he, of course, will waive any and all rights to further litigation. Now that we're agreed upon that, please sign yours." He scribbled his name on Dana's contract and then passed it across the table. She signed in large flowing cursive, adding a quick sketch of a roller skate next to her name.

"That's it?" she asked.

"That's it, you're done. If you need anything else, you can contact any of the offices on this card." He handed her this one last parting gift, a white business card with a list of five phone numbers for various agencies. "And with that, I'm gone. I'll send in the officers outside to escort you off the base."

He winked as he picked up the now empty large briefcase. He tapped his fingers against the handle as he picked it up.

"Government property."

"Joshua, wait," she commanded, standing and putting herself between him and the door. "The Atomic Juggernaut. Where is it?"

He froze. "I can't tell you that."

"I need to know where it is. That nobody can use it. That no one else is hurt by its existence. I can't let you leave until I know."

"Dana, I can't tell you that. It's confidential information," he said firmly. He reached around her for the door but then stopped. He leaned in close to her ear and dropped his voice. "Just know it's been taken apart. The power plant has been neutralized. Homeland Security already has the remains packed to bury what's left. This is what the government does."

She relaxed her posture. "Then get me some proof that it's buried or destroyed or whatever. I want a photo, something. You can do that. *Please.*"

"I can't make any promises on that, but I can give you my word that I will try. That's all I can give you. On the lives of my family, I give you my word." He reached into his wallet and pulled out the photo of his family, holding it up to her face. "Take this. It's my family. And that's my oath to you, this is over."

As she stared into the details of the picture—he was pale in his Hawaiian shirt, his tanned wife in an orange sundress, a beautiful baby on her lap—she knew he meant want he said. Before she could say more, he was gone and the door had closed. Dana stood alone and looked down at the briefcase left for her. She laid the gold bar on top of the papers inside and closed it. While it should have felt very heavy, it somehow felt light in her hand. The door opened again, and an officer indicated it was time for her to go.

Director Jameson leaned against a door in the hallway with her arms crossed as Dana walked past her, dangling the briefcase. The two women, juxtaposed in career, clothing, and age, gave each other a mutual nod as the younger woman left the elder one behind in the hall. Joshua emerged from an unmarked door across the hall.

"That felt good," he declared as he loosened his tie. "It's nice that we did the right thing and gave her some closure. Things got pretty crazy there, but probably par for the course for our black book operations, right?"

Director Jameson sighed and put a hand on her hip. "Joshua, what is our job?"

"Well, we run forensic accounting to reconcile and detect rogue activity—"

She halted him with her hand. "We protect the United States of America. That's it. That's what we do. There's a good chance the members of One Hundred Roads believed they were doing the same. Rhodes just lost control with his own idealized version of protecting the country. Whether what we did 'felt good' is immaterial. We protect this country, no matter the cost."

She slipped a pack of cigarettes out of her coat pocket and tapped it against the palm of her hand. She smiled when she became aware of his inquisitive look. "Didn't know I smoked, right?" She placed the pack back inside her pocket. "Certainly not inside. Just getting ready for the walk to the car."

"Director, are you saying you don't get *any* joy out helping out a girl like this? She's got her legacy now. I know that sounds a bit dramatic, but she now she can move forward knowing what her family did, what sacrifices they made. And in the end, she helped stop this program. God knows what could have happened if the juggernaut fell into the wrong hands. She's got a more secure future ahead, and the mysteries of the past behind her." He drew a long loud inward breath and then sighed a long exhale. "Doesn't that feel good? Dana Jefferson knows the truth now. Her truth. That feels good to me."

Director Jameson met his gaze with one eyebrow slightly raised. "When we do it right, we sow seeds that can bloom in the desert." She turned and walked down the windowless hall accompanied by the clacking and echoing of her shoes against the cold tiles. She stopped and spun around for a final note.

"Joshua, I'll see you back in DC in one week. You've earned some time off. Spend it with your family. Your child. Your *wife*. And thank you for your service."

Chapter 52

Solsbury Hill – Peter Gabriel

Dana stood on the porch of the Andrews's house and stared at the doorbell. The effort and motivation needed to push the button had evaporated over the past two weeks after Nick was shot. She knew she needed to just rip off the bandage and face Nick's father, and that started with pushing the doorbell. Mary Beth, who had been waiting in the car, suddenly stood by her side.

"I'll do it," she declared as she rang the bell.

Mr. Andrews promptly opened the door. He looked well, Dana thought, given the circumstances. He immediately breached the silent wall between them.

"Hi ladies. Just got off the phone with the hospital. Everything looks good. Just gotta get over there and deal with a heck of a lot of paperwork. Please, come in." He gestured toward the kitchen table where Mary Beth seated herself with a gracious smile. "Dana, I took your things out of the garage and put them in Nick's room. Oh, and I figured you could use a proper bag or two, so there's an old duffel next to your things."

Dana continued to stand just inside the entry, her head starting to ache. She felt unworthy of any kindness for what she had inflicted on this fragmented family, undeserving of Mr. Andrews's graciousness and consideration. Her hands trembled and her breath quickened as she pulled less and less air into her lungs. Her knees started to buckle before she realized what was happening.

"Mr. Andrews, some help," Mary Beth shouted as she ran to Dana's side and caught her as she began to collapse. Mr. Andrews reached her other side just in time, and he and Mary Beth carried her to the couch, where they sat her down. Mary Beth gently positioned Dana so her head was between her knees. Dana gasped and shook in fits, clutching her chest and ripping at her jacket zipper.

"Oh God, oh God, I'm so sorry, Mitch, I'm so sorry," she panted. "I almost killed Nick. I'm so sorry."

Mr. Andrews put a hand on her back as Mary Beth ran to the kitchen for a glass for water. Dana clutched the glass when it arrived and drank slowly, trying to slow her breath.

"It's okay. It's not your fault," he reassured her. "He made a choice, a big choice, but it was *his* choice. He *followed through*. And I'm proud of him." He rubbed his hand soothingly in a small circle her on the back. "He decided to fight for a person he cared about. You understand that, right?"

She looked up at him, her watery eyes matching his own. "I almost got your son killed. I didn't listen. I thought I could keep him out of it to keep him safe, and he just followed me into danger."

"Nick did this because he cared more about you than himself. And you tried to do the same. That's where you need to place your thoughts. And your heart. There was a point in time where I could have lost him, because of choices that *I made*. Sobriety gave me back time with my boy." The words caught in his throat. "But since he met you, he's become the man I dreamed he would be."

She stared into the almost empty glass in her hands, watching the surface as she swirled the contents. Her breath had returned almost to normal; her mind started to clear. She knew what she needed to do.

"I'll be back in a second."

Mr. Andrews looked at Mary Beth in confusion as Dana jogged to the car outside and retrieved her backpack. She laid it on kitchen table with a loud thud and opened it carefully, pulling out the gold bar inside.

"Mr. Andrews, this is for you. Nick's hospital bills are going to be taken care of with some monetary assistance from Big Brother, and so is his college tuition, but you, you shouldn't have to work until you drop dead. You should enjoy your time with your son. I almost took him away from you, and this is the least I can give you," she trailed off as she thought about her own parents. "And what's left over can pay for a few dates with the lady of your choice." She winked at Mary Beth.

"I can't take that, Dana."

"It's on the table; it's not going back in the bag."

"When Nick gets out of the hospital, you guys should figure out what to do with that," he countered.

"I did. It's mine. And now I'm giving it to you. Hey, I'm settling the bill on my room and board and a few dozen pieces of toast. I'm going to go pack my stuff. Thank you for the duffel bag."

She strode to Nick's room feeling lighter and began to transfer what she could fit from her trash bags into the faded green duffel. On the bed sat Nick's gray sweatshirt. She folded it carefully and placed it on his pillow. There were several tempting souvenirs she considered but decided to take nothing and leave nothing. She just wanted to disappear.

She lugged the bags to the front door and turned about to face Mitch once more. "I think this is the best way for me to leave. Thank you, again. For everything you've done for me. And your son."

Mr. Andrews wrapped his arms around her and said nothing. When they broke their embrace, he held up his hand in a mock salute. Mary Beth was already loading the bags into the car. Dana smiled at Mr. Andrews once last time and walked out to the car. He closed the door behind her.

"I think my truck is still parked on a side road by the bunker, assuming the raccoons and squirrels haven't stripped it for parts," she joked, but Mary Beth did not laugh.

"Are you okay with all of this?" she asked Dana, gesturing toward the rancher house.

"Honestly, no, but I have to be okay with it."

Dana's mind flashed through a slideshow of the escalating encounters of the past few weeks. She remembered the blood on her jacket from Trooper Sanchez. The images of Angela's stab wound, Nick's gunshot. Even the cold face of Olsen gurgling after his body was broken by her own hands. The sparks that singed her face as she broke open the juggernaut and entertained seriously hurting, even killing, Mr. Rhodes.

She remembered Stephanie, the sad little girl outside of the burger joint who asked if she was a superhero. Would she grow up to be strong because of her experiences, maybe become an Angela, or a Dana, or become a battered and defeated woman unable to fulfill whatever potential burned inside of her tiny frame?

"I have to be okay with all of it," she repeated to Mary Beth.

Chapter 53

Love Don't Come Easy – White Lion

T he afternoon sun cast long shadows from the buildings that lined the boardwalk, throwing them across the planks and onto the dunes lining the beach. The offseason foot traffic was light in Asbury Park. Dana watched the few elderly couples walking arm in arm to destinations unknown as the salty wind whipped her hair across her face. She looked out over the ocean and then over to the convention hall where the Asbury Angels had competed the night before, without her on the roster. It had been several weeks since the events at the airport, but she still could not find the heart to rejoin the team and her friends.

She finally got up to the courage to see Angela face-to-face early yesterday afternoon. When Angela arrived in the locker room, first one there as always, Dana was waiting for her. Dana apologized to her for everything, from the hurt she had caused when they broke up to all the chaos in the bunker. Angela had taken the apology with grace, and even thanked Dana for the opportunity to unleash her fighting skills and her bottled up anger. She showed Dana the long scar from the stab wound. Angela felt it was the best parting gift she could ask for from Dana, something that would show her next girlfriend where the relationship bar was set. For a moment, Dana had wanted to kiss her goodbye but knew that would only muddy the closure she and Angela both needed.

A sandy gust of wind whipped across the boardwalk with a skittering din. Dana checked the time on her phone and then the last text message from Nick earlier that morning. She put her phone away and walked to an empty bench that faced the expanse of the Atlantic Ocean. *I've never taken the time to just stare at it and stand still,* she thought. She put her feet up on the railing and watched the waves advance and retreat gently on the gray sand. An inquisitive seagull wandered toward her, cocking his head as he inspected her perimeter for fallen food.

"I don't have anything for you, big guy," she told him, and he stopped as if he understood her, then lifted both wings and emitted an angry caw to express his disapproval before disappearing over the dunes. She followed his path with her eyes, then turned them back to the sea. A voice drifted over her shoulder, carried by the wind.

"Making new friends?"

Nick appeared next to the bench, hands in the pockets of his work coat, a new growth of blond stubble covering his cheeks and chin.

"Thank you for finally returning one of my calls," he said with a small chuckle. Dana quickly stood up and hugged him. He winced slightly, some pain and soreness still lingering, but his smiled assured Dana that her presence was not the cause of his discomfort.

"Nick, I'm sorry. I'm sorry I did all the things I did that hurt you. Physically, mentally. I haven't been able to forgive—"

He raised a hand and then gently rested it on top of hers, which was clutching his arm.

"Dana, I made my own decisions. There's no apology needed." He looked into her eyes, which began to water. She averted her glance and drew a deep breath to steady herself.

"Nick, I don't belong here. I don't know where I belong, but it's not *here*." She waved a hand in general at the air around here. "There's nothing for me to find here anymore. I need to go. I'm leaving for New Mexico." She met his gaze again briefly, then turned back to watch the ocean. She nodded toward the backpack sitting on the ground next to the bench. "I'd like you to take care of the girls. Shirley's still in pretty sad shape, a little funky, but I know you can get her back in working order."

"You're not taking them with you?"

"No," she muttered.

Nick lifted the bag, hearing the rattling of loose parts inside the canvas, and slung it over his good shoulder.

"Did you enroll in a college for the semester yet?" she asked, eager to change the subject.

"I talked to the transfer offices. Thank you for arranging the funds. But that wasn't necessary."

"Well, it's the least I could do. I mean, you literally took a bullet for me." She forced a laugh but couldn't stop a tear from rolling down one cheek. She crossed her arms, feeling her lip start to quiver as she thought of the words she needed to say. Nothing was coming to mind. She bit her lip to stop the shaking.

"Nick, you've helped me *breathe* again these past weeks. I needed that. I *need* that." She broke away when she saw his eyes started to water. He cleared his throat as he fiddled with his coat zipper.

"You know, there's a couple good engineering schools out in New Mexico. I could enroll there." He put his hands on the boardwalk railing.

"You'd leave New Jersey? For real?"

"I think . . ." He paused as his voice wavered. "I'm ready now. My dad has been poking me about 'starting my own journey' and 'becoming a man.' Not that he's trying to kick me out, but he's, you know, he's giving me permission to move forward on my own path. He told me it was better to have a bird leave the nest on his own than to kick him out."

"Yeah, he's a wise old owl, isn't he?" she said affectionately.

"He is. Plus, with the sudden fortune he's attained, he has the chance to figure out what he'd like to do for himself. And New Mexico is only a plane ride away if he misses me. Of course, I'd need a place to crash before I got my own pad. Unless you know someone out there with a spare room. Got a spare room on those ten acres?" he asked coyly. He adjusted the strap on his good shoulder. "I could work on these girls while I wait for school to begin out there."

Dana stared at the dune grasses, watching the faded yellow and green strands whisk in the wind. At the edge of the water, a sandpiper skittered across the wet sand, stopping for a moment to peck at a shell before running off to join a small pack of fellow wading birds. A pair of seagulls on the roof of the convention hall squawked before taking off together and dissolving into the air over the horizon.

"Nick." She put her hand on top of his. He turned his palm up and interlaced his fingers with hers. She felt a warmth spread through her as a windy gust whipped her hair away from her face. She looked down at their hands and then up at her friend, and smiled.

"Dana." Nick pulsed her hand, and she returned the gesture.

"Let's go."

0:00   3:13

Epilogue

The Chauffer – Duran Duran

Marcus Hardy read the last page of the contract on his kitchen table one more time. He ran a manicured finger under a short section that contained a large number and sat back. He smiled broadly before his brow twisted into a serious knot.

"Okay, I think we have a deal, Olsen," he declared in a loud voice. Olsen had been looking out the back door, and his wheelchair squeaked as he turned back to face Marcus. The afternoon sun bounced off the glossy weave of the lapels of his black suit. His necktie rested in a loose knot to accommodate the bandages still adhered to the sides of his neck and upper chest. Olsen reached into his inner coat pocket with an unsteady hand to produce a silver pen. Marcus stood to reach for the writing implement.

"Thank you." Olsen clicked the pen and signed his name, a more ragged version than he the one he had adorned his business checks with prior to the swelling and bandages that constricted his hands.

"Once I lost the One Hundred Roads contract, I thought that I'd be belly-up in a month. I'm glad the government figured out how to cut out the middleman and just buy me out." Marcus beamed as he accepted the pen.

"Well, we know a good business deal when we have one," replied Olsen, looking at the chronograph on his wrist, watching the silver armature waltz through five, ten, fifteen seconds. "Anyway, you get the money, and we get everything from the barns to the carport."

"You mean the *garage*, I assume?" Hardy raised an eyebrow.

"Sorry, that's the Australian in me," replied Olsen. "Can we take a look at those barns now?"

"Well," Marcus hesitated, "there's just some old family stuff in those, boring things like furniture, cabinets full of old tax forms, the like. I'll get them all cleaned out by tomorrow morning."

Olsen slid the contract over to his side of the table. "The ink may not be dry, but as of now, we own them, so if you don't mind, I'd like the security code."

A tall woman wearing a gray trench coat stepped into the kitchen from the parlor, her tactical boots falling loudly against the tile floor. Her short blonde haircut accented her crisp cheekbones, centering around her dark-blue eyes that glared under penciled eyebrows at Marcus.

"I'll ask once," she purred. "What's the code to access the barn, Marcus?"

He opened his mouth to reply but froze as she dropped her coat. She wore a black sleeveless jumpsuit, which was tucked into her boots, but it was her arms that made him gasp. They were covered in a metallic skin tracing the lines of each muscle from her deltoids to her fingertips. As she moved them, a faint buzzing and whirring came from each joint. Marcus shot a worried glance at Olsen.

Olsen shrugged. "I'm not in charge of her, so I can't really do anything." He leaned forward and placed his fingers on Marcus's trembling hand. "I'm sorry. It's not my call."

The woman leapt over the table and seized Marcus by the throat. She lifted him upward, holding his flailing body a foot above the floor. "The code," she repeated.

Marcus held up his trembling hand and gestured with three fingers, then five, then two. His tongue protruded as he gagged. Olsen nodded at the woman, who promptly dropped Marcus to the floor. The woman swung her leg back with a ratcheting clatter and swung her foot into Marcus's chest, punting him across the room. His body smashed into the sheetrock and he rolled on to his back after the impact, eyes wide and unblinking. Olsen let out a defeated sigh and shook his head.

"That really wasn't necessary."

"Let's go out back," she countered with a smile.

She effortlessly pushed Olsen in his wheelchair out the back door and to the barns. The low-hanging sun glinted on her arms. The faint mechanical tones were drowned out by the chittering of beetles and cicadas in the century-old trees around the house. The woman gingerly lifted him up so he could input the code Marcus had so graciously shared. The door slowly began to slide open.

"Round up the remaining boys from the other assignments," Olsen instructed her. "Once the funds are transferred, reroute them again through the Caymans and kill and wipe the account. Then route a half million immediately to the New Mexico account I just set up."

"New Mexico?"

"That's where the operation is headed next."

The woman nodded. Impatient with the slow-moving door, she clasped one side and wrenched the door from its frame, crushing the metal like dry leaves in her grasp. The banding around each of her biceps whined and clanked as she pushed Olsen's chair inside.

"Did you talk to Silver about fixing your back?" she asked as they stopped in front of the large sarcophagus in the middle of the cavernous space. He set her query aside as he studied the coffin, identical to the one that housed the Atomic Juggernaut in the bunker. He allowed himself a smile. The dust had been wiped away around the circumference, and he reached up and placed his hand over a small handprint by the portal.

"The doctors think I'll get some, if not most, of my mobility back. The nerves weren't severed. And for the record, I'm not going to entertain talking to Silver." He studied her mechanical arms and soured his face. "Silver's price is too high."

"That's what I thought, too, once upon a time, but I'm happier now."

"Your daddy's money paid for your procedure. I don't have that same luxury." He rested his chin on his hand and gazed at the sarcophagus. In the distance, a truck rumbled slowly up the Hardy Farms driveway, on time as Olsen demanded.

"They're here. Shall I open this thing up?" She tapped her steely fingers on the juggernaut's container.

"Yes, see if you can tear it open. We've got a lot of work to do, Nina."

Dana and Nick will return in

Photograph

and the

Daughters of Invention

Acknowledgments

My Wife:
Thank you for supporting my leap of faith into this endeavor. There's so much more to say, but there are not enough words to express my love and gratitude for you every single day. Thank you for letting me be your foster cat.

Amy Reeve:
Your instruction, your firm but fair feedback, and your hours of work helping to make this become a reality are beyond words. Thank you for marrying one of my best friends and being a lighthouse protecting me from crashing against a shore pocked with poorly chosen words and phrases, and the wreckage of plot points covered in the tangled seaweed of unwieldy metaphors. I hope that sentence makes you cringe.

Ed Pratico:
You've been by my side on my most creative endeavors. You were the first person to bring Dana Jefferson out of my mind and into the world, and I will never, EVER, forgive you for that. I needed someone I could trust to read the first words as I brought Dana to life, and you were my Doctor Frankenstein. Damn you to Hell. And thank you.

Linnea Weber, Michael Leahy:
There were moments in conversation where you each turned a word or phrase in your feedback that gave me hope when I was in the darkest of creative places. As I continued working through the pages, I kept these pockets of time handy so I could breathe and push forward. Thank you for reading.

Nicole Bunnell:
Your friendship has been a true gift over the years. You helped guide me through dialogue and diagnosed my characters in this world I've built. Thank you. For everything. I hope I can someday pay back the hours of free therapy I've stolen.

About The Author

Michael Blatherwick was born and raised in New Jersey. He is a graduate of Villanova University and worked in the world of finance for over twenty years. This is his first fiction novel after several years in the trenches as a technical and business writer. He currently resides in Bordentown, New Jersey, with his wife, their dog, a menagerie of cats, domestic and feral, and a rotating roster of foster kittens.

Website: michaelblatherwick.com
Twitter: @blatherwords
Instagram: @jackowick

Made in the USA
Middletown, DE
25 October 2022

13402059R00175